THE ULTIMATE

X-MEN ®

WOLVERINE

THE ULTIMATE

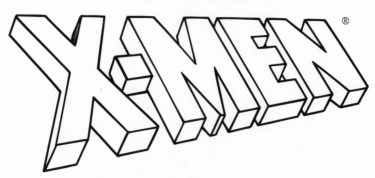

X-MEN

STAN LEE

Editor

MARVEL COMICS

BYRON PREISS MULTIMEDIA COMPANY, INC.

NEW YORK

BOULEVARD BOOKS,

NEW YORK

THE ULTIMATE X-MEN

A Boulevard Book
A Byron Preiss Multimedia Company, Inc. Book

Special thanks to Ginjer Buchanan, Lara Stein, Stacy Gittelman, the
gang at Marvel Creative Services, Peter Sanderson, and especially Steve
Roman and Keith R.A. DeCandido.

PRINTING HISTORY
Boulevard paperback edition / October 1996

The Putnam Berkley World Wide Web site address is
http://www.berkley.com

The Byron Preiss Multimedia Company World Wide Web site address is
http://www.byronpreiss.com

ISBN 1-57297-217-3

BOULEVARD
Boulevard Books are published by The Berkley Publishing Group
200 Madison Avenue, New York, New York 10016
BOULEVARD and the "B" design
are trademarks belonging to Berkley Publishing Corporation

CONTENTS

CONTENTS

INTRODUCTION

Stan Lee

Illustration by Joe St. Pierre

Why?

Why are the X-Men so popular worldwide? Why are they comicdom's best-selling super hero series?

There are countless gaudily costumed super heroes and super hero teams in their skimpy, skintight spandex suits, racing around the pages of more comic books than ever before. Some of them are bigger, stronger, and more powerful than our own mighty mutants. Many of them wear costumes that are far more abbreviated than anything our X-Men and women would dare to don. Almost all of them offer as much fighting and smashing and running and jumping and flying and yelling and snarling and rampaging as the X-Men.

So I repeat—why? Why are the X-Men far more popular than any of the other proliferating teams of comic book heroes? Why has the X-Men series thrived, grown, and prospered for more than three incredible decades while other super hero groups have fallen by the wayside?

In other words, what's the reason for the phenomenal appeal of the X-Men?

Before we expose this most closely guarded of all secrets, you must take an oath never to reveal what you are now about to learn to any representative of a competitive comic book company. Best of all, you needn't even come to our offices to take your oath. You can do it yourself at home in front of a mirror. We trust you. After all, anyone reading this book can't be all bad.

And now the answer you've been waiting for!

The secret of the X-Men's unparalleled popularity is— it's basically *a super hero soap opera!*

INTRODUCTION

Please be aware that the phrase *soap opera* is not used in a derogatory manner. In their purest sense, soap operas are about people: their relationships, their problems, their frustrations, as well as their hopes, dreams, and aspirations. Most comic book super hero stories are concerned with characters who are ever in action. Marvel's super hero mags are concerned with *people we care about* who are ever in action! A subtle difference perhaps, but anyone brainy enough to have bought this book will surely have no difficulty in recognizing the fact that it's the X-Men's *relationships* that keep us glued to the edge of our seats, that won't let us dare to miss an issue, and that have enabled us to outsell any and all of our competitors' comics in every part of the country and virtually all over the world!

Luckily for me, I won't have to spend too much time proving my point. The stories you're about to read will do that for me. Sure, each is replete with spine-tingling suspense and pulse-pounding danger, but the most important element of all—the element that'll keep you glued to your seat, unable to leave till you've read the last page—that element is the carefully crafted portion of *human drama* which is so unique to the award-winning mythos of Professor Xavier's mighty group of mutants.

Despite their incredible powers, each member of the X-Men has his or her own Achilles heel. Each and every one of them is troubled in some way or other, just as you and I so often are. Each has some degree of vulnerability. Each has known moments of frustration, fear, and weakness. Yet each has managed to overcome those weaknesses and to triumph at the end.

And what triumphs they've been! In the thrilling roster

of tales that await you you'll find yourself cheering the exploits and victories of some of the most popular X-Men of all. And while you're reading each and every one of these titanic tales and rooting for your favorite heroes, you'll notice a most interesting fact. You'll notice how right we were in referring to these stories as "soap-opera themed." For, though the operative words have always been *fantasy* and *action*, you'll find that it's our characters' personal problems that keep you and countless other readers steadily coming back for more.

As you know, the ranks of the X-Men are continually growing and changing. Since it was impossible to include them all in this collector's-item anthology, we opted for choosing the most dramatic, the most complex, and the most multifaceted of our luminous list of players. While every reader has his or her own favorites, it's unlikely that anyone would fault us for featuring highly dramatic tales starring these very special mighty mutant super heroes (in alphabetical order so that no one's pride is hurt!):

Archangel. Beast. Bishop. Cannonball. Cyclops. Gambit. Iceman. Jubilee. Phoenix. Professor X. Psylocke. Rogue. Storm. Wolverine.

If ever there was an all-star cast, you'll have to admit that this is it! Though we have neither the time nor the space to discuss each of our leading men and women, there is one character who deserves at least a passing nod. . . .

It's no secret that Wolverine is far and away the most popular of all the X-Men with readers both young and old, which certainly lends credence to our soap opera theory! Just think of it—here is a man without a clear memory of his past, with no knowledge of how he became the way he is. Twice in his life he has lost the one he loved; once to a mysterious death, and once to another man. Though the most charismatic of all the X-Men, he lives in the shadow of fear, fear that someday his bestial, savage nature may take control of his body, and if and when that day should come, no one he encounters would ever be truly safe!

By the way, if you reread the names of the X-Men featured in this tome, you'll notice that five of them are females. Actually, we had a plethora of female mutants to choose from, because Marvel Comics has always been in the forefront of the battle for female rights. We have countless other heroines who might have been included in this book as well, but we ran out of pages. However, we're sure you'll agree that the days of comic books casting women as nothing more than victims is long since gone, and we're proud that the X-Men have always treated females as full-fledged partners in their battle to save humanity.

Therefore, in an effort to show no favoritism, it doesn't matter if you're male or female, young or old, big or small, or anything in between: we welcome you! May you enjoy reading these terrific tales as much as we enjoyed collecting them for you.

Excelsior!

Stan Lee

IT'S A WONDERFUL LIFE

eluki bes shahar

Illustration by Tom Grummett

Forty miles north of New York City in the northernmost tip of Westchester County lies the small town of Salem Center, New York. Here vast tracts of gently wooded greensward cradle the sprawling estates; they are still mostly private houses, though one of the stately homes that once boasted a secret dock for smuggling Prohibition-era booze and still can claim an unrivaled view of the Hudson River has become a five-star restaurant, and another is now a thriving bed-and-breakfast. The town of Salem Center is the kind of place that driven Manhattan professionals like to escape *to*: surrounded by riding academies and private schools, all the grace notes of a life of wealth and privilege, it is a community that values privacy, where secrets are jealously guarded.

Although some secrets are bigger than others.

On Greymalkin Lane the houses are set far back from the road. Their existence is proclaimed only by the pillars flanking the iron gates of the widely spaced driveways. On one gate in particular, as if identification of what lies within is particularly important, there is a small brass plaque:

"The Xavier Institute of Higher Learning."

Once I had a normal life. The running man clung to that thought as if it were a place he could go to hide. He'd had a normal life, a quiet life, a life where men with guns didn't come to his door, and then—and then—

His foot hit an exposed tree root and he was knocked sprawling. He lay facedown, sucking the wet-earth-scented air into burning lungs and wondering where he was. His last ride had dropped him north of New York City somewhere; he'd thought it was safe enough to hitch again. The running man had never heard of Professor Charles Xavier or his school, although he'd certainly heard of the X-Men. He had no idea that he was less than a mile from possibly the only people on earth who could help him. The running man had given up hope of help long ago.

He'd been standing at the edge of the road when he saw the black sedan with the government plates cruise past him in the southbound lane and then pull into the "Official Vehicles Only" turnaround. He'd taken off cross-country; when the landscape opened out into woods and fields, he was sure he'd lost them.

His breath rasped in and out of his lungs with a desperate gasping sound as he lay there. His throat felt as if he'd swallowed dry ice. Thoughts spun through his mind like angry hornets.

Have to get up.

Almost finished.

Get up, *dammit!*

But he couldn't. He could only lie there. A matter of minutes now and Black Team 51 would have him.

If only he could be sure they'd kill him.

But they wouldn't. That was the special hell of it. They wanted him to work for them. And he was afraid, afraid of what they would make him do. . . .

Once upon a time, the running man had possessed a name. He'd been David Ferris; twenty-nine, unmarried, and—according to his now ex-girlfriend Alicia—looked a lot like Fox Mulder on *The X-Files.* Until a week ago he'd been just another teacher at Penrod High School in Indianapolis, Indiana, brass buckle of the Corn Belt.

A normal life. Once he'd had a normal life.

IT'S A WONDERFUL LIFE

* * *

It was August, and so it was hot, and the four men and one woman could easily have sought the sanctuary of the air-conditioning inside the sprawling mansion—or even the pool on the other side of the house. Instead they sat in a casual grouping upon the shady flagstoned terrace at the back of the house, concealed from accidental view with a caution that had become habit long since. The only sound on the hot summer air was the rattle of ice in the tall lemonade glasses and the desultory sound of relaxed talk among them. These five had passed through Life and Death together, and the most important things they could express to one another had already been said long ago.

They were all in their twenties, all at that peak of health and conditioning that marks the professional athlete, whose success or failure depends entirely on the educated body's response to the demanding mind. But these five were not professional athletes, though one of them, at least, had arrived at that peak of fame and adulation that only sports stars and rock stars—and super heroes—know.

Once he'd stood with the Avengers, Earth's mightiest heroes, in the days when there were no East or West Coast Avengers, no first or second team. But before that his allegiance had been to another assemblage, in the days now long past when that supergroup's roster could be counted on the digits of one hand: in that twilight moment between their discovery that they were different from the rest of humanity, and the moment the world learned to hate and fear them.

His name was Henry P. McCoy, and he was the X-Man known as the Beast.

Of the five heroes gathered on that shady secluded terrace, Hank McCoy looked least human, though all five of them had been able to pass for human once—had in fact passed for human during one of those dark periods when the X-Men were driven underground by a prejudice so deep that even some of their fellow heroes turned against them, and Hank McCoy had left them to pursue his first love, biochemistry research. There, youthful pride and an experiment gone wrong had trapped him forever in a shape as bestial as his code name—the form of a burly blue-furred monster with long, gleaming fangs. Since his transformation Hank stood upright only with the greatest of effort, though he could bound along on his knuckles and toes faster than a racehorse could run.

At the moment Hank McCoy reclined in a specially reinforced lawn chair, the dark glasses balanced on the bridge of his nose adding a note of absurdity to his broad inhuman countenance. He perched his slippery tumbler of lemonade on the tip of one taloned finger and studied it meditatively.

"I hate to mention this, Warren m'boy, but you're interfering with my tan," Hank said.

Behind the Beast stood his teammate, bio-mechanical wings spread to block the sun. When Hank spoke, he spread them wider, then turned aside so that his shadow no longer fell upon the Beast's blue-furred body.

"Oh, well, excuse *moi*," Archangel said with a grin, making a big show of getting out of his teammate's light.

Born Warren Worthington III, he had called himself the Avenging Angel when Professor Charles Xavier invited him to join the X-Men—and convinced him to shorten his name to simply Angel. But the man now called Archangel had drifted nearly as far from human as Hank had. Once great white-feathered wings had sprouted from his shoulder blades when the hormonal changes of puberty had brought his mutant gifts to flower—though those were gone now, irrevocably damaged in battle and amputated. In their place Archangel now bore glittering metal wings, as intricately feathered as his natural ones had been, and so bound into his nervous system that he could launch their razor-feather darts at will. The same dubious benefactor who had engineered this transformation had also turned Warren's skin a cyanotic blue: stronger and tougher than ordinary human—or even mutant—skin, it provided a great advantage to Archangel in battle; at the same time it irrevocably marked him out from the rest of humanity. Different. Alien.

David Ferris had always known he was different—

get up you have to get up

—but when he'd been a child a quarter of a century ago the world had been different, too—

get up it isn't that hard they'll be here soon

—the superteams and lone costumed avengers that were so much a part of modern daily life now—

you can't let them take you

—were a thing of the future, or dim past-era memories in the minds of those who had fought beside the more-than-human in World War II—Captain America, the Sub-Mariner, the first Human Torch—then called the Invaders. The bitter enmity between *homo sapiens* and *homo superior* was still years in the future—

come on; it isn't that hard

—in those days, growing up in rural Shelbyville, David

had known that other people bowed to the inevitable, accepted the fact that choosing one thing made all the others impossible—

if you can't walk, crawl!

—realized that life was a process of choosing one thing and forsaking all the rest.

But David Ferris didn't have to.

Years later, in his reading, he came across the words that explained what he had known, instinctively, from birth: that there wasn't one reality, but millions—that every possible choice that could ever be made was made *somewhere*, in one of the parallel worlds that, to David's mutant perception, were as tangible and accessible as the books on the rack at the soda fountain downtown. David could spin the wheel of fortune and make those different worlds *real*.

Worlds where Hitler had won World War II. Worlds where humanity had never evolved. Even worlds where humanity was the only known sentient species—no Atlanteans nor Kree, no Skrulls, not even Galactus to threaten sleep.

He might, with his mutant gift, have grown up to don a gaudy costume, taken a romantic *nom de guerre*, and gone on to fight crime and/or evil, as Benton Harper—Chicken-Man—used to say on the radio. But David just didn't have a world-famous sort of nature, and when ultimate evil came to the Midwest, the Avengers or the Fantastic Four were almost always only half a jump behind.

get up
hands and knees
crawl
c'mon David you have to keep moving

No one needed him to save the world. Not when others were available to do it.

"Do you ever wonder why we do it? I mean, we could have had normal lives," the young man said pensively.

And in fact, the speaker looked normal—a slight twentysomething with brown hair and brown eyes and a faintly mocking smile—save for the thick coating of frost that covered his hand and turned the liquid in his glass to gelid slush.

"That's something you'd never have to worry about, Robert m'lad," the Beast said. He regarded his glass meditatively, tossed it up, caught it, and drank.

Bobby Drake—Iceman to his teammates and enemies—slid his free hand unobtrusively below Hank's line of sight. At a mental command, snow began to form in his palm, created from the moisture in the air by Iceman's mutant power: the power to create ice and project the cold needed to keep it from melting under even the most adverse conditions—like a hot August day.

"Knock it off, Bobby."

The snow turned to water before Iceman could consciously react. Save for his heavy dark glasses, Scott Summers looked ordinary enough to be Bobby's older brother, but as Cyclops, he had been the X-Men's first team leader, and after so many years, the habit of obedience that had saved Bobby's life countless times was ingrained in the younger man's mind well below the level of conscious thought.

"I wasn't doing anything," Bobby protested, more out of habit than any hope of getting away with it.

"Yet," the fifth member of the party finished for him.

Cool and eye-catching in white tennis shorts and sleeveless turtleneck, Jean Grey was a regal redhead, with a model's poise and flawless skin. Both a telepath and telekinetic, she was also now married to Scott Summers.

"Bobby, when are you ever going to grow up?" she asked with an amused, long-suffering sigh.

"When somebody makes him," Archangel drawled in his silver-spoon accent. The sunlight threw flickers of light off the silvery metal of his wings. "And I think I just might—*What was that?*"

All of them had heard it. A short, sharp, odd sound, brief and loud.

Archangel turned in the direction the sound had come from, his wings mantling for flight. "Maybe I'd better—" he began.

"It was probably just somebody's arugula steamer misfiring," the Beast said lightly. "Warren, old friend, you really should—"

"I'll just go check it out," Archangel said quickly. Stepping away from the others, he spread his wings to their full span, and, with one powerful downbeat, Archangel was airborne.

Hank sat up a little straighter in his chair and regarded the others quizzically from beneath furry beetling brows.

"Did it ever occur to anyone that we may be a wee bit too hasty in borrowing trouble?" he asked.

"There's never any need to borrow trouble," Scott Summers answered grimly. "They give enough of it away free."

"Besides," Bobby Drake quipped, "what else do we know how to do?"

* * *

The running man crawled now. He didn't know what else to do. He was already half delirious with exhaustion; the image of a long-ago Indiana summer came to him, of a day on which any heroic dreams he'd had were quenched forever. He'd been eight years old, and his dog had died. . . .

The flashback came easily, pulling him back into the past when he knew that what he had to do was to get up, to *run*, even though there was nowhere to run to. Even if he Spun himself into one of those other worlds whose ever-shifting reality he could sense, Black Team 51 might be waiting for him in almost any of them, and he wouldn't know they were there until it was too late.

Grimly, David Ferris forced his body forward, though the movie in his mind played on unchecked. He thought about little else, now, but that moment when his life had undergone an irrevocable . . . mutation.

It was August, and so it was hot. . . .

Penrod High School was a racially homogenous blue-collar Indiana high school, proud of its football team and with no more in the way of alcohol, drugs, firearms, and teen pregnancies than plagued most American schools these days. PHS was an old building, dating from the early 1940s. Later architects could have told its designers of the unwisdom of putting such a tempting ledge outside the fourth-floor windows. Just six inches wide, purely ornamental.

Snow days had made the school year run all the way into July, and the start of summer school had been correspondingly delayed. It was twelve-thirty. Lunchtime. And David, who was teaching English Comp in summer session, had been heading for his car, thinking of nothing more exotic than the local Pizza Hut cuisine, when he heard a girl's shrill scream behind him.

He turned and looked, then looked where she was looking.

Up.

From inside the classroom the ledge looked wide enough to walk on. Until class cutup Martin Mathers actually got out onto the ledge, away from the refuge of the classroom window, and looked *down*—

David Ferris needed only a moment to take in the situation; he could already hear the distant wail of the fire engines coming to the rescue. They'd be here in a few minutes, only Martin didn't have those few minutes. Already David could see him teetering at the edge of the ledge.

You can save him.

Was it some perfidious serpent that whispered those words in the depths of David Ferris's mind, some lingering ambition to be a hero? Perhaps if David had dreamed bigger dreams, he would have had the skill and control when it mattered. Or maybe the tragedy had been foreordained from the moment that the baby Spun apple juice to orange juice in its bottle.

I can save him.

Was it some primal hatred of *homo superior* for *homo sapiens*? Was it the need to justify his existence to a world that saw his kind only as a threat? For two decades he'd been careful to hide his mutant power, until now. Until once again the stakes had been life . . . and death.

Was it an act of heroism? Or genocide?

No one would ever know. The only thing that was certain, on that bright summer day, was that David Ferris reached into the shadows of possibility to Spin a safer refuge for Martin Mathers—a ledge that was wider, a world in which the boy had never gone out the window at all—

And missed.

Because in all the myriad worlds of possibility, David had forgotten that there was one in which no ledge existed at all. . . .

Archangel lunged skyward with powerful beats of his deadly silver wings. Like some fearsome bird of prey, he instinctively sought the air currents that would pull him higher into the sky. *Hank was probably right,* Warren mused, catching a thermal that swept him a dozen yards higher in seconds. He felt the corresponding pull in the muscles of his back as his wings spread and cupped the rising air. Almost absently, his eyes searched the ground below for the source of the sound, picking out with ease the flagstoned terrace of Professor Xavier's school and the four figures still seated there. *It probably* was *an arugula steamer misfiring. Not a job for the X-Men.*

It was just that Archangel couldn't resist any excuse—even a lame one—for taking to the air. The others just didn't understand. Couldn't. None of the earthbound could understand the glory of unaided flight.

Warren's train of thought abruptly broke off and he smiled wryly. Old habits died hard; in his teen years as a student at the school, such thoughtless musings would have earned him a severe rebuke from the X-Men's mentor and taskmaster, Professor Charles Xavier. From the very first,

Xavier had insisted that his X-Men think of themselves as *human*, not *homo superior*, as Magneto and some other would-be mutant messiahs would have it. Human. Not better. Only different.

But some differences were basic—as fundamental as the difference between walking . . . and flying. His fellow X-Men didn't really understand that their teammate's need to fly was as basic as theirs to walk. Archangel banked, spreading his wings wider and gliding in a slow spiral. His overflight of Salem Center and its surroundings wouldn't compromise site security; he was high enough up that anyone watching from below would probably take him for a kite or a plane. He'd stay up here long enough to be able to say he'd checked out the area and then go back. It was the least he could do, considering that his reconnaissance was really only an excuse for a little harmless exercise.

Then Warren looked down at the ground below, and what he saw made him fling his wings forward, spilling the wind through his pinions and bringing his body to a shuddering halt in the warm summer air.

The Indianapolis police kept him for endless hours before deciding that they could not prove responsibility in Martin Mathers' death; could not prove that he had actually been involved; could not even prove what everyone at the school now knew to be the truth . . .

David Ferris was one of *them*.

He came home to an apartment that had been violated, the furniture destroyed, the walls painted with slogans that had used to be familiar only from the evening news. *Die*

Mutie Scum—genejoke—read the letters in dripping paint, and in that moment David knew that his life was over.

But his dying had hardly begun.

This is it. I'm through. He'd finally managed to stand, clutching at a tree trunk for support, but he knew that forcing his exhausted body to run was beyond all possibility. And the part of David Ferris that wanted to pay for his crimes—*rebellion is as the sin of witchcraft*—welcomed the hunters who followed him so relentlessly.

Black Team 51. Their names were Gilman and Egan, and they'd come into his life a little over a week ago, while he was still staring helplessly at the wreckage of his apartment. They'd told him their names, but they hadn't told him anything else. Except the most important thing.

"There's a man who'd like to meet you. He wants you to work for him. You're special, David. He's interested in your special abilities. And face it, after yesterday how many choices do you have?"

Come with us, and Spin dross into gold, into fire, into blood . . . And all across the Multiverse, a thousand David Ferrises refused and died.

But David Ferris knew more about choices than any other man alive. He'd played along, played for time, and when they'd let their guard down he'd given Egan and Gilman the slip and fled to New York—hoping to get out of the country—only to find that Black Team 51 had second-guessed him, just as they had at each step down the line. They'd been waiting at the airport.

He'd panicked and run, hitchhiked, anything to find a reality that didn't place him in the back seat of that black sedan. And for a few hours he'd thought he'd won, but every time he reached the road it seemed the car found him again within minutes. Content to follow, playing some sadistic game of cat and mouse, waiting for the moment when David Ferris could run no longer.

Waiting for this moment.

Why were they so cautious? Were they expecting him to fight back? David smiled without any particular humor. It was true that they didn't know what he was capable of, but the real joke was: *he* didn't know what he was capable of. And it didn't look like he was going to live long enough to find out either.

There was a sound of tires on gravel on the road behind him. David turned on unsteady legs to face it. The black sedan's side windows were tinted, and the windshield was some sort of one-way glass. The car might be full of Martians, for all David could see, but in some universes the windows weren't tinted, and he knew it was Egan and Gilman. Who were through playing. David heard a faint hum as the powered side window rolled down and some monstrous and evil machine of chrome tubes, flashing lights, and wicked flanges poked out.

It looked as if it had been dropped here from some alternate reality, like something out of a *Star Wars* movie, something that could not possibly function. David stared at it in disbelief. As it sighted on him a thin keening grew louder, sliding out of audibility until it was only an ultrasonic pressure against his skin. And in a moment of despairing clarity, David Ferris realized that he did not want to die, that he would do anything to stay alive—and free.

He'd even do what they wanted him to do.

The Wheel that hovered at the edge of his consciousness

every waking moment came sharp. David reached for it, Spun it into manifestation with the last of his mutant stamina, braiding all the possible realities together as the power surged through him into the world. His body cracked like a whip as living flesh completed the circuit, and David Ferris reached out from What Was to What Could Be—

And in the blink of an eye, Could Be became Was.

The summer sunlight went flatly yellow, and the stench of burning sulphur seemed to hang on the air. Beneath the wheels of the black sedan, the asphalt pulled and turned to tar and stretched like hot taffy . . .

Until it burst.

Ropy tentacles the color of rotting eggplant slithered through the tarry chunks of broken road, writhing themselves around the car, tightening and beginning to *pull*. The hood gave a sharp *ping!* as it buckled, and under the unrelenting pressure the tinted windows crazed, then shattered, then spilled over the doors of the car like dangerous candy.

Someone screamed. The weapon in the car slewed crazily about, then fired, and for a brief instant David Ferris's body was outlined in a corona of multicolored light.

"He's been gone too long." Bobby Drake's voice was hard and decisive. He stood up, taking a step toward the edge of the terrace as though that would tell him where Warren had gone.

"Jean?" Scott said.

I'll scan, the redhead answered through their psychic link. Jean Grey got to her feet and closed her eyes, searching telepathically for the imprint of Warren's thoughts through the background static of thousands of other minds.

It had been less than ninety seconds since Archangel had departed on his aerial reconnaissance, but the outcome of battles had been decided in far less time. Their former teammate Kitty Pryde had once said that being an X-Man was like wearing a psychic sign that read, *come and kill me*, and those who had been X-Men longest had that worldly wise paranoia burned into their very bones.

"Forget that. I'm going to look for him," Bobby said.

Like some illusion wrought by time-lapse photography, a puddle first of frost, then of ice, spread beneath his feet, broadening into a frozen wave that became an ice-slide sweeping him aloft.

"Bobby!" Scott snapped in exasperation.

"Wait!" Jean Grey said. *Scott, there's*—

And then everything happened at once.

There was a blinding flash of sunlight on silver wings— Archangel's return flight. There was warning in his very bearing, from the low, fast flight barely above the tree line to the way he kept looking behind him.

With a faint frosty crackle, Bobby Drake's clothing froze into brittle glassy shards and fell from his body. Iceman's body transformed into a glittering form of ice that melted and reformed a thousand times a second over his entire body, giving the unyielding ice the illusion of flexibility. The sun glinted from his frozen form in a heliographic display, and a wave of arctic cold cut through the baking August heat.

At the same moment on the terrace below, Scott Summers got to his feet. From the table beside him he lifted what at first appeared to be a pair of fancy sunglasses; a gleaming gold visor echoing the helm of a knight of old, bisected horizontally by a thin line of brilliant ruby quartz. A more delicate instrument than the blast goggles he had been wearing, the battle visor allowed him to wield the full force of his incredible optic blasts with the delicacy of a surgeon. Closing his eyes tightly, the wiry and supremely ordinary-looking young man first removed the bulky goggles and slipped the gold-and-ruby visor into place. As the cybernetic contact points touched his temples, the X-Man known as Cyclops opened his eyes, and the annihilating blood-red light of his destructive optic blasts washed over the inside of his cybernetically controlled battle visor.

"Let's go, folks," the X-Men's team leader said.

Beside him, Jean Grey's body began to glow, and she telekinetically launched herself into the summer sky.

As for Hank McCoy, he had no need for a flashy transformation or display. He merely set down his lemonade glass and removed his glasses as the shimmering figure came crashing through the trees at the edge of the lawn.

Assuming they'd still been alive and in a talkative mood, Egan and Gilman could have told David what had hit him—and was about to cause the X-Men such trouble. The Moebius Lance was, in fact, a weapon that had been specifically designed to subdue supernormals with powers classified as parapsionic, such as Gambit or the Scarlet Witch. It had been developed during experiments conducted on the mutant known as Angar the Screamer before his death, and was supposed to scramble a parapsi's nervous system, setting up a feedback loop that would render them the victim of their own power for a short but undetermined period.

There were only two problems.

The Moebius Lance had never actually been tested on the people it was supposed to control.

And its effects weren't anything like the ones its designer had predicted.

Thoughts and memories spilled through David Ferris's mind as his neurochemistry reconfigured, wiping memory and personality from the intricate architecture of his brain. All that he was drained away, the tangled skein of memory unknotting into smoothness once more.

Above the other X-Men, Archangel braked and veered groundward. He didn't know what connection the glowing man below him had with the wrecked car he'd seen back on 9A North, but he did know that the car looked as if it'd been bear-hugged by the Hulk and that even in Westchester normal people didn't glow in the dark.

Archangel and the former David Ferris broke through the trees at about the same time.

A moment ago he'd been hungry, tired, and afraid. Now he was none of those things. He no longer remembered that he'd been fleeing, or from whom. The running man stopped when he reached the edge of the trees. He didn't, in fact, remember being David Ferris very well at all.

Probabilities cascaded through David's mind like a winning hand of solitaire on Windows 95.

say something you have to

So many ways to go, so many paths to choose, and who he was had been lost forever, buried in a thousand might-be-maybes, and who was he?

you have to remember it was important you were—you were—

"I am the Wheel of Fortune!" David Ferris shouted.

"In that case, I'd like to buy a vowel, Vanna," the Beast replied smoothly, loping forward. The glowing man was a threat, but possibly not the main threat. In torn jeans and ripped shirt, their little glowworm looked more like one of the victims than like the vanguard of an attacking force—but it didn't pay to take chances...

"For God's sake, Beast, be—" Cyclops shouted.

The glowing man flung out his hand.

—killme goingtokillme extremism in the defense of liberty is no vice—

And that was the last thing Hank McCoy saw.

In this world, at least.

"I said, ya gotta get over yerself, Torchy."

Henry P. McCoy twitched ever so slightly as the unmistakable gravel voice of Benjamin J. Grimm cut through his concentration.

There was a crash from the room beyond and the sound of a rushing *whoosh* of flame. Hank sighed and pushed his glasses farther up on his nose. Working as Reed Richards's research assistant was a wonderful opportunity, it was true, and if not for Stark International's continuing-education program, he wouldn't have had it.

If only it weren't so . . . stressful.

"Look here, brick-face—" Another crash.

Hank winced. He sincerely believed that violence was

the last refuge of the incompetent; he abhorred physical brutality and shunned strife in every form. He'd managed to forget that in addition to being one of Earth's foremost scientists, Dr. Richards was a lightning rod for trouble. Usually super-powered trouble.

And me without a supernormality to my name, Hank thought mournfully. A little agility hardly counted. In fact, it was a positive prerequisite for his current assignment.

The building shook. Hank leapt to his feet with a yelp of dismay. While he'd been distracted, the chemical he'd been timing had boiled over and was now foaming greenly across the lab bench.

What you need, Henry old son, is a guardian angel . . .

A thousand presents, a thousand worlds; each as real as the next. . . .

And the Wheel was Spinning. . . .

Cyclops was the farthest away of any of the team: Archangel, Iceman, and Phoenix were airborne and in all the years he'd known him he'd never been able to persuade Hank that a full frontal assault wasn't the best way to assess a new and unknown threat. In the instant that the Beast disappeared in a flash of light, all the rules changed, and the glowing man calling himself the Wheel of Fortune went from potential victim to certified threat.

Making sure his teammates were out of the fire line, Cyclops opened his visor far enough to emit a thin ruby lance of raw power.

Split-second calculation raced through Scott's mind:

Should be enough to KO him if it hits; he looks *human enough—*

There was a grinding crash from above. At the same time a tree beside the stranger's head exploded in a shower of splinters. Chunks of ice fell out of the sky. A dozen different things clamored for Cyclops' attention all at the same time.

Bobby?

Missed!

How?

"X-Men—pull back!" Scott shouted.

Phoenix had chosen to come at the glowing man from behind. She heard Scott's shout through the link they shared, and her automatic running assessment of the danger they were in spiked. Hank had vanished, but the clean abruptness of it told Phoenix that it was probably some sort of teleportation—

And if it weren't, the years ahead would be time enough to grieve.

There's something wrong here. And whatever it is, it's getting worse.

When he'd first appeared, the stranger had been surrounded by a chatoyant nimbus of biogenetic energy, almost a halo. Now the area of affect began to spread; the figure inside it to blur, to multiply—and as it did, its psi-signatures did as well. The sensation for Phoenix was similar to being in a rapidly filling auditorium where everyone was talking at once. Ten, a hundred, a thousand: the force of his multiplied thoughts was drowning all other thoughts in a wave of telepathic static.

How does he—? There are more of him every instant.

Above and ahead there was the sound of an explosion; Jean Grey swerved groundward to avoid the flying chunks of ice. What had happened to Bobby?

What had happened to all of them? She could no longer "hear" her teammates, nor any of the ordinary human minds that made up the community of Salem Center—and in fact, she was no longer sure any of them were there at all. But above all things, Jean Grey was a professional, and the Mission Objective came first. Stop the intruder; shut him down.

Seconds before, Iceman had been twenty feet overhead. Trained always to fight as part of a team, he'd kept a running check of where the others were—Warren was above and on his left, Jean should be coming up from the bogey's blind side. Hank and Cyke were somewhere on the ground; not in his attack path. Now was the time to put a set of ice handcuffs on their unfair unknown and have him wrapped up and ready to deliver.

Bobby angled his ice slide groundward—

—and smashed directly into Archangel below him, also coming in for an attack run.

But that's impossible—he was behind *me—*

"Drake, you—moron!" Archangel shouted, silver feathers chiming faintly as he battled desperately to stay airborne.

But Bobby Drake had troubles of his own. The collision with Archangel's wings had shattered his ice slide; Iceman was four stories up with no visible means of support.

Where's Hank? Bobby wondered as he fell. He didn't

want to nail him with an ice pylon if Hank was moving into position to catch him, but at the same time, he didn't want to *crash*—

Snow. Just the thing on a hot day. With reflexes honed in a thousand Danger Room sessions, Iceman flung out both hands, making the air beneath him cold, colder, coldest . . .

It was only too bad that what was beneath him wasn't ground at all.

No! That's impossi—

The rest of his life was going to be measured in seconds if he didn't time this just right. Bobby Drake drew a deep breath and launched himself into space. A terrifying moment of free fall, and then the crossbar smacked into the palms of his calloused hands. He was glad he'd taken the time to apply the extra coat of rosin to his hands; it was August, and sweat and high-wire acts didn't mix. He pulled himself up and over, taking a moment to steal a glance at the audience in the seats far below.

The Big Apple Circus was one of the few tenting circuses still working. Five years ago Bobby Drake had signed up as a rigger. It was exciting to work a hundred feet above the ground, but Bobby craved excitement the way a couch potato craved junk food. He was always looking for the next thrill.

Case in point. Bobby Drake, boy aerialist. He launched himself from the trapeze to the slack wire ten feet below. To the ringside audience, it looked as though he were jumping to his death. *Angel bait,* the others called him.

Bobby Drake always worked without a net.

* * *

It was the unexpectedness of the sound that made Cyclops turn toward it. What he saw made his eyes widen with disbelief behind their ruby-quartz firewall at the sheer . . . idiocy of it. *Funny. I didn't remember the swimming pool being on this side of the house,* Cyclops thought inconsequentially. But if it hadn't been, it was now; Scott could even see the place on the concrete lip where Wolverine had etched graffiti years before.

But what was by far the most interesting thing about the swimming pool at the moment was the fact that every drop of water it contained had been turned into a filtered, pH-balanced, chlorinated block of solid ice. And Iceman was frozen into the middle of it, entombed like a fly in amber.

Chipping him free would have been a delicate task at the best of times, but as Cyclops turned back from his split-second assessment, he realized that time had run out.

He was alone, facing the Wheel of Fortune.

And then he wasn't there anymore.

And the Wheel of Fortune was Spinning.

I know every sound my ship makes. Scott Summers looked out across the bridge with the satisfaction that came from the awareness of being in his proper place. All around him, overlapping holographic screens showed him images of a starfield adjusted to compensate for redshift distortion and modified with the data feed from the navigational computers.

What season was it at home? Scott shook his head, smiling at the foolishness of wondering about a homeworld he'd left while still a child. The glory of that day was something that would burn in his memory like a nova until the day he died: Alex, the orphanage, the great golden god dressed in polychrome buccaneer's leathers, striding in to claim them both, take them away . . .

Christopher Summers. Their father.

Still, Earth was his home; Scott had been born there, in the Midwestern United States. He might go back there someday. It was summer there now, he thought. What was the name of the month? *August,* that was it . . .

"Shi'ar raiders detected by long-range sensors, Captain!" the helm said.

Scott Summers brought his mind back to the present with a jolt.

"Battle stations, everyone—go to Condition Red. Okay, Starjammers, it's time to break up this little party—"

A moment before, there had been five of them; now Phoenix was alone. She reached out for the mind of the intruder. A moment later she realized her chosen tactic was wrong, and four seconds after she began her intervention, Jean Grey knew that she'd just made a potentially fatal mistake.

In her years as an X-Man, she had probed the minds of aliens, madmen, and demons, linked together members of the team across both years and light-years, travelled from the far side of the galaxy to a future that never was.

This was different.

This was like all of them at once.

With a dim, fading part of her mind, Jean Grey could feel the earth beneath her feet, the warmth of the sunlight beating down on her shoulders, the roughness of the tree bark beneath her fingers. They were part of one reality.

But not the only one.

* * *

"If I had the wings of an angel—" The melodious baritone came to a distracted halt as the singer tried and failed to remember the next line. *Oh, well. Hardly matters,* Warren Worthington III told himself philosophically.

Below him the green of the Hudson River Valley unrolled in an immaculate carpet, and Warren almost felt as if he could taste the wind on his face. This little flight up to Albany was just what the doctor ordered to chase those boardroom blues away.

Making a small adjustment, Warren maneuvered the Piper Cub into a showy sideslip. He'd always loved to fly . . .

I've always loved to fly. Why did that simple statement fill him with panic? Of course he did; been flying since he was sixteen; his father had bought him his own plane for his twenty-first birthday. Sailplaning; hang gliding; Warren had always loved anything that would take him into the air.

My wings! He could feel his heart hammering in his chest, racing faster and faster. Black spots danced before his eyes and the Piper Cub's stick slipped forward, taking with it the nose of the small plane. Falling forward in an uncontrolled dive, the small plane began, lazily, to spin.

Where are my wings?

The scream of air past the Cub's cowling roused him to his immediate plight. Frantically Warren clawed at the controls, trying to pull the plane out of its deadly dive. He heard the singing in the guide wires as the ailerons snatched at the treacherous air. The surface of the Hudson rushed closer with each passing second. Only the wings of an angel could save him now.

But Warren Worthington III didn't have wings.
He never had.

And as the surging tides of David Ferris's mind closed over her, Jean Grey was linked to a universe in which every possibility was just as real as every other.

Every one.

August in New York, and even in the 1990s, some addresses are still more fashionable than others. Submitted for your approval: a particular Park Avenue penthouse, somewhere in the East Seventies.

She called herself Jeanne Grey, having changed the spelling of her first name to the more exotic French form when she reached adulthood. She was born with the power to read people's minds—and cloud them too. She grew up in a small town—Annandale-on-Hudson—knowing what people were going to say before they said it.

Sometimes it was an advantage.

"Mrs. Byrne, how lovely to see you again. I'm so glad you've heard from your son—didn't Kra Tho tell you everything would be all right?"

The regal redhead took the arm of the older woman, and led her from the vestibule of the lavish penthouse to the drawing room where the others were waiting for their Wednesday-afternoon sitting. She smiled inwardly as Mrs. Byrne's surprise and awe reverberated through her mutant senses. Amelia Byrne believed absolutely in the power of Kra Tho, a disembodied being from ancient Atlantis who spoke through his contact, Jeanne Grey, to bring messages of hope and purpose to the modern world.

Kra Tho did not exist, though he was a very lucrative fiction. And an easy road to travel, for a young woman who had never heard of either Professor Charles Francis Xavier or his unique private school.

No. That isn't me.
    Although she knows it is.
    I have to change it.
    But how do you change the present?
    That isn't me. . . . Thrust into an alternate universe, her ego merging with her body double's, Phoenix fought desperately to free herself from the trap of David's thoughts. But she was only one person, trapped in only one possible present. The Wheel of Fortune turned for them all. . . .

He'd been sorry to have to leave the party, but he'd promised Barry he'd put in some hours this weekend. Too bad he hadn't been born rich instead of so good looking.

Scott Summers smiled at his own feeble joke and shifted the briefcase to his other hand. Among his other regrets was that there wasn't a subway stop nearer to his job than West Fourth Street; it was a long walk in this heat. Too bad he hadn't been born lucky instead of smart; luck would at least have arranged things so he didn't have to go in to work on a Sunday afternoon in August. But the presentation to the client hadn't gone at all well, and Barry had promised an entire new ad strategy by Monday. And that meant overtime. A weekend full of it.

Scott sighed, welcoming the coolness in the lobby as he went through the revolving doors at 375 Hudson. August in New York wasn't for sissies. The guard knew him and waved him through, proof that he was putting in too many hours at the job. And for what? Athletic shoes. An account as ordinary as the rest of his life . . .

Everything about him was ordinary, Scott Summers thought to himself.

Horror lent her strength. *He's shuffling us farther and farther away—into realities where mutants don't exist at all—I can't let him blot us out this way—David! David, listen to me! We aren't the enemy. We don't want to hurt you . . .*

". . . net profits down every quarter for the last six years, eaten alive by Korea and Japan; what did I expect?" Bobby Drake sighed.

Not this. He scanned the "Help Wanted" columns of the Sunday *New York Times* again, although he knew he wouldn't find anything there. The available jobs for obsolete middle-management former programmers were few to nonexistent, but nobody'd thought that IBM would make the cuts it had.

Now he was out in the cold. Despite the August heat, Bobby Drake shivered. He wasn't even thirty yet—his life couldn't be over.

Could it?

Deliberately closing her mind to Ferris's perception of the world, Phoenix turned her thoughts away from the present, sinking deeper into Ferris's psyche. Into the only place that help could come from. Into the past.

* * *

His name was Davey Ferris, and he was eight years old. Starbuck had been his companion and best friend for as long as Davey Ferris could remember, which was, why, it was years and years. Starbuck was no particular kind of dog—a Heinz, as Davey's father liked to say, because he contained fifty-seven varieties of dog within his rangy frame—but that didn't matter to Davey.

And then one day Starbuck died. Hit by a car.

"Daddy, where's Starbuck gone?"

"I'm afraid he's dead, son," Davey's father told him. But in hundreds and hundreds of universes right next door Davey's dog was still alive . . .

"But he doesn't have to be, Daddy!" Davey Ferris had tried, for the first time, to explain.

"Hush, son. No one can bring back the dead."

"But, Daddy, he isn't all dead. Not everywhere."

Davey Ferris wasn't quite sure why his father said Starbuck was dead, when Davey could see him, alive, in the universe next door. He supposed that Starbuck had tracked mud in or broken something, and as he was a good boy, he thought he wouldn't bring Starbuck back until they'd gotten over being mad. But he was only eight, and eventually he forgot . . .

His father's fear had bridled David's use of his mutant power more effectively than any prohibition could, but he hadn't been able to bear to give it up entirely. Instead he'd only used it for little things.

Until it was too late.

In his mind . . . the car . . . Black Team 51? Another government agency or private corporation that desires to enslave the supernormal for their own purposes? Weariness and anger threatened to break her concentration: when would governments and would-be governments stop treating paranormals as mind-less puppets to be exploited for some nationalistic agenda? *All we want is our own lives . . .*

But David Ferris hadn't been given the luxury of autonomy.

The Moebius Lance—energy weapon? Drug-delivery system? Whatever it is, David didn't mean to fight us at all—now, if I can only make him see that!

Phoenix's battleground was a world where will and desire were weapons; where passion took all and good intentions were the best defense. She no longer knew where she was at all, in this psychic realm where every possibility was as real as every other. All she knew was that she *must* succeed.

Come with me, David. Come back with me—

But the lure of Might Have Been was strong. . . .

Let's get this over with so I can go home.

Parts of Long Island were scenic and pleasant and delightful to visit. Stark Industries wasn't built on any of them. Though it had been years since this location was a particularly important manufacturing plant—or even the main one, Morgan Stark having moved most of Stark Industries assembly overseas—most of the administration for the Stark financial empire was still located here. Despite the fact that the corporation had been deprived of its guiding genius with Anthony Stark's death a decade earlier, Stark Industries continued to hold thousands of lucrative patents, and a number of top-secret industrial processes too confidential even to patent.

That was why she'd come.

It's too bad my telepathy is so short range, Jean Grey thought as she made her clandestine way as close to the fence as she dared. *If I had more range, I could do this from a hotel room in Montauk and avoid all this mess.*

But the fact of the matter was that telepaths were in short supply in the competitive world of industrial espionage, so as she sent her mind out to tap the minds of others and began to speak her findings quietly into the small tape-recorder she carried, she reflected that this truly was the best of all possible worlds.

The helicopter that hung motionless in the sky over the mansion on Greymalkin Lane was the same one that had been following David Ferris all morning. It was stealth configured, sonic suppressed, and transparent to nearly every form of tracking and monitoring device that could be matched against it by the major players in the field, but in the end, technical superiority had come down to a simple matter of looking out the window and keeping in radio contact with the chase car below.

Sometimes the old-fashioned methods worked the best.

Ashton and Keithley were the sort of faceless professionals who populated the field arms of an uncounted number of alphabet organizations from SHIELD to A.I.M. to SAFE. It didn't matter to them whether they were sent out to retrieve David Ferris or a quart of milk from the corner deli; they did what they were assigned, collected their security clearances, and, if they were lucky, their pensions.

As Egan and Gilman would not.

Ashton and Keithley's first warning of trouble had been the mirror flash of light that zeroed every bean counter in the bird. They didn't see what happened to the chase car, but when the light was gone, it was easy to see that the car below had been crushed like a paper cup and sunk into the roadway.

"Did they use the lance?"

"Do I look like a mind reader, Ash?" his partner said.

Once the sensors started mapping again, TechInt told them there was no one left alive below. Their quarry was gone, but, flying a standard search configuration, they found Ferris again without trouble—rather too easily, in fact.

"Who's that guy with the wings?"

"Wait one . . . congratulations, Mr. Ashton," Keithley drawled. Like his partner, Keithley wore a dark suit and dark glasses, his only concession to individuality being the silver gargoyle earring dangling from his left earlobe. "You've just won yourself your very own Archangel. Known to be affiliated with both X-Factor and the X-Men, the database says; also known to operate solo."

"You mean there's more of them," Ashton said resignedly.

"Look down there, off to the right," Keithley said helpfully. "One, two, three more that I can see. We're blown."

"Time to phone home."

A shielded zip-squeal transmission to base, and a few moments later the surviving members of Black Team 51 had their new orders.

"It's over. Shut him down."

Slowly the blurring of possibility faded, leaving Phoenix alone in her own mind once more. And with the lessening of that psychic din, the sound of other minds that was a normal part of Jean Grey's daily existence became audible once more.

The sense of deadly purpose from the craft hovering above her was unmistakable.

She looked upward through the trees, and instinctively stepped away from David Ferris. When she used her powers against the helicopter, she didn't want him fried by the backlash.

"Shut him down." She shook her head at the weird doubling effect of hearing the words and hearing someone hear them. Where were Scott and the others?

Then the helicopter fired, and she had her answer.

The bolt was as instantaneous as light and as colorless as air: a carbon-dioxide laser, enabled for only one shot. Not really that powerful—it wouldn't even have slowed Rogue down—but powerful enough. There wasn't even time for a scream.

As an X-Man, Phoenix had seen death too many times to count, but murder never lost its power to horrify her with its very casualness. At the same moment that the laser pulse reduced David Ferris and all his spectrum of possibility to a smear of greasy ash, Phoenix launched herself skyward. Intent on the copter and its cargo, she barely registered the reappearance of the other X-Men or the reestablishment of the psychic rapport that allowed her to brief them in the space of a heartbeat on what she'd gleaned from David Ferris's mind.

It seemed wrong that it was still afternoon, still summer. To live so many different lives should have taken more time than this. But that didn't matter now. She was nearly there.

The skin of the helicopter was so close that her outstretched fingertips almost skimmed it, and Iceman and Archangel were only a second or so behind her. She'd tear the helicopter apart; they could catch the passengers. A maneuver the teams had rehearsed a thousand times in every possible combination of heroes.

But Ashton and Keithley—and their faceless masters— had other ideas, and the black budget toys to implement them.

The ultrasonic whine of the warp-gate enabling skirled up past the range that bats and dogs could hear, crossed the threshold of pain, and vanished into the hydrogen song of space. The skin of the black copter began to crackle with heat as its fusion generator ran flat-out, powering up for Jump. The amount of energy that had to be wasted into the environment when space-time was folded made the warp-gate of very little use except as a last resort.

Or a weapon.

She felt the radiant heat of the helicopter's skin on her hands and face, and intuition deep as instinct made Phoenix recoil. *It's a trap!* she cried mentally, just as the chase copter gave up its local space-time referents in an incandescent pulse of energy.

The shock wave gathered Phoenix into its superheated embrace and flung her backward. Protected from physical harm by her telekinesis, she nonetheless crashed through Bobby's already-melting ice bridge, sending him flying as well. Disoriented, she couldn't see where her teammates were, or even be sure in which direction the ground lay.

But Phoenix had shielded Archangel from the brunt of the explosion. With less than five seconds to intercept both his teammates before they hit the ground, Warren spread his wings wide, angling each pinion for maximum drag as he surfed the wave of sweltering air, and reached out to snatch Iceman's falling body out of the sky.

One.

Reaching out with the blind instinct of a seasoned aerialist, Bobby grabbed Warren's reaching hand.

Two.

Muscles and wings both creaked with the strain of absorbing the momentum of Bobby's helpless plunge, and in a moment more both men would fall.

But the air was Archangel's element.

Three.

"Heads up, Hank—catch!" he shouted. Using Bobby's own momentum, Archangel made his own body a fulcrum to swing his teammate over and down into the Beast's waiting arms.

Four.

Converting the braking maneuver into a forward glide, he slid forward with a raptor's casual grace to intercept Phoenix's falling body less than a dozen feet above the ground, carrying her safely to earth.

Five.

Down and safe.

"It's *wonderful* to have wings," Archangel said fervently. He straightened out of his landing crouch, setting Jean Grey lightly on her feet. She smiled at him and reached up to brush back a stray curl of blond hair from his forehead.

"I know," she said gently.

"How come I end up with you and Warren gets the girl?" Iceman complained to the Beast.

"Because, Robert m'lad, some things never change," Henry McCoy said absently. He set Iceman down and stepped back, staring skyward with a frown and absently brushing melting frost from his coat. He looked toward Cyclops, brows raised in puzzlement.

Scott Summers glanced at his watch. It was a quarter after three; less than five minutes had elapsed since Archangel had gone to investigate a peculiar noise.

And then. . .

And then *what?*

Cyclops looked around, but as far as he could see and hear, the threat was over. He allowed himself to relax slightly; Bobby and the others were all right. None of his team killed—*this time*, the ever-present fear reminded him—no one captured, no one hurt. As fights went, that was the best the X-Men could expect these days. The only definite casualty of the engagement was one might-be innocent man, the so-called Wheel of Fortune.

The faint wail of a siren in the distance warned that the alarms and excursions at the mansion on Greymalkin Lane hadn't gone unremarked by the citizens of Salem Center.

"Just another Pleasant Valley Sunday," Archangel said derisively. "Business as usual for the X-Men, the Hard-Luck Harrys of the super hero trade."

Scott Summers glanced toward the edge of the trees,

where the only evidence that anything had happened at all was one splintered tree and a charred spot on the ground.

No. Not the only evidence, Scott corrected himself. With a profound sense of unreality, he stared at the swimming pool, now located inexplicably at the foot of the terrace. The water was liquid—had Bobby really fallen into it, or had that been some bizarre sort of hallucination? He shook his head in bafflement.

"Come on, team, let's take this inside before the authorities come looking." He turned his back on the unaccountable swimming pool and started up the steps. The others followed as he opened the French doors and went into the house.

The welcoming quiet of the mansion's interior told Scott that any alarms triggered by the intruder hadn't disturbed the mansion's other inhabitants. The flash had been visible for miles, though, which meant he'd better have some kind of an explanation ready for any of the teams that were heading home because of it.

"What the hell *was* that?" Bobby Drake demanded indignantly, breaking into Scott's thoughts. "Another nutty government agency? A crazed multinational? Girl Scouts?"

"We'll probably never know," Cyclops answered. "Go and change, Bobby," he added out of habit.

"Not if we're lucky," Iceman muttered under his breath. He headed for the stairs to find his room and a change of clothes.

The other four looked at each other.

"It's a strange world," Archangel said finally. The words sounded hollow even as he spoke them.

"Maybe," the Beast answered, as if Warren had said more than he had, "but it's a wonderful life."

GIFT OF THE SILVER FOX

Ashley McConnell

Illustration by Gary Frank

o far enough north and the roads run out.

Go far enough north and you get to a place where it doesn't know it's springtime.

Here the snow still lies thick on the ground, and the sun's up only an hour a day, if you can call that thin piece of disk "up." The Northern Lights paint the sky all the time, shimmerin' veils of red and green and blue, so even the long night gets bright as day. The mountains are high and grand, the tundra stretches on forever and ever and ever. Ain't nothin' out here but me an' the wolves, caribou and hare, ptarmigan, eagles, bear. . . .

Come to think of it, it's downright crowded.

And crowded not just with life, but memories. I've got a lot of those, tied in to this part of the world.

I wonder sometimes why I came. To find something, I think, but I'm not sure what; something important, maybe. It's not like I can get away from anything up here. No matter where I go, I'm still Wolverine; still mutant, still a killer.

Maybe that's why. Up here, I fit right in, claws and all. The claws just mean I fit on the predator side o' the scale, and I can take care of business just as well as any polar bear. I don't have to worry about anything except eating and sleeping and staying warm. Real basic stuff, living and dying, right along with the rest of the predators and prey, wolves, ptarmigan, foxes . . .

Been tracking one o' those for a while now, or maybe she's been tracking me. Just curiosity, both sides. She's a pretty little vixen, beautiful silvery white fur. Couldn't even see her against the snow, 'cept those bright wise eyes and little black nose. And black on the tip of her tail, too. They give her away.

She showed up looking for a meal, picking up leftovers from an old caribou cow I'd taken down. She was careful, real careful, but she's in pup and the hunting hasn't been too good lately. I spotted her staring at me, one paw curled up against her chest, ready to run. But the caribou was still warm, steaming up into the icy air, and I could see her nose twitching at the good smell of blood. My smell, too. She might not ever have seen a human being before, and my smell'd be strange, and dangerous.

Not that I'm much of a human being.

I stepped back, away from the kill, inviting her to eat her fill before the wolves showed up. We both heard the howls, far away, as they caught the scent. That cow was going to feed a lot of us over the next couple of days.

She waited until I was far enough away for her to feel almost safe—maybe a dozen yards—and then dove in, almost disappearing into the body cavity, getting her coat matted and red. I was almost sorry I'd already taken the liver and heart, but I was hungry too, and I'd done all the work, after all. I picked up snow and started cleaning up. Hate doing it that way—the damn stuff's *cold*—but I hate dried blood in my hair more, and the stink of death. Mutant healing factor takes care of frostbite. Good thing too—I don't have a pelt quite as thick as the little one's.

The howls were coming closer. I glanced over at the carcass; the vixen had slowed down a little, was lookin' up between bites now. Hungry as she was, she didn't eat much. I wanted to take some steaks before the rest got there, but I could afford to let her finish. This time of year, mostly she'd be living off mice, and they're hard to find under six feet of snow. A meal like this one . . . well, animals didn't have Christmas up here, but it was close enough.

She pulled herself out and looked at me.

"Well, whaddaya waitin' for?" I asked. She jumped a yard away at the sound of my voice, then stopped again and watched me, tryin' to figure me out. I hoped she was havin' better luck than I was.

"Better get home," I advised her. "They'll look at you and think you're just another snack."

The howls were real close now, and she glanced in their direction. Whether she understood the words or not, she knew what I said was true. In less than the blink of an eye she was over a hummock of snow and gone, heading for her den.

I grinned and went back to the caribou. I didn't need a knife to get what I wanted—the claws took care of it just fine. There wasn't going to be much left of the hide, but I wasn't hunting for hides, and the scavengers would eat that too.

I took forty pounds of tough caribou flank and shoulder, and left the rest for the pack circling around at a distance. We traded respectful growls—I didn't want to mess with a whole pack, particularly, and they sure knew better than to mess with me—and I headed back for my camp, for fire and clothes and something almost civilized. I'd eat well for a couple of days, make jerky, keep wandering. I hadn't found what I was looking for yet, and every few hours the Lights bloomed across the sky, mocking me, telling me I better find it soon or lose more than I ever wanted to. Always assumin' I haven't done *that* already.

Two days later I went back to the kill to see what was what. The sky was dark for once, heavy clouds sayin' the Arctic wasn't through with winter yet, pilin' up, gettin' ready to dump another load of the white stuff. I guess I was hopin' the fox had had another chance at a meal before it hit.

The wild had been busy—there were cracked red bones scattered around rucked-up snow, the big bones not even a wolf's jaws could devour, and a couple of ribs sticking up, still attached to the spine. That was all; not even the skull was left of what had been, two days before, a wise and wary and beautiful animal. The spoor showed the wolves had done most of it, though I found the brushed-up snow from an owl's landing, and the vixen had come back. Hadn't got anything this time, though—the trail showed where she'd come up, stopped, then run like hell from something bigger and hungrier than she was.

I backtracked her a ways. Must have been an owl or an eagle; no tracks of pursuit 'cept mine. But no signs of struggle in the snow, either, and her spoor led across tundra to a little stream that later on in the year would turn into a whole river with the melting of the snow. I crunched on, curious to see if I could find her den.

I'd just about spotted it—a nearly invisible hole in the side of a ravine, just above where the water would top out— when I heard something thrashing around, and the sound of somebody else's snowshoes. I followed the racket around the side of the hill, movin' with the wind, to see the little vixen getting herself untangled from a trap and held up in the air, just about to get her throat cut by a knife held by somebody who was so wrapped up in a parka I couldn't tell *what* it was, except human. Whoever it was had laid a gun down careful in the snow nearby.

"*No!*" I yelled. The trapper spun around—never a good idea when you're wearin' snowshoes—and dropped the struggling animal. The vixen scurried off, limping, leaving red marks where her foot'd been caught. It was broken, probably. Only mercy was, she couldn't have been in the trap very long, and she'd eaten real well recently. She might heal by the time she littered, and before she starved.

The trapper'd got balance back, snatched up the rifle. Wasn't pointing it at me, though. Smart move, though the guy couldn't know just how smart, o'course. Couldn't really see the face: the parka hood was pulled up, had a thick rim of wolverine fur around the edge so he could just see out. Wolverine fur doesn't frost up from the moisture on your breath like other kinds do. That's just one of the ways we're different from the usual, me an' the big weasels.

"What the hell d'you think you're doin'?" The voice was muffled, angry. Rightfully so, I guess, though I hate seein' things caught in traps. The barrel was still pointin' down, though, so there was a chance he was sensible—not going to try to kill a man over one fox pelt late in the season. I've seen some who were that crazy.

"She wasn't worth it," I said. "An' I been followin' her—"

"What are you, some kind of nature freak?" He reached up and pulled back the hood, taking off the ice glasses to get a better look at me.

Gave me a better look at the trapper, too. Wasn't a man at all, but a woman. Young one, too, maybe thirty, thirty-five—hard to tell, the little lines around her eyes might be from starin' over the long distances, or from laughin'. The wind shifted, and I got the scent of her, finally, sorted out from the furs she wore, the smell of metal from the gun and blood from the fox.

"Look, buddy, this is my trap line. You're trespassing."

I raised my hands, palms open. "Hey, no argument. I guess I just got caught by s'prise. Didn't think anybody'd bother to trap fox in spring. 'Sides, she's gonna litter soon."

The woman looked kinda embarrassed. "Yeah, well. It's been a bad season." She picked up the trap, looked at the blood and the scrap of fur caught in it. "Barely even had this one. She'd have pulled out of it if I'd been half an hour later. Probably didn't even break her leg."

Good, I thought.

"I hate these damned things anyway," she said. "I'd like to get some of the other kind, but they're expensive." Instead of re-setting the trap, she shrugged out of her backpack and stuck it inside, alongside a bunch of others. When she was done, she looked up at me. "What're you doing out here, anyway? I haven't seen another human being for eight months."

I lifted one shoulder, let it drop. "Wanderin'."

She gave me a searching look, like she saw more than just a short guy with maybe too many muscles and a whole lot of hair—like she saw a person inside, and was considerin' what she thought about that. Her look reminded me of somebody—one of those somebodies I didn't much want to think about. I nodded and turned to go my way, when she said, "I got some preserves, back at my cabin. Storm's coming, too. You might want to get in out of it."

I stopped in mid-stride. I could wait out a storm just fine, den up like any predator would, but she didn't know that. It was a generous offer. Besides, it'd been six weeks since I'd tasted anything sweet, and I'll admit my mouth watered. "Peach?"

"Strawberry."

"Even better."

She grinned. Had a nice smile. "Let's go, then."

I grinned back, then had a thought. "Give me a second —got to take care of some business."

She nodded, blushed a little and turned away while I stepped discreet-like out of sight.

The hole in the side of the ravine was the den, right enough. I could smell her, deep inside, scared and hurt and with pups comin', growlin' real soft. Still had a lot of fight left in her. Wasn't ready to give up, not by a long shot— made me proud of her. I stopped some way away, marked out a margin for her to keep the wolves away from the smell of blood, and divided up the jerky I'd spent two days dryin' and slung half up so it landed just outside the entrance. That'd be more than enough to keep her goin' for a while, and still left me with a decent contribution to dinner.

The trapper was waiting, bundled up again, gettin' a little impatient to get goin'. Couldn't blame her; the wind was pickin' up and the clouds were just about close enough to touch, and little flakes of snow were spittin' out of the sky. We set out at a pretty good clip, trying to beat the weather, following the stream bed south.

I was kinda disappointed, in a way. Seemed like you couldn't get away from people anywhere these days. Sure, I'd gone nearly five weeks without coming closer to another human being than the contrails streaking the sky, flyin' the transpolar route, but I wasn't quite sure I was ready yet. I still had some things to work out.

But I hadn't made much progress yet, and this'd be different, anyway. So I followed. She knew her way, I had to give her credit. It's easy to get lost up here. No trees, and it looks flat but it isn't really. The stream was our only guide, and sometimes it just flat disappeared. Couple of times she stopped to get her bearings, but in an hour and a half we heard barking.

Came around one last hill and there it was, neat little log cabin, a cache set up high where bears couldn't get at it and solid so they couldn't knock it down, drying and tanning shed with skins staked out. Not too many of them; either she'd bundled up her winter's take already, or it really had been a bad season.

There was a generator shed too, stinking of oil, with a good-sized tank nearby, an outhouse a decent distance away with a lost-man line going from the front door of the cabin to the generator and then to the outhouse door. But she wasn't just burning oil—she'd managed to get a decent load of wood for the winter; I could tell from the space cleared beside the cabin. She must have spent most of the summer bringing it in from where the woods started, fifteen or twenty miles south. This time of year, she was getting down to her last couple of cords.

Her team was staked out around the cabin, seven mean-lookin' brutes that looked mostly wolf. They didn't like the smell of me and made sure I knew it. I almost snarled back at them, but the woman was telling me not to worry, they'd settle down soon. I could've told her better, but that would have taken some explaining I wasn't ready for. She made sure I could see she could control the dogs. Don't know if I was supposed to be impressed or maybe reassured; I could already see she knew what she was doing. She'd have to, living up here all alone.

She was alone, too, except for the dogs. The inside of the cabin was just as neat, one room with a stone fireplace and hearth at either end, one for warmth and one for cooking, with an oven and stove, vented into the chimney, at one end. No refrigerator, o' course. Hardly needed one up here. There was a sink of sorts, a stack of buckets, and a tub big enough to sit in. She must have water stored somewhere.

The fireplace at that end of the room had a banked fire, and there was a pot on the grill set over it, bubbling, filling the place with a smell that made my mouth water and almost overcame the other scents of hot wax, oil, burned wood, woman, baking. The other side of the room had a rope-sprung bed piled deep under furs and a cabinet and chest for clothing.

A wooden table with four chairs took up the middle of the room. One wall was all shelves, floor to ceiling, with all kinds of supplies, sacks of flour and beans, jars and cans, one shelf full of books. The wall, on the door side, had pegs for guns, and a guitar hanging up ready. Things were stored away proper.

There were a couple of oil lamps, and an electric ceiling light, and a lot of candles scattered around. She had a window, too, covered with glass and oiled paper, but by that time it was so late, it didn't make any difference. I could hear the wind outside and, far away, wolves, but in here there wasn't any wind at all. When she lit the lamps, the place glowed golden. I liked it right away.

She thumped down her backpack with its load of traps into a corner, peeled out of her parka with a sigh, and fluffed out her hair—medium length, dirty blonde, a mass of natural curls that hadn't seen a big-city stylist in a real long time. She was wearing a leather tunic that hung down to her knees, leggings of leather too, laced up snug. It wasn't the kind of stuff you could find in a store.

I was glad, and kinda amused, to see that she set aside her gun with a whole lot more respect than she did her pack, and made sure it was handy. She didn't look my way to make sure I saw; she didn't have to. The woman wasn't a complete fool, invitin' a stranger into her home in the middle of nowhere. Between the gun and the dogs, she probably felt pretty safe. Well, I sure wasn't no threat to her, though she didn't know that. She must have liked what she saw, in that long look.

I stripped off my own parka, watched where she hung hers up on a peg, and put mine next to it. I'd forgotten what it was like to be really warm; the inside of the cabin was toasty. I let go a long breath, savoring it.

She turned at the sound, as if she'd almost forgot I was there. I could see how that could be, if she'd been by herself for most of a year.

"My name's Gayle," she said, sticking her hand out the way somebody does when they're shy and don't quite know what else to do. She had a firm grip. I shook the hand quickly and let it go; no problem.

"Logan," I said in return. "Gotta thank you. Sounds

like a bad one out there tonight." The wind was really howling now.

She smiled and turned to stoking up the fire under the pot. I was right; those lines around her eyes were from laughter, not age. She might have a little gray in with the blonde, but not much. "Last big storm of the season, I hope."

"Ice ought to break on that stream anytime now," I agreed. I indicated my pack, still sitting on the floor. "I didn't come empty handed—got some caribou, just dried, if you'd like some."

She raised an eyebrow, looking at what wasn't there. "Caribou? How'd you lose your gun?"

I wasn't gonna tell her I didn't need a gun when I hunted. "Oh, things happen." I hoped it was vague enough that she wouldn't push it, and it was. She had good manners. I pulled the pack out, unwrapped it. "More'n enough here for two." *Three,* I thought, remembering the vixen. I hoped the little fox was okay. I'd prob'ly never know. I'd done as best I could for her, and now she was better off than she would've been if I hadn't come along; had no reason to feel guilty. Hell, if it hadn't been for me, she'd be a pelt pegged out for scraping right now, that lovely silver fur limp and dead.

"It looks good," she said, putting the pack on the table and unwrapping it. She separated out a fair share, checked it over careful.

"It was a healthy cow," I assured her. "I got lucky."

Gayle nodded and added the meat to the pot. It wouldn't flavor up like it would've if it were fresh, maybe, but it wouldn't be bad either. Sure enough, the smell from the stove was changing already, and I had to swallow back saliva. The woman sat down and started taking off her boots, looked up at me, and pointed with her chin at another chair. "Rest your hands and face," she said. "I'll set up a bed for you on the floor tonight, if you don't mind an air mattress."

I chuckled. Mind? I'd been sleeping on cold ground for too long. I liked the way she set the rules, too, real clear but without a heavy hand. This might not be what I'd been planning when I came up north, but it wasn't so bad. "Don't mind at all. I'm grateful."

It felt good to get out of that top layer, down to jeans and a red flannel shirt and socks. I'd been out of more than that quite a bit, of course, but sure hadn't been *warm*. Gayle fussed around with food, putting more on here and there until I protested that she was doing too much. The dishes didn't match, but they held enough, the stew thick with potatoes and meat, canned green beans, even bread still warm from that morning's baking, spread thick with the promised strawberry preserves. There was only water to drink, though she offered to mix it with some powder or other for flavor; I took it straight, and she chuckled.

I ate like a man starving, but only because she kept piling it on, watching me and giggling. When I tried to tell her no, I was cutting too deep into her supplies, she just laughed and said there was enough and more to last her to the thaw, and she was enjoying the sight of it.

After, while she was cleaning up, we talked a little, trying out the sound of our own voices.

"Not usual to see a woman on her own up here," I said. She could take that up or not, as she wished.

Apparently she didn't mind too much. "I suppose it isn't. We emigrated from Alaska ten years ago. My husband and I built this place. He died three years ago. Heart attack."

"Sorry to hear it." I wanted a cigar in the worst way; it would've made the evening perfect. I hadn't felt so relaxed in weeks, even though I never quit watching for trouble. Doubted I *could* quit, after all these years. But this—this place was peaceful. Sitting here, I felt almost civilized. Almost human.

She wasn't laughing for a minute—took a deep breath and let it go and then smiled again. "David was a good man. I buried him here; I couldn't leave and go back to the cities. This is our place. I go down to Gensitka every year to sell furs and buy supplies, and the bush pilots stop by every once in awhile to check on me. This year has been bad for that, though. I can talk to them on the radio if I need to. So I'm not really alone."

She was warning me again, not that it would have done her a bit of good, and askin', too. She was entitled to something, for the hospitality. I'd say what I could.

"I'm Canadian," I told her. "Been knockin' around the world awhile." Well, that was certainly true. "But I miss the wild. Things get too complicated, I come back, roam around getting the kinks out." And this place was sure doing it, though not, maybe, in the way I'd thought when I first came up here.

"What kind of complicated?" she asked, too casual.

I smiled. "I'm not on anybody's wanted list, if that's what you're wondering," I said. Not quite true, maybe—damn, I was going to have to quit that, testing every statement. It was a leftover habit from one of the people I was trying to figure out, or forget. "I'm retired military." Subject to recall and remobilization, unfortunately.

She nodded, accepting. She was an accepting kind of woman. Maybe a place like this, miles from the madding crowd, was the safest place for her. Kinda funny, that: the most civilized place was the one with the fewest people. Just reinforces my opinion of most people, really.

We talked some time longer, played a couple of hands of gin rummy, then she set up the air mattress and a healthy pile of furs. Had to get back into parka and boots again— at least she did; the cold wouldn't have bothered me none, but it would've taken too long to explain that—for our respective trips to the outhouse. The lost-man line came in handy; snow was coming down like a northern version of forty days and forty nights, and there wasn't no Ark in sight.

By the time she came back from her turn, I was rolled up in fur, staring into the dying fire. She made quiet noises, moving around to get ready for bed, and then the place got real quiet except for the sound of breathing and the crackle of the fire. Finally my eyes closed, and I slept.

It was Jubilee, again. She was crying, hurting, doubled over, and all around her the Northern Lights were rippling, flowing. I was trying to reach her, but my claws were out, and I couldn't make them retract; every time I touched her I hurt her worse. After a while she looked up to me and flinched away at the sight of me. But I couldn't quit trying, couldn't stop clawing. She was bleeding all over, and I was the cause.

The dream changed. It was Mariko, asking, begging for a *coup de grâce*. And I gave it to her, gave her peace and freedom from pain, but my hands were covered with her blood and it wouldn't go away.

Then Storm. Rogue. Psylocke. All of them, and every time I reached out, my claws came away bleeding.

And not just the women; the men too. I couldn't fight next to any of them without turning on them. I cut them all down, Cyke, Bishop, Gambit, Beast, Archangel. Not just fighting; in my dream, I took out the Cajun over a poker game, and his cards were nothin'. Even Xavier himself wasn't safe. No one was safe with me.

I woke up, and it took a minute to realize where I was. The fire had died down, and it was beginning to get chilly, the cold air freezing the sweat on my skin. I got up, quiet-like, and looked out the window, bending the oiled paper back.

There wasn't much to see. Snow had piled up on the windowsill, and it was still comin' down. If I'd been out there, denned up somewhere, I'd have rolled right over and gone back to sleep till spring thaw. Dreams or no dreams. Animals dreamed of killin', after all.

There was a sound behind me—a good thing, it gave me warning. When she touched my shoulder, I didn't turn around and gut her.

"Logan?"

It had been a mistake after all, coming here.

"You were dreaming—nightmares—can I help?"

I shook my head, not looking at her. "No. Nothin' can help."

"I can help," she whispered. "I can."

Saliva was filling my mouth again. Swallowing, I shook my head.

"Then maybe you can help me." I could feel her lips on my shoulder. "It's awful cold, Logan. Warm me."

"I can't," I said, barely recognizing my own voice. But then she touched me, and my own body made a liar out of me. I couldn't breathe.

"I don't know you," I managed to say. "You don't know me."

"It's better that way," she said, and moved around between me and the window. "I'm not looking for anything but comfort. Sounds like you could use a little comforting too." Leaning forward, she kissed me, very lightly, on the lips.

I felt as if I were a man made of stone, stone with a molten core beginning to bubble deep inside. I couldn't kiss her back, but couldn't push her away either. She chose to take it as encouragement—I didn't encourage her, I didn't. She slid her hand down my face, my neck, began unbuttoning the flannel shirt, placed the palm of her hand against my chest, looked into my eyes.

And I looked into hers, and saw no tears, no fear, only kindness and knowledge. She knew what she was asking for.

She knew. She looked inside my soul, and she wasn't afraid.

When I woke again, it was to the smell of flapjacks on the griddle. My body ached in a way I hadn't felt for a long time. Over by the stove, Gayle had set up the tub, and stockpots piled high with snow were melting on the hot surface. As I watched, she manhandled another pot off the stove and poured the contents, steaming, into the tub. She was wearing jeans again, and her boots, and a plaid flannel shirt.

"They're done," I said.

She gave me a quick smile and flipped the pancakes over, took the empty pot to the door, and stepped outside for a moment. When she came back, it was filled with already melting snow.

"Let me help you with that."

Giving me a droll look, she pointed to the pots on the stove. "Trade you a decent breakfast for an indecent bath."

"I've heard worse offers."

The snow came from the path along the lost-man line, making it easier to move around outside and providing bathwater at the same time. I fed the dogs while I was at it, settling the matter of just who was the toughest animal around in short order. The lead dog backed off fast enough, then took it out on the next dog down so he wouldn't lose any more status than he had to.

Breakfast was good. The baths were better. Big as it was, it would only take one of us at a time, but it helps to have somebody around to add hot water when it's needed.

Afterward we emptied and filled the tub again, a process that took a while, and then it was my turn. Being clean all the way to my toes felt as wonderful as anything else that day, even Gayle kneading at my shoulders till I was dozing in the hot water. By the time the water had cooled and it was time to wrestle the tub out the door and empty it again, I had to admit I was feeling pretty good.

The snow had stopped around noon. There wasn't no point in my leaving then, with only a couple of hours of daylight left. So I stayed the night through, only this time there wasn't any question about the air mattress.

Next morning, I woke up late again. I didn't have to say

anything as I got dressed; Gayle knew. She watched me dress and didn't say anything until I sat on the edge of the bed to pull on my boots.

"Thanks for the help with the tub, Logan," she said. It sounded real inconsequential, but something in her tone made me stop and look at her. "I can never get that thing out the door by myself. Have to use the pots to pour out the water."

"Glad to be able to help." I smiled back at her—couldn't help it. That was when I realized I'd finally slept the night through, without dreams.

Without dreams. Without fear. Gayle had accepted me completely. As another human being. Not as Wolverine, not as a mutant; as a man.

And I hadn't hurt her. She was smiling at me over the now-empty tub.

"I don't know that I'll ever be back to do it again, though." Fair's fair; I had to say it out loud. There was more than one way of hurting someone. I didn't want to spoil it now.

"I know." There wasn't any anger or hurt in it. Maybe some regret—or maybe I'm just flatterin' myself. Man does that, sometimes. "I'm glad you were here. More than you know."

"I could say the same thing, darlin'." I finished pulling on my boots, got up, and reached for my parka and pack. I could whip ten times my weight in polar bears on a bad day—today, well, there wasn't anything in the northland could stand in my way. Pausing by the door, I looked back at her, still huddled in the furs, smiling at me. "Would you do me one favor, though?"

"I could probably manage that." She was still smiling, the kind of smile a woman gets when she's contented. She'd earned those little lines around her eyes, far as I was concerned.

"That little silver fox I found you with? Could you let her and her cubs be? I'd kinda like to think she's all right, out there."

She chuckled, snuggling the furs up to her chin. "Yeah, Logan, I could do that for you. It's little enough for what you've done for me."

One more look, that was all. "Good-bye, Gayle. Thank you."

"Thank *you*."

I carried with me the memory of her smile. It kept me warm for a long time, traveling under the Northern Lights.

That was all. I stepped out again, heading north, into the Lights, flowing and glowing across the sky. Into the cold.

Only this time I carried with me a spark I'd nearly forgotten I had, and a new memory about mercy and comfort and laughter, with no one getting hurt, no one being betrayed.

It *was* possible . . . if I could only figure out how to get past the rest of it.

Maybe that was possible, too.

STILLBORN IN THE MIST

Dean Wesley Smith

Illustration by Ralph Reese

he swirling mist off the Mississippi gripped the narrow streets of the French Quarter in a deadly blanket of silence as her body was dumped out onto the black, damp cobblestone like so much garbage. The last of her blood dripped from the slash across her neck, adding only slightly to the bloodstain on her white prom dress.

She rolled once, ending up against the shallow curb, eyes open, staring unseeing up at the moss- and vine-covered buildings around her.

"Hurry," a hoarse whisper said from the driver's seat of the black insides of the dented old Caddie.

"Done," another voice from the black interior said. "Go."

The rear door on the passenger side of the old car slammed, sending a hollow echo down the narrow street. Then, tires spinning on the damp surface, the car fishtailed forward, disappearing into the mist like a fleeing ghost, leaving behind only the echo of its passing.

The mist swirled in the faint light over the young woman, closing down over her white face and dress as if trying to protect her from being seen in the night. Only the blue orchid corsage still pinned to her new dress marked her location like a flower on a grave.

Two blocks away Remy LeBeau walked almost aimlessly through the mist, not seeming even to notice the pre-dawn night around him. His long brown raincoat was pulled tight across his chest, the collar up as if protecting his neck from unseen rain. A black headband held the long, unruly brown hair out of his face. A lit cigarette drooped from his lips, the orange glow of the ember giving his face sharp, deep shadows. In his left hand he carried a long staff, using it almost as a cane.

His eyes seemed blank, as if he were walking the street at a different time. In a sense, he was doing just that. He was living the time of his youth. The time of his marriage. The time of his banishment from this, his hometown.

The memories of those days swirled around him, mixing with the mist, filling the streets and buildings with his past life. This was his first night back in New Orleans in a very long while, and he wasn't sure why he was even here now. Somehow, he just knew he was needed here. Over the years he had learned to trust that feeling.

So now he walked in the mist through the streets of the Quarter in the hours just before sunrise, the only time *le vieux carré* ever was truly quiet, thinking of the past, of his life as it had been, and paying very little attention to the present.

Suddenly he stopped and glanced around. A few blocks to his right a group of drunk tourists on Bourbon Street laughed too loudly, sending echoes of their party through the sleeping Quarter. Otherwise, the streets were empty.

Yet suddenly the present called to him, pulling him from his memories of his wife and his family. He didn't know how, exactly, but he knew something was happening.

He turned away from the tourists and toward the edge of the quarter where it was bordered by the projects. At a fast run he followed his instincts, his raincoat flapping behind him like wings.

It was only moments before he found her.

"Oh, no, *chère,*" he said, kneeling beside her.

He ignored the gash across her neck and gently picked

up her head, looking into her open, staring eyes. Again his memories took over and he went back to the moment he'd last seen those eyes, beaming from the radiant face of a sixteen-year-old girl standing beside her father while they waited to board a plane back to New Orleans.

Cornelia Hayward, daughter of Julian Hayward, the most powerful man in New Orleans, and one of the ten most powerful people in the country. Rumors were that he controlled the powers of the night, as well as the businesses of the day. Even the assassins' and the thieves' guilds didn't cross Hayward and he in turn left them alone. But Remy knew him and had helped him a number of times.

That day in the airport Remy had taken Cornelia's hand and kissed the back of it, and she had almost blushed. Her father had smiled and shaken Remy's hand. He had invited Remy to visit, even though he knew Remy was an outlaw in his own hometown.

Remy would never have guessed he had been drawn back here because of Cornelia.

As if picking up a rag doll, he lifted Cornelia's thin young body from the damp street. Her head started to roll back, exposing the huge slash across her neck, and he quickly braced her head against his arm, making her seem more like a lover passed out from too much drink.

He didn't know how, but some way he needed to get her to her father. Hayward owned a large home in the Garden District, near where Remy used to have a home. A home he had hoped to settle in with his wife. A home he lost when he lost his city.

"Put her down, LeBeau," a voice said from behind him.

He spun and again her head lolled back, showing the huge gash.

His hand under her quickly grasped the cards in his coat pocket and waited as a figure stepped from the shadows of a courtyard door.

Remy almost staggered back as the face of the intruder came into the faint light.

Julian Hayward stopped a few feet from Remy, never taking his gaze from the Cajun X-Man.

"Your daughter?" Remy said, lifting the light weight of Cornelia slightly.

"I know, son," Hayward said. "But you are not the prey we hoped to catch with this bait. Now put her down and step in here with me. I will explain."

"You killin' your own children, *homme*?"

Hayward laughed. "Corey, honey. Reassure the poor man."

Suddenly in Remy's arms the girl's body moved. It so startled him, he almost dropped her.

Somehow she lifted her head, closing the huge gash across her neck as she moved. "Thanks for caring," she said in a whisper. "You are a dear and I would enjoy staying in your arms, but I can't. Now please put me down."

Then her head rolled back and she was again the body of a dead girl. No pulse, no blood, no life. A huge gash sliced across her neck.

Remy stared at the now lifeless body in his arms, his mind not believing what he had just seen. Yet, it had happened. He glanced at Hayward and the father nodded, indicating that Remy should put her down.

Carefully, Remy placed the body of the young girl back in the gutter and stood.

"Now, quickly," Hayward said. "Come with me." He turned and moved back into the courtyard and the black shadows beyond.

Dazed, Remy followed through the courtyard door. There had been a number of times over the years in New Orleans when he knew someone he had once thought dead to be still alive. His wife, Belle, was one. But he had never had a corpse come to life in his arms. At least not until tonight.

And Hayward had used the term *bait?* His own daughter as bait? And what was he trying to catch with a dead girl? Who or what would *want* a dead girl?

Too many questions.

Remy, with only a glance at the body in the mist, stepped through the dark courtyard door and was instantly blinded by intense white light. One hand came up to shade his eyes while the other went inside his pocket for his cards. He had the ability to change the potential energy in an object to kinetic energy, creating an instant bomb.

Crouching, he blinked hard and fast, forcing his eyes to focus on his surroundings more quickly than natural.

There seemed to be no danger.

Slowly, he turned around. The door he'd stepped through was nothing more than a black archway. He couldn't see anything through it, let alone the cobblestone street and the girl's body that he knew was only a few feet away.

"Over here, LeBeau," Hayward's voice said.

Remy hesitated while glancing around. The huge room

was filled with thousands of computers and machines and at least fifty people, all wearing white lab coats. Only Hayward and Remy and the computers broke the stark whiteness of the room. Every person in the room seemed to be focused on their own task. No one paid him the slightest attention.

With one more glance at the blank door into the street, Remy moved over where Hayward stood behind a row of white lab coats sitting in front of computer screens. On the one directly in front of Hayward, Remy could see Cornelia's body in the street.

Other screens showed the road and the surrounding buildings. It was clearly a very sophisticated surveillance system, one Remy bet even Wolverine would have been interested in studying.

Remy was about to ask Hayward what in the hell was going on when a white-faced man in a white lab coat at the end of the row said, "I have contact from the east."

"Good," Hayward said.

Remy leaned forward as out of the corner of the screen a shadow moved. And then another and another.

"There are nine of them," another white-faced man in front of a screen said.

Suddenly, figures appeared out of the shadows around Cornelia, almost as mysteriously as Hayward had appeared. Remy had been raised in the thieves' guild, trained in not being seen. And he was impressed.

"Who are dey?" he asked.

Then he saw. They were children. The oldest didn't look more than sixteen; the youngest he guessed around ten. They were all dressed in black and moved smoothly, almost as if they were floating. But he knew they weren't. They just knew how to move silently and quickly.

They surrounded Cornelia's body and one of them picked her up, her stained white dress a stark contrast to their black bodysuits.

One of the older children motioned that they should go and almost as quickly as they had appeared, the children and Cornelia's body disappeared into the shadows.

Beside Remy, Hayward let out a deep breath, as if relieved. "They took her. Good."

"You wanted dis?" Remy asked.

Hayward nodded, glancing away from the screen and looking directly at Remy. "You look as if you could use a drink. And I know I do." He put a heavy hand on Remy's shoulder and turned him away from the monitor toward a door on the far side of the room. "I will explain. But only after a drink."

Hayward's private office looked nothing like his lab. Oak shelves filled with leather books covered two walls. Expensive paintings under spotlights dominated the other two. A large desk filled one corner, but Hayward directed Remy to the overstuffed couch and then asked him for his choice.

"Nothin' 'til I get a few answers."

Hayward nodded and punched a small button. A panel and picture slid back and a well-stocked bar slid forward. In silence he poured himself a Scotch and took a good portion of it straight away. Then he refilled his glass and turned to Remy.

"You almost destroyed my plan tonight, son."

"I was t'inkin' I was helpin', me."

Hayward laughed, then dropped down into a large chair that faced the couch. He took another sip of his Scotch and then sighed. "Remy, you remember the last time Cornelia and I saw you?"

"Airport."

Hayward nodded. "We were returning from the best specialists in the country. Cornelia had only two months to live at that point."

"What?" Remy almost stood, but instead moved to the edge of the couch.

"Nothing anyone could do. Hereditary illness, the same that killed her mother. I had always feared it would take my daughter, too, and it did."

Remy didn't know what to say, so he said nothing as Hayward again sipped his Scotch.

"I spent most of Cornelia's life working on a way to save her. When you last saw us, I had determined that I had failed. There was no cure. So I went the next step. I figured out a way to bring her back after she was dead."

"De Elixir o' Life?" Remy asked. For generations both the thieves' guild and the assassins' guild had fought over the Elixir of Life. It was the very reason Remy had been banned from his hometown.

Hayward laughed, dismissing Remy's question with a wave of his hand. "Not hardly. You and your family made sure that wasn't possible. Besides, there was too much baggage with that Elixir."

"Den how?"

Hayward laughed, but this time his laugh sounded hollow and strained, as if directed at his own personal demon.

"I mixed science with black magic," he said. "Simple, actually."

"Voodoo?" Remy asked, his stomach sinking at the thought of zombies.

"Not really," Hayward said. "I just studied the principles behind the voodoo and the zombie legends and applied science to them. By the time Cornelia died, I had the answer. I brought her back."

Remy nodded. So the young girl he'd picked up in the street had actually been dead. But somehow reanimated with life. Science or black magic, she was still a zombie. One of the walking dead.

Hayward downed the last of his Scotch and stood, moving over to the bar to make himself another. With his back to Remy he continued talking. "I can tell you don't understand. I loved my daughter more than anything. The thought of her dying was impossible for me even to consider."

"She still dead, *homme*," Remy said.

"Only technically," Hayward said, spinning around to face the X-Man.

Remy held the intense, blazing gaze of Hayward for a moment. The man was obsessed with this topic, that much was very clear. There seemed no point in arguing it. Inside Hayward knew his daughter was dead and that knowledge was eating at him like maggots in a coffin. And Remy knew that the children, once zombies, were monsters. They might look like the children they used to be, but they were just dead flesh walking. Nothing more.

Remy stood and stepped toward the door through which

they had entered. "So why slit her t'roat an' put her out, bait for de other child'n? What went wrong?"

"My formula was stolen," Hayward said. His shoulders sagged and he moved over and sat down heavily in his chair. "It was meant only for Cornelia. No one else."

"Who stole it?"

"A lab tech," Hayward said, almost laughing. "A nobody who is now dead and will remain that way."

"But dose childr'n out dere de walkin' dead."

Hayward sipped at his drink, as if deciding to go on or not. Then he asked, "You ever hear of the Arrington?"

Remy felt himself shudder at the mention of the name. Arrington was a combination gang and family. Their leader, a gentleman named Lang, claimed that the Arrington, under old deeds dating from before the War between the States, had title to most of the area where the newer sections of the city had been built. Years ago the courts had rejected the family claim. So the family and their friends, back before Remy was even born, had gone underground, working to retake what they claimed was theirs without much caring how, or who got killed. But for the last five years they had been fairly silent members of the New Orleans crime world.

"Yeah," Remy said, "I hear o' dem. I don' much like what I hear."

Hayward nodded, staring down into the golden liquid in his glass. "I agree. The stupid lab tech thought he could sell my formula to them. They killed him and took it before I could retrieve my property."

"So why children?"

"My formula only works on children or young adults."

Remy stood and began to pace, trying to give himself a

moment to think. He'd just had two run-ins with the Arrington, and both times people had been killed. There was
no telling what they'd do with the ability to raise dead children. But one thing for sure, they'd use the children to take
parts of the city back by force, parts they felt belonged to
them.

Remy stopped his pacing in front of Hayward. "What
exactly dey plannin'?"

Hayward looked suddenly tired, his eyes glazed over, his
mind a long distance away as he slowly shook his head. "I
don't know, but two weeks after they stole the serum, children started turning up missing. Lots of children, mostly
from the projects. I never meant for my work to kill children." He took a deep, shuddering breath and then, in a
very soft voice, as if he were only talking to himself, said, "I
just wanted to save my own daughter."

Now Remy understood even more. Not only were the
demons of his daughter eating at Hayward, but the deaths
of other children now rode his mind, smothering him slowly
but surely.

"So what's Cornelia doin'?"

Hayward seemed to shake himself and glance up at the
X-Man standing over him. "She's locating their operational
headquarters for us. I have a force ready to move in when
she's in place."

Remy knew where the Arrington were mainly headquar-
tered. It was a huge old building just outside the French
Quarter. At one time it had been a warehouse, and from
the outside it still looked that way. He'd been inside and
had no desire to return. But he said nothing.

Hayward stood. "I think it's time we go back to work, don't you?"

Without waiting for an answer, he moved through the door and into the white lab beyond. Remy followed. There was nothing else for him to do.

Twenty minutes later the signal came in.

"On the big screen," Hayward said, and on a nearby wall a map of the city suddenly appeared. After a moment a blinking light showed.

"That's not possible," one tech said. "That's outside our door."

"What?" Hayward said. He stared at the huge map for a moment and then made for the black arch leading into the street. But Remy was faster and he broke through and into the humid night air first, his hands on his cards, ready.

The mist still filled the dark street; again his eyes took a moment to adjust to the extreme difference in light. He moved against the building and crouched, letting all his senses cover the area while his eyes adjusted.

There was no one moving. Nothing.

Hayward blundered into the street, followed by two of his guards. It was then that Remy saw the head.

Cornelia's head.

It sat on the shallow curb, blank eyes staring at the doorway and her father.

Clamped in her teeth was a small golden button, most likely the bug Hayward had been using to track her.

Now she was truly dead. There would be no bringing her back this time. Not even the walking dead could continue when their heads were cut off. No magic was that powerful.

Hayward slumped to the sidewalk and picked up his daughter's head, cradling it against his chest as he sobbed.

There was nothing more Remy could do here. Hayward and his men were out of the picture, at least for the moment.

Remy had discovered why he'd been pulled back to New Orleans. Silently, he stepped back into the shadows and moved away. As with any good thief, no one saw him go.

The mist covered the old cotton warehouse district like a thick film. The biggest warehouse in the center loomed like a block in the fog, massive and very dangerous. The wood of the loading docks had decayed and rotted away. Someone long ago had boarded over the high windows on all the buildings. For the untrained eye, the warehouse district looked as if had been deserted for years, just another example of the decay of the city, standing amid many other deserted buildings.

But Remy's eye was not untrained. Through the cracks in the old wood he could see the reinforced steel and concrete walls of the main Arrington building. Hidden cameras covered every inch of area around the building. Invisible laser beam sensors crisscrossed the streets a block in both directions. Even a rat couldn't move in this area of abandoned buildings without being tracked.

But Remy had been trained in the thieves' guild, his skills honed as Gambit with the X-Men. He was much, much better at getting in somewhere unseen than any common rat.

Carefully, slowly, an inch at a time, he made his way along a wall, passing over and under laser beams while never moving fast enough to trigger a motion detector. He stayed in the shadows of the wall knowing that, to anyone watching a camera, he would be nothing more than shadow.

After leaving Hayward, he had considered just barging into the main building, fighting. That was more his style, more his recent training. But he didn't know exactly what was going on with the children and he couldn't take a chance of any of the live ones getting hurt until he knew.

It took him over an hour, but he finally made the rear door of the building immediately next to the Arrington headquarters. He knew of a tunnel leading from each of the neighboring buildings into the main one. It would be his best way in.

With an easy twist, he picked the complex lock of the door and slipped inside. The place smelled of mold and decay. It was the building closest to the river and farthest from the normal traffic patterns of the French Quarter and the main areas of New Orleans. It would be the least-used building for entering the main compound. He counted on that.

He crouched against the wall, waiting for his eyes to adjust. His senses told him instantly he was not alone. "So much for goin' in unannounced," he said softly to himself.

"Remy LeBeau," a voice said, echoing through the darkness. "Nice of you to come back to see me."

Remy stood, his hands in his pockets on his cards. The voice belonged to Lang, the fat, chipmunked-faced leader of the Arrington. But it had been broadcast. Lang would never risk himself in the open like this. Remy could see ten outlines in the dim light, all holding machine guns. Lang had sent his goons. But he had underestimated Remy by sending only ten.

"I'm so sorry, however," Lang's voice continued. "that we won't have a chance to chat."

Remy jumped, hard and fast, while at the same time sending glowing cards at where he'd spotted the shadows.

First the explosions of gunfire, then of Remy's cards filled the huge, empty warehouse.

In a tight ball, Remy flipped over twice in midair before landing and rolling behind an old column.

The bright orange flashes quickly showed Remy that he'd taken out most of the men with his first throws.

But he needed a diversion for just a moment longer.

Flipping energized cards at the remaining Arrington men as well as at distant walls and camera locations, Remy moved quickly into a cloud of smoke from the explosions.

Then between explosions he slipped down the stairs.

At the bottom of the stairs two men with guns ready stood guarding an open tunnel. He was on them so fast, they didn't even get a shot off before he rendered them unconscious.

Taking both the guns from the men, he quickly kineticized the energy in them and then, with all his strength, threw the guns down the dark tunnel toward the main Arrington building.

He stood to one side as the explosion sent an impact blast back his direction so hard, it destroyed the old wooden stairs he'd just come down.

At a full run, flipping energized cards ahead of him into

the smoke as he went, he crossed through the tunnel and under the main building compound.

A main staircase led upward, but it was blocked by a huge steel door at the top. Five of Lang's guards already lay unconscious around the bottom of the stairs and still no sign at all of the children. Or the zombies.

He needed to think of them as zombies, but somehow he just couldn't get the image of children out of his mind.

He glanced around, then picked up a metal folding chair from a guard station. There was no point in being subtle now, not after this explosive entrance.

He quickly changed the potential energy of the chair into kinetic and, with a quick spin like a hammer throw, flung it at the steel door at the top of the stairs.

The explosion sent the door smashing inward.

Immediately on the other side machine guns opened up a deadly rain of fire.

Remy dove for a nearby tunnel and waited, tucked against a wall, as the area under the building was riddled with hundreds of bullets.

Finally the firing slowed and stopped. Six men, obviously more of Lang's stooges, appeared at the top of the stairs and looked down.

Spinning out six energized cards with a quick flick of the wrist, Remy took all six out. Then, flicking cards through the opening above, he went up the stairs and to the right, rolling to stay out of the line of fire, all the time flipping card after card.

The firing stopped in a dozen explosions as he came up hard against a concrete wall. He remained crouched, letting his senses scan the smoke-fogged room. This assault felt like an evening in the Danger Room back at the Xavier Institute. Here, just like there, you never knew what was going to come at you at any moment.

Then, through the smoke, there was movement. Someone was slowly coming toward him. Remy crouched, ready for anything.

It took a moment for his mind to register what was coming at him, then a moment longer to get past the shock of it.

What appeared to be a young woman in a white prom dress stumbled through the smoke directly at his position.

It was Cornelia. Or, more accurately, Cornelia's body.

Her head was missing.

Her body stumbled forward, as if under mechanical control of a bad director in the worst B-movie.

Remy stared for a moment at where her head should have been, remembering her smile at the airport and how he had kissed her hand.

Then he realized that in her hands she now carried two very large and very live explosive charges.

With a quick flip of two energized cards, he hit both charges, while rolling as fast and hard as he could away to the left.

The concussion from the huge explosion smashed him against the wall. He banged his head hard on the concrete, but managed to come up running. Ahead was a wide double door made of ornate wood.

At a run he hit the door with both feet, sending it smashing inward. If he remembered right, behind this door was Lang's personal office.

He had remembered right.

Six guards flanked Lang, but before any of them could even get off a shot at the intruder, Remy flicked energized cards against their chests, sending each smashing backward in a muffled explosion.

The explosions also knocked Lang backward and Remy was over him in a flash, pulling him back to his feet and holding him up above the desk. In the two years since Remy had seen Lang, the man had gained another hundred pounds. Now he seemed to be more a ball of flesh than anything else.

"Dat any way to greet a guest?" Remy asked with a smile.

Lang shook his head no, his fat chipmunk cheeks folding and unfolding with the motion.

Remy dropped him into his overstuffed chair and with one foot shoved him hard back against the wall. Lang's head banged the wood and then lolled forward. His eyes were glazed and blood dripped from his mouth where he'd bitten a fat cheek.

"My motto," Remy said, bending down right into the fat man's face, "is live and let live. *Comprendez-vous?*"

Lang took a moment, then finally nodded, his beady eyes focusing on the X-Man.

"I'd never be here, but now I hear tell you take children."

"None of your business, thief," Lang managed to say, spitting blood as he did.

"Ah, dere you wrong. Children is all our business. Harmin' children harms me. Harms my family. Harms my city. Now where are dey?"

Lang just spat out blood. "All dead and waiting to kill you, LeBeau."

Remy grabbed the fat man by the collar and picked him up with one hand, holding him pressed up against the wall. With the other hand he took out a charged card and waved it in front of Lang's face before tucking it carefully into the rolls of blubber around the fat man's belt.

At the sight of the card the man's small eyes grew large and he swallowed. "We can talk, LeBeau."

Remy nodded. " 'Til my arm gets tired, fat man. But if you give me a wrong answer, my arm gets real tired. Now, de children?"

Remy saw the fat man's eyes flicker in the direction of the main door. With a quick flick of the wrist, Remy sent five charged cards spinning in that direction. The explosions and a short, cut off scream made him smile at Lang. "You a fat one. I t'ink I drop you now. Yes?"

"No!" Lang said. "The children are in the next building over, toward town. But they're all dead. All zombies."

Remy pretended to almost drop Lang and the fat man squeezed his eyes closed, then opened them again.

"Sorry," Remy said. "You sure need to lose de weight. Now what else?" As he asked he took another charged card out of his pocket, waved it in front of Lang's face, and slipped it into the fat man's belt beside the first.

Lang's eyes got even wider than before. "Without another dose of the formula real soon, they won't even be zombies. They'll just be dead."

"So where de medicine?"

Lang swallowed and glanced to the left at a wooden door leading into a back room. "Back there, in the lab."

"You lyin' to me, *homme?*" Remy said, pretending to drop the fat man.

Sweat poured from Lang's face as he shook his head. "LeBeau, I'm telling you the truth. They're already dead and will be for certain in thirty minutes unless I take them their next dose."

Remy nodded and, with a flick of his arm, tossed the fat man in a swan dive over his head into the center of the office. The guy let out a short scream before he hit.

The resulting muffled explosion made Remy smile.

Without looking back, he went through the door into the lab. The fat man had been telling the truth. The place looked like a chemistry lab, with one large table running down the middle. Beakers full of fluids filled the table. Remy stood in the door studying it all, then stepped inside and picked up a metal stool. Holding the stool up, he energized it until it glowed brightly.

And for a moment, he hesitated, thinking of the children. But now they were already dead. All he was doing was stopping monsters like Lang from using their walking bodies for what ever purpose they wanted. Remy hated with his deepest passion anyone who could hurt children.

With as hard a throw as he could manage he spun the metal stool at the center of the chemicals.

Then he tumbled backward and out of the way of the explosion.

Glass and smoke filled the room and he turned and ran. There was no telling what sort of poisons were in there burning now.

He paused in the outer area only long enough to make a quick call to the police, telling them there was a fire and where they could find the children.

At least this way their parents could give the kids a decent burial. That was more than Hayward would be able to do for Cornelia.

Remy waited outside in the shadows of a nearby empty warehouse until the police had fought their way inside.

Then Remy LeBeau turned away, heading back to the X-Men, once again leaving his hometown. But this time he left it just a little better than when he'd found it.

And, as with any good thief, no one saw him go.

X-PRESSO

Ken Grobe

Illustration by Dave Cockrum & John Nyberg

ooking back, I'd say the second most exciting thing that happened to me today was getting hit in the gut with a fastball special. Well, maybe the third most. Y'see, being an X-Man and all, improbable, unpredictable stuff happens to us all the time. It's just as likely that one of us gets spirited away to another dimension as rip a pair of dungarees. But what happened today was different. It was special. Still, I don't mind saying, it didn't start out too pretty.

It began with a letter from my momma. She wrote to tell me that my younger brother Josh had left the farm to go to Nashville. I swear, when I read that, I felt my jaw hit the floor. Y'see, since my daddy died and I went to study with Professor Xavier, Josh has sorta been the "man" of the house, helping out my momma and the younger kids on the farm. Up until I got that letter, I thought Josh'd always stay on the farm, on account of he took such pride in it. More than once when I'd come home for a visit, Josh'd go out of his way to tell me that he 'n' momma had the farm well in hand, thrusting that fact in my face like a badge of honor he'd won in a war I'd never fought. 'Course, he was always a little jealous that our sister Paige and I had gotten to leave the farm and go to private boarding schools. But at that same time, he'd always take great pride in the fine job he 'n' Momma had done in taking care of the farm and our younger brothers and sisters. Besides, Paige and I only went away for school because we'd discovered that we had mutant powers, and going away to the Xavier Institute and the Massachusetts Academy was the best way to deal with them. Josh was pretty relieved that he didn't have that particular curse.

'Cept maybe his singing. Lord, he has such a lovely singing voice, like no one I'd heard before or since. Oh, 'cept
for Lila. Or Alison Blaire. 'Course, they're professionals.
What the heck did my dangfool brother know about "making it" as a singer? How could he leave the farm to go on
some merry chase to be the next Garth Brooks? I love my
brother. But if he was standing in front of me when I got
the news, I swear I would've boxed his ears. How dare he
leave Momma alone to run the farm for something as frivolous as this? College I could understand. But a singing
career? With poor Joelle probably still recovering from
her run-in with that cult and the rest of the young'uns still
not big enough to handle the farm by themselves, and
Momma . . . well, I just couldn't stop thinking about it. I had
to figure out what to do.

Now mind you, I ain't ashamed to say that I had one or
two other things worrying me on a fair to regular basis—
not the least of which was my recent promotion from leader
of the X-Force team to a full-fledged member of the X-Men.
But dangit, family's important. I couldn't stop thinkin'
about Josh leaving the farm. And I couldn't stop thinking
about my momma workin' herself to the bone, with me
gone for years, Paige havin' left only recently, and now Josh.
And I couldn't help but feeling a symphony of guilt that
started as soon as I discovered my mutant powers and took
Professor Xavier's offer. But most of all, I couldn't stop
tryin' to figure out what I could tell Josh to make him give
up this damnfool idea and get him to go back to the farm
where he belongs. And that's what I was thinkin' about
when the Beast threw Gambit at me.

For most of the week, Professor X had seen fit to pit

pairs of us X-Men against each other for practice. For this particular Danger Room session, the Professor put the Beast and Gambit on one side, and Archangel and myself on the other. Two flyers against two walkers. Heck, I had Archangel on my side, and he's one of the original X-Men. I figured we had it all over Hank and Remy. Of course, I didn't account for how distracted I'd be over that letter.

The X-Men call it a "fastball special": one member throws the other one to take out one or several opponents. Well, that's all well and good if you're fighting against the Marauders or the Genoshan High Guard, but I guess I didn't expect it in a simple Danger Room sequence.

I'm invulnerable to dang near anything when I'm using my blasting power. Gambit knew that, and it gave him free reign to cut loose. Remy charged up his quarterstaff, filling it to bursting with energy, and, with the force of the fastball special behind him, brought it full-tilt into my solar plexus. Now, it didn't exactly hurt. But it bounced me off a couple of the Danger Room's walls and shocked me out of blasting. I hit the floor, dislocating my shoulder.

Now, these Danger Room sessions are rough on purpose. Professor X says it's the only way to keep ourselves sharp for real missions, and he's right. But, damn, did my shoulder hurt! Remy apologized, even though we both knew we're supposed to give it our all in the Danger Room. And the Beast was even kind enough to reset my shoulder, which didn't make it hurt any less, but at least I could move it around some. Then I went back to my room to nurse my arm and my pride. I wouldn't have minded a bit of time to myself.

No such luck.

"Guthrie!"

I could hear my girlfriend hollering all the way from the other end of the East Wing. For a pretty little thing of five feet four or so, there was a danged good reason even aside from her mutant powers that she took the code name Meltdown. Even when she wasn't trying, she was goin' critical. And this time, she was trying.

She burst into my room without knocking. "Where the hell have you been? I do hope you realize that you just stood me up for lunch!"

I slapped my head with my hand. "Tabitha, honey, I'm sorry. I forgot. But we weren't goin' out for lunch or anything . . ."

"That's not the point, Sam! We hardly get to see each other as it is without you forgetting little things like 'meet me in the commissary at two.' How hard is that to remember?"

I caught on quickly that there wasn't no way I could blast myself out of this particular doghouse. "Tab, I'm sorry. I've got a lot on my mind and—"

"Yeah, Sambo, I'll just bet you do. I see you looking at the other women on your team. You think I don't notice you and Psylocke making eyes at each other in the Danger Room?"

And I thought I could only get blindsided in the Danger Room. "What?"

"I've got eyes behind these shades, Guthrie. Don't you dare try putting anything over on me. And don't think I didn't notice that you were watching every move that she made, that tramp . . ."

Now, I know a lot about Tabitha. I know how she needs

a lot of attention, 'cause she's real insecure and all that—problems with her dad and all. I also know that our relationship's taken a few hits by my getting promoted to the X-Men and her staying behind in X-Force. We go on different missions most of the time and just can't see each other as much as we'd like to. But this just wasn't a good day to address it. And she obviously wasn't in the mood to listen—or even to stop talking!

My shoulder ached something fierce, my head throbbed from the morning's events, and it got harder and harder to listen to Tabitha's ruckus. Now, I don't like to speak ill of anybody, least of all my girlfriend, but, well . . . she got irritating. Too irritating. So irritating that I found myself getting up, grabbing her by the shoulders, and forcibly placing her on the other side of my door. Then I slammed it right in her face.

Of course, I used my bad arm, which made me even madder. Bad enough I'd failed my family and embarrassed myself in front of the other X-Men. But I wasn't about to stand there and listen to Tabitha's paranoid rants. I can only coddle her so much, you know? Sometimes I needed understanding. This was one of those times and I just couldn't deal with Tabitha's crazy accusations today.

I'll never understand us. Meltdown 'n' I've fought side-by-side against aliens, forces of nature, cold-blooded killers—you name it. We've been through more together than most couples dream of. But one little domestic squabble and both of us just go to pieces.

Well, I could hardly figure out what to do with myself after that. I wanted to just take off through the ceiling, blasting through floor after floor of the mansion and out into the sky. 'Course, I stifled that urge pretty quickly. I like to think of myself as a strong man—heck, I'm a mutant, after all. But that don't seem to mean much in the face of family troubles, girlfriend troubles, and dislocating your shoulder, all in the space of a few hours. I didn't want to talk to anybody. I wanted to be alone with my thoughts. And getting out of the mansion seemed like a pretty good idea. The Institute's getting more crowded all the time, and as for the woods outside the campus, well . . . Wolverine's taken to living out there these days. And he's been scaring me lately.

I was on a train bound for New York City within the hour. Now, you might wonder, *What the heck was Sam thinking, going to the biggest city in the world when he wants to be alone?* And if you are, then you must not have been to New York much. 'Cause there's just so many people there, rushing around, each in their own world. That makes for millions of little worlds in one city, and I figured it wouldn't mind one more. Besides, I wanted to be around normal people and maybe, just maybe, not worry about being a mutant for a while.

I started by just walking around downtown. I didn't much feel like going to any of the museums, and I like the Greenwich Village area quite a bit. It's kinda, well, alive. Everyone's in their own little world in New York, but the Village is the best place to sit and watch 'em go by.

Another thing I like about the Village is it always looks the same. I've seen pictures of the Village from the 1950s and 1960s, and, well, there's not much important about it that's changed. The buildings are all there, and even some of the clubs and theaters are the same. But most of the storefronts are flashier now, and today there's a lot more kids from the Empire State University campus running around.

Now, while the Village isn't exactly the best place for solitude, it's an ideal spot to lose yourself in a crowd. After walking around aimlessly for a while, poking my head in stores and checking out vintage record shops for old George Jones albums, I decided to head up to Washington Square Park. Washington Square Park isn't exactly a park like we had in Kentucky. After all, it's mostly concrete, and the places that have grass also have KEEP OFF signs. But there's no place better in the Village to entertain your eyes for free. On a crisp, just-after-a-light-drizzle day like that one, people from all walks of life hang out to meet, relax, perform, or watch passersby, as I was doing that day. As I entered the park, I heard dogs barking as they chased their masters, their tennis balls, or each other in the fenced-off dog run just to my left. Right in front of that was a group of musicians playing and singing old Beatles songs. Way over to the right was a man in a three-piece suit buying a hot dog from a street vendor. Just past them was a single guitar player singing love songs, surrounded by a few pretty young college girls. Listening to that boy sing made me think of Josh's own glorious voice. I remember him even as a young'un, using that voice of his to charm us all: singing "Amazing Grace" in church, leading the family in sing-alongs by the fireplace on cold winter nights, and entertaining his friends at the soda shop like this young fellow in front of me was doing. In fact, I got so caught up in the flow of memories that I didn't even notice until too late that my pocket had been picked.

I felt light fingers cross my back pocket and immediately

reached to discover my wallet was missing. Looking up quickly, I saw a kid in a yellow T-shirt and baggy jeans running away. "Stop!" I yelled. I screamed for the police, but there weren't any around. Typical, ain't it? So I took off after the kid. That is to say, I ran after him. No sense in using my mutant power in broad daylight, I figured.

Does anyone really think that yelling, "Hey! Stop, thief!" at a thief is really going to make them stop running from you? Well, I did it anyway, and of course it didn't work. 'Course, after chasing him for a few blocks, I realized that I wasn't going to catch up to him, and no one was willing to help me. Maybe I looked too much like a tourist. I sure don't look like no New Yorker! I felt my heart beating faster and I started to get a stitch in my side. But there was no way I was gonna let that kid get away with my wallet.

Just my luck, the kid turned down a side alley. An empty side alley, mind you. So I figured, what the heck, and took off. I mean, really took off.

Lord, do I ever love flying. I so rarely get the chance to really take off, to really soar. I feel such a rush from using my powers. I guess regular folks find it scary that there's someone like me around, who can fly like I do. But if I could give them the power for a day, I would, just so they could experience the pure joy that goes with it. Sometimes I feel sorry for them, 'cause they don't get to shoot through the air like me. Speeding through the air, seeing clouds and rooftops whipping past—I tell you, it's true freedom, if only for a moment. But not that day. At that time, I just wanted to teach this guy a lesson—Cannonball-style—for picking my dang pocket.

Using my Cannonball powers, I caught up with him in

a second, yelling, "Surprise, sucker!" as I grabbed him by the waist of his baggy pants and took off into the air. He began yelling in Spanish and twisting around so much, I thought he might fall right out of those pants. I'd figured it might be fun to put a little scare into him, but he wasn't scared at all. Also, my arm hurt like crazy. So I made a snap decision and deposited him on the rooftop of the nearest apartment building. I grabbed the wallet out of his hand and took off just as he tried to throw a punch at me. *So that's how he wants to play it?* I thought. I blasted back down to the alley and went looking for a phone to call the police. It had occurred to me that they might be interested in a trespasser on the roof of that apartment building. Hell, there were a lot worse things I could've done to him.

I could hear him swearing and yelling to beat the band as I flew down from the roof back into the alleyway. I'm pretty sure I looked around to make sure nobody saw, but I don't completely recall. I didn't really care at the time, 'cause, dang, after all that'd happened already, I didn't rightly care.

I came out the other side of the alley onto a street I didn't recognize. I thought I'd walked down most every street in this area, but didn't recall this one. I walked into the first storefront I found. The words COFFEE A-GO-GO were stenciled on the storefront window in a cut-paper style that reminded me of movie posters from the 1950s. I could sense coffee and conversation before I even opened the door. But there wasn't much that could have prepared me for what I saw when I walked in.

Across from the front door lay a small stage that barely held five empty stools and a microphone stand. Next to it

hung a sign that said FREE VERSE POETRY READINGS FRIDAYS
AT 9. Why would they need so many people onstage for a
poetry reading, I wondered?

Then I took a look around the place. Colorful Guate-
malan weavings, which I recognized from my art history
courses, hung from the walls next to wild canvasses that
looked like something Jackson Pollock painted in a bad
mood. People of all ages sat at the tables, mostly wearing
berets, porkpie hats, or black turtlenecks. Above them hung
strangely colorful mobiles composed of geometric shapes.
Many of the men had goatees and the women had long,
straight hair. Boy, did I feel uncomfortable in my slacks and
plaid shirt. I'll tell you, it felt like I'd walked straight into
Greenwich Village in the 1950s. From the little I'd remembered from movies and old magazines, I seemed to have
walked into a picture-perfect slice of beatnik culture. A
woman kept yelling for someone named "Chester" until I
turned around and realized that she meant me.

The lady who had finally caught my attention was
older—forty or so, it was difficult to tell. She wore a white
men's oxford shirt over a black leotard. She didn't wear any
makeup and kept her dark hair, streaked with gray, pulled
back in a ponytail. The tray under her arm tipped me off
that she worked there. The one raised eyebrow told me that
she regarded me with some amusement. I tell you, that's
the blessing and curse of being a mutant: I have this incredible power inside me, but on the outside, I still look
like a gangly farmboy. To this lady I must have looked like
I'd wandered in off the street, which, well, I had.

"What's the Odyssey, Homer? You here for cheer or you
just come to do the pet shop window thing?"

What language was she speaking? "Um . . . I, uh . . . is there a phone here?"

She eyed me coolly. "Smoke signals for paying Indians only. Buy a cup or take your dime elsewhere."

I sighed. "Okay. Fine. One cup of Earl Grey, please."

She nodded. "Phone's in the back next to the Che Guevara collage."

I said thanks and made my way to the back of the café. The air was thick with cigarette smoke, incense smoke, and a couple other kinds of smoke I wasn't sure I recognized. I caught snatches of conversation where words like words *classism, paradigm, Mugwump,* and *yage* stood out to my virgin ears. Also a name that I didn't expect to hear. Mine.

"Sam."

I turned to see him sitting at a dark table in the far corner. Truth to tell, he was the last person I'd expected to see in a place like this (aside from me, of course). He had been in the first class at the Xavier Institute, back before my time. And while I'm pretty much the last X-Man to date, he's the first, the best. But for the life of me, I couldn't figure out what he was doing sipping coffee in the back of a beatnik coffee shop.

He waved me over. I joined him. Even his clothes, while surprisingly stylish, seemed out of date. He wore a suit nearly the color of the wet pavement outside, with a thin tie, and while I hate to say it, he looked like a character out of those *Man from U.N.C.L.E.* episodes my friend Roberto likes so much. Mind you, it fit right in with the mood of the café. But it seemed odd not to see him in his traditional blue-and-yellow battle-duds, or in the sweatshirts and jeans that he wears when he's fixing the planes or the machinery in the Danger Room. Come to think of it, this was the only time I could remember seeing him not working. A stray beam of light glinted off of his red sunglasses as he took a sip from his coffee cup.

As I walked to him, the café seemed to brighten up a little, as a strange place only can when you spot a friendly face. Although *friendly* generally isn't the first word I'd use to describe Cyclops. I found him a little intimidating. 'Course, if I had the power to kill people just by lookin' at them the wrong way, I don't suppose I'd want to make too many friends either. In many ways, the X-Men've never had as capable a leader as him. But friendly? Heck, he's always been nice enough to me; just distant is all.

I shook his hand, always respectful of his authority as leader of the X-Men.

"Scott. What're you doing here?"

"Same thing as you, I suppose. Care to sit down?"

My eyes flicked to the phone. Scott sat within spittin' distance of it. "Um, in just a minute. I have to make a phone call."

Well, there was no way around it, sure enough. I didn't want Scott to know about my momentary lapse in judgment. But I couldn't leave that kid up on the roof to hurt himself or cause who knows what kind of trouble. Facing away from Scott, I placed the call to the police, trying to keep my voice as low as possible without sounding too suspicious.

So much for that. I pretended to cough over my shoulder and caught a glimpse of him, staring at me intently. *Busted!* I thought to myself. Not for nothing has he been the field leader of the X-Men since I was in grade school. He sussed the situation out pretty quickly. He had his lips pursed and his arms folded, staring at my cup of Earl Grey across the table from him as I approached.

He didn't apologize for eavesdropping. He didn't need to. "You want to tell me how you know about this trespasser on the roof?" He asked, catching my gaze and (I think) looking me straight in the eye.

Briefly, and somewhat ashamedly, I told him what had happened with the pickpocket. Cyclops isn't one to show emotion, but I did notice the corners of his eyes crease like most people's do when they go into a deep frown. Boy, just seeing that made me feel lower than a Morlock in a cistern.

My head sank between my shoulders as I waited for a reprimand from my team leader. I knew exactly what Cyclops was going to tell me: that we should only use our powers in dire situations, that random displays of them only elicit fear in the general populace, that if the wrong person took a picture of me or even saw me flying that boy to the roof, it could seriously compromise my privacy and that of the X-Men as well. In my mind I pictured Scott and Professor Xavier calling me into the Professor's office and telling me that I just wasn't working out with the X-Men, that I'd made too many mistakes and would have to go back to X-Force. I braced myself, practically feeling my shoulders touch the bottoms of these big ears of mine. Scott aimed an accusing finger at me and opened his mouth to give me the lecture I deserved. But then he took a good look at me (at least I think he did; it's tough to tell behind those red sunglasses of his), lowered his hand, and let out a long, low breath.

What came from him didn't sound like a scolding. It came across as softer, more patient. "What you did wasn't too smart, Sam. Someone could have seen you. I thought you knew better than that.''

"I know, sir. But I just haven't been myself today. My brother's leaving the family and my girlfriend hates me and I'm not measuring up and . . .''

Well, I try not to get to emotional in front of a senior X-Man. Shucks, I'd only just been promoted to the big team recently, and I still had to prove myself. But I couldn't help it. It all came pouring out: my brother, my screwups in the Danger Room, my argument with Meltdown. I just couldn't help but tell my problems to a familiar face. Scott listened to every word, brow slightly furrowed about those ruby specs, his chin resting in the crook between thumb and forefinger, aiming the whole of his concentration at my tortured monologue.

I talked and talked until I ran out of things to say. Then I looked up at Cyclops, and caught him actually smiling. Or was it a smirk? It's difficult to tell with Cyclops. He doesn't smile much.

"Sounds like a pretty bad day.'' His voice was even and calm.

"Yes, sir. It sure is.'' I said, unsure. Here I'd poured out my heart to the man—the leader of my team—and he responded by smiling? I wasn't rightly sure whether or not he was mocking me. And like I said, he wears those ruby quartz sunglasses all the time, so it's almost impossible to read his face. I decided to give him the benefit of the doubt.

He raised his hand to signal the waitress. "Zelda! Another espresso, please, and refill my friend's tea. And some *biscotti.*''

Zelda smiled and nodded across the restaurant to him.

"You got it, Slim," she called back as she stepped behind the brass espresso machine and began to pull levers.

Neither of us said a word as we waited. Scott folded his arms again and stared straight ahead at me. I noticed that he'd clenched his jaw and hadn't said a word for what seemed like a full two minutes. The whole effect reminded me of the sort of expression one makes when trying to plot a course on an unfamiliar road map.

I didn't say anything either—heck, I didn't have nothing left to say. I looked at Scott's glasses and thought of the power behind them, how his optic beams could flare out and tear the head from my shoulders before I could blink. It's not easy living with the X-Men. As many times as they might save your life or you theirs, there's always a possibility in the back of your mind that Wolverine might snap, or that you might accidentally touch Rogue and lose your identity. I've been with 'em in one capacity or another for some years now and I still find that hard to shake.

Zelda came over with a tiny coffee cup and a larger tea mug, each with an Italian biscuit placed in the saucer. "*Uno espresso a-go-go, bello*—with nutmeg and cinnamon, just how you like it. And some more Earl Grey." I reached for my wallet. Without looking at me, Zelda said, "Keep it in the holster, cowboy—if you're a friend of Slim's, the bevvies're on the *casa*. Enjoy."

Then she fixed Scott with a mocking smirk. "And as for you, Slim, how's it I hardly see your pan these days? All this time and you're too good for the A-Go-Go?"

Scott's manner, while unsmiling, was easygoing. "Come on, Zelda. You know it's not like that. It's just that after the last time, we wanted to spare you the ruckus."

Zelda's eyes turned upward. "Don't remind me! The last time you people showed up, Drake brought some walking, talking Mighty Joe Young-looking thing in here—and I don't mean Topo Gigio, *shatz*. He nearly caused a riot in here with that animal."

I realized that Zelda was talking about the Beast. I don't know how, but I could tell Scott was holding back a grin. "Now, Zelda, no harm done. Didn't Bobby promise not to bring pets in anymore?"

"Yeah, and I haven't seen his carcass since. What's he doin', starting the next ice age early?"

"Something like that. I'll let him know he should come by soon."

"You do that, Slim. Tell him all is forgiven. Don't think I don't remember how he used to be warm for this form back in the days." Zelda patted her hip, winked at me and sauntered back to the counter, tray nestled under her arm.

She knew Iceman and—in a way—Hank too? Had they come here before—and often? Why hadn't I ever heard about it? I couldn't wait to hear the story. But even above that, one nagging, burning, tantalizing question tugged at my curiosity above all others.

I couldn't bear not asking. I cleared my throat, turned to him, and, with as much tact as I could muster, I asked, "Slim?"

"Old nickname. I know Zelda from way back."

Way back? My mind instantly rang with question upon question. How in the heck does the stoic leader of the X-Men know this strange beatnik woman? It made me want to imagine Scott before the X-Men. I couldn't.

Scott could tell. He leaned toward me and said, "I take

the train in to New York fairly often, when I have time. Sometimes I come with Jean, sometimes I go alone. The mansion's a great piece of land, but it's not the best place to take your mind off of your problems." I nodded my head in agreement and took a couple of sips of my tea. I realize that anyone who actually knows Cyclops would have trouble believing that he's anything but businesslike, stoic, and, well, cold. But I swear to you, sitting in that coffeehouse, sipping from that tiny cup, he was downright gregarious. For him, anyway.

Scott looked around the café and continued on. "This café has a special place in X-Men history. Bobby and Hank discovered it years ago, when we were just starting out at the school. After a while, we all started coming here. As important as our training was, we tended to lose track of the real world. Coming here, we could let off steam—as people—and feel like we had a part in the real world too. It wasn't like anyplace we'd ever seen before. It was so free and accepting.

"You should have seen it then, Sam. Wall hangings and Picasso prints, the whole place filled with smoke and wild performances. On any given day you could find poets, dancers, musicians . . . the place looked like, well, much like it does today. The credit goes to Zelda for bringing back the look of the place. She was just a waitress at the time. Now she owns it.

"Eventually, the four of us graduated, and the new team of X-Men came in, and the place was bought by new owners and turned into a diner. Then, when Jean . . . came back and we started X-Factor, we returned to the old spot to find that it had become a sushi bar, of all things. A year ago, that place went out of business. God bless her, Zelda got some money together, bought the place herself, and restored it to its former glory. Jean and I've both been coming back ever since. As you heard, Bobby and Hank haven't been here in a while."

That was the most I had ever heard Scott say at one time—to anyone. I was flabbergasted. I think I was a bit too obvious about it, as usual, because Scott looked a little taken aback, and a little embarrassed, probably for having gone on like he did. He cut himself off with a bite of his *biscotti*, and gave me that road-map look again.

"But let's see what we can do about your problems. The first one's easy: Fastball Special."

"Yes, sir."

"The next time an opponent tries that on you, use your shoulders to sort of sidestep it in the air." He made a swinging motion with his shoulders to illustrate. "Quickly grab your opponent and ride his momentum from behind. Then he's yours to drop or do with what you will."

Of course. "Gee, Scott, you make it sound so simple."

"No. You and I both know it takes hard work. I also know that you're no slouch. Schedule extra Danger Room time and practice. You'll get it. Let me know if you need help and I'll have Warren work with you."

Now his voice started to fill me with confidence. This was the Cyclops I knew. He was truly the best an X-Man could be. For a moment, I couldn't believe I was sitting in Greenwich Village drinking with him.

He chewed and swallowed another bite of *biscotti*. "Second of all, forget about making your brother change his decision. If my experience is any indication, you have no hope of telling your brother what to do."

I'm not one to argue with someone like Scott, but what he said just didn't seem right. "He's making an absolutely wrong decision! This—this Nashville thing—it's idiotic! As the eldest Guthrie male, it's my responsibility to talk him out of it. And I'll tell you, Scott, I'm not the only member of this family who—"

He shot me a look that I could feel through those ruby quartz lenses of his. "No, Sam, you're not."

Hearing him say that shut me up and made me feel like a wet sack of feed. Y'see, I know about Scott's past from the computer records. And it's just plain sad. He grew up in an orphanage, not knowing he had any family to speak of. He only found his brother after ten years, and his father and his grandparents after twenty. And that's it. 'Cept for his in-laws, that's all the family Scott has, unless you count the X-Men. And Scott'd had more than his share of trouble with his brother. His brother ended up discovering mutant powers as well, powers even more dangerous than Scott's.

"What you've got to understand, Sam, is people aren't going to change just because you want them to. My brother's spent half his life running around the world, trying to figure out his place. And there wasn't a single thing I could do to change that. He's doing a fine job heading up the X-Factor team now, and I'm proud as hell of him. But if he decided to leave tomorrow, nothing I could say or do would change that. Sam, if you love your brother, the best you can do is stand back and catch him if he falls. If you're lucky, he'll make the change himself, or ask for your help. Or maybe, just maybe, he's made the right decision after all.

"Look at Magneto. How may times has Charles tried to reform him? Wolverine? Sabretooth?"

He raised an eyebrow above its ruby lens.

"You?"

He was right. When I first discovered my powers, I threw in with Donald Pierce, an old enemy of the X-Men, because he paid well and I had to support my family. But when the Professor uncovered what a rat Pierce was, the Prof invited me to his school and welcomed me with open arms. He's helped my family and me out ever since, and the farm's thrived besides. I made the best decision of my life when I joined the Xavier Institute. And here I was trying to stop my brother from making his own decisions.

"You don't want to lose your brother, Sam."

"You're right, sir. Point well taken."

He drained his espresso cup. "Third: Meltdown. Apologize to her."

That suggestion set me aback. What did he mean, "apologize to her"? Didn't he realize all the neurotic trash she was talking to me? Obviously he didn't, so I related the rest of our argument—or should I say her argument—to Scott, point by point, and I really would have gotten my dander up if Scott hadn't raised his voice just enough to cut me off and say,

"Sam."

I heard a bit of irritation in his voice. "Yes, sir."

"Do you love her?

I let out a sigh or resignation. "Yes, sir."

"Does she love you?"

"I believe so."

"Then apologize, dammit. Life's too short to waste your time with laying blame and pointing fingers. You're an X-Man, Sam. Live your life the best you can with no regrets. When you go on the kind of missions that we do, you can't afford those luxuries."

I hate to say it, but he made a brick of sense. I really did care for Tabitha, and when it came down to it, none of that little stuff should've mattered. Suddenly I couldn't wait to find her and tell her. Scott must've picked up on this because he was already standing up and pulling money from his wallet for the tip jar.

"C'mon. If we catch the six-thirty, we can make it back for dinner. Gambit's making gumbo. Bobby's doing dessert."

Zelda waved us out with a wink and another reminder to bring Bobby the next time we came. As we stepped out into the crisp fall air, I felt just a little bit different. Nothin' to scream about. But I had learned a lot about myself, and more than I'd ever hoped about the man whom I'd always passed off as the most dispassionate X-Man.

We walked the thirty-odd blocks back to the train station, talking all the way.

We missed the 6:30 and had to catch the 7:05 local instead, but it was okay. That's what happened to normal people. And for once, there were no emergencies, no problems. No superpowers. Just a couple of friends killing time. And feeling every bit as human as we had a right to.

FOUR ANGRY MUTANTS

Andy Lane & Rebecca Levene

Illustration by Brent Anderson

ogan's car was like Logan himself: brash, aggressive, and powerful. Bobby Drake could hear it thundering along the drive toward the Xavier Institute long before he could see it. There was no doubt in his mind that it was Logan. Who else would drive a car like that?

As he stared out from the window of Professor Xavier's study, a sense of foreboding weighed Bobby down for a moment. Of all the X-Men who could have returned to the fold at that time, it had to be Logan. There would be no sympathy for the ordeal Bobby was about to go through. No understanding. Just sarcasm and a continual barrage of jokes. Jean would have understood. So would Hank. But not Logan.

There was a fine mist of rain in the air outside. Without thinking, Bobby reached out through the window and felt the shape of the water molecules, caressing them, altering their energy levels until they sought each other out for company. Snow began to fall outside the window, each flake unique.

Just like mutants: each cursed with his or her own singular abilities.

The car finally cleared the treeline and raced toward the mansion, belching smoke from its exhaust. Crimson and yellow flames had been painted along its sides. Logan had the top down, despite the rain, and his abundant black sideburns were whipping back behind him like a scarf as he drove. He was smiling ferally, and Bobby could see the glint of his too-white teeth in the morning sunlight.

"Bobby, you're worried," said a calm voice from the room behind him.

"With respect, Professor, it doesn't take a telepath to spot that," he replied. As he turned away from the window, the last thing he saw was Logan's car slewing to a halt, throwing up an arc of gravel, and the man himself vaulting over the side and loping towards the door to the mansion. "I just don't see how I can do this and keep the X-Men out of it. I've lied once already. If the authorities find out—"

"I understand your concerns, Bobby," the Professor said. The light from the roaring fire in his study gleamed off his hairless scalp, making him look like he had a crimson halo. "But remember, you will be serving your country."

"Professor, I've put my life on the line for my country more times than I can count. I just—"

The door slammed open and Logan strode in as if he owned the place, almost glowing with health and animal vitality. "Hi, Charley," he interrupted, "hi, Bobby-boy. How's tricks?"

"I'm glad you're back, Logan," Xavier said. "I would like you to drive me down to town tomorrow. There's a case starting at the Westchester County Courthouse I want to sit in on."

Bobby suppressed his anger at the change of subject, although he knew that Professor Xavier must have spotted the slight drop in temperature in the room.

Logan's eyes gleamed. "Somethin' to do with mutants, huh? Warren been caught flyin' past women's bedrooms at night?"

"Nothing like that," the Professor said in his infuriatingly calm way. "Bobby has been called up for jury duty, and I want to see how things go."

Bobby cursed silently. He'd been hoping that the Professor wouldn't tell anyone.

Logan's gaze flicked across to Bobby. "Weeeellll," he drawled, "defectin' to the enemy, eh, bub?"

Bobby immediately felt his temper rise. "Hey, Canuck, this is my civic duty, if you don't mind. At least I've got some feeling of moral responsibility!"

"Well ain't we on our high horse?" Logan switched his hunter's gaze back to the Professor. "Somethin' 'bout the way you're talkin' gives me the feelin' there's a problem, Charley."

Xavier nodded. "Your senses are as finely honed as ever, my friend. We were hoping that Bobby's case would have nothing to do with mutants and he could sit on the jury with no conflict of interest. Unfortunately, during the empanelling process yesterday it became obvious that the accused was himself a mutant—a man named Arthur Streck. All the jurors were asked to declare whether or not they themselves were mutants. Bobby had to lie, of course, given that his powers and his identity as an X-Man are not widely known."

"I asked the Professor whether or not I should find another reason to get kicked off the jury," Bobby interrupted. "After all, I can fake a cold better than anyone—but he said no."

"One juror did declare himself to be a mutant," Xavier explained. "He was immediately excused. The reason given by the assistant district attorney was that a mutant would be automatically biased in favor of another mutant. I find this line of reasoning specious, and I wanted Bobby to remain on the jury so I can monitor how fair the deliberations are."

Logan nodded. "Most all juries I ever came across were biased to the core," he said. "So, what's this Streck guy charged with, anyhow?"

"First degree murder," Bobby said.

"Should you be tellin' us this?" Logan frowned. "Ain't you supposed to keep quiet 'bout what goes on in court?"

The Professor looked a little discomfited. "Bobby is indeed bound by an oath not to discuss the case outside the courthouse, but I have persuaded him that his primary duty is to justice, rather than to the letter of the law."

"And besides," Bobby added, "the case hasn't actually started yet. The jury were sent home today while the judge considers points of law."

Logan considered. "Y'know, I think I will drive you down to the courthouse tomorrow, Prof. Might be interestin'."

Bobby sighed. This was exactly what he'd been hoping to avoid. It was bad enough having to be on a jury, worse having to lie about it, but to have Logan sitting there in the public gallery—that was almost too much to bear.

Logan leaned back in his seat and hooked his hands behind his head, suppressing a smile as he felt the woman beside him shuffle surreptitiously farther away. He looked around the chamber, assessing it and the people within it. The oak-paneled room wasn't grand, but it was trying very hard to be, like a hick cousin dressed up for a night at the opera. The people were the same—all the petty officials puffed up with their own self-importance. Making the most of a small-town case that had suddenly made the big time.

Almost unconsciously, Logan had chosen a position that gave him a good view of the court proceedings while leaving a clear escape route to the door. Something about the silence in the chamber made him nervous. It was an expectant rather than a peaceful silence, charged up with all the things people weren't saying.

Xavier, sitting calmly beside him, had seemed to understand his motivation and hadn't protested. Or maybe courtrooms made him as uncomfortable as they made Logan. There was certainly an animal edginess about this one. He could smell the ghoulish interest of the press gallery behind him, the animosity of the public, and the fidgety nervousness of the jury.

Bobby didn't look any happier than the rest. His usually amiable face was pinched and worried. He constantly ran his fingers through his sandy hair, while his eyes roved the courtroom, carefully avoiding those of Logan and the Professor. In fact, they settled most often on one of his fellow jurors: a stately dark-haired woman Logan judged to be way out of Bobby's league—and Logan was an expert at these things. Bobby was looking at her when the assistant DA rose to make his opening statement, and at the squeal of the prosecutor's chair he jerked his eyes away with a start. Logan gritted his teeth. Drake was acting so guilty you'd have thought he was the one on trial. Why didn't he just wear a sign? MUTANT IN DISGUISE—PLEASE LYNCH.

"Alan Wydell, a man with no few political ambitions," Xavier said quietly, nodding toward the ADA.

Logan studied the man. Medium height, middle-aged, paunchy—not much good in a fight, but could probably talk himself out of one. "I guess winning this case wouldn't hurt those ambitions none."

The Professor smiled very slightly, his expression then changing to a thoughtful frown as he gave his full attention to the prosecution's opening remarks.

"... heard a lot about the mutant menace. And maybe we've been told there isn't such a thing. Well, if there isn't a mutant menace, there sure as hellfire are mutant menaces, and this—" Wydell spun round dramatically to point at the defendant "—this is one of the worst of them. Five good family men, sons and fathers and brothers, have been killed. Torn to shreds by the savage claws of a freak of nature that some might say should never have been born. Murdered in cold blood by this—this man, Arthur Streck."

The emphasis didn't escape Logan's attention, and he felt anger surge within him at Wydell's blatant manipulation of the court.

Streck shifted uncomfortably, as if the scores of eyes resting on him exerted some real physical force. Logan's scalp prickled with the fear he could sense emanating from the defendant. Fear and, even more strongly, anger. The press had dubbed Streck the Dinosaur Killer. His green-yellow scales fitted this image, but Logan was put in mind more of a cat. Streck's frame was slender and looked agile. His face, beneath the scales, was narrow and intelligent. Beside him, the tip of a prehensile tail twitched its irritation. A cat, and not a tame one.

The ADA had paused to stare at Streck, and Streck returned the stare full force, his lips drawn back in a sneer that was halfway to being a snarl. Wydell shifted away slightly, his expensive lawyer's suit rumpling as the muscles beneath it unconsciously tensed for action. All around the courtroom Logan could feel the same reaction repeated. The million-year-old fight-or-flight instinct of an animal confronted with a threat.

"You may ask why we're so sure we've found the right . . . man," Wydell continued after a moment in his deep, reassuring voice. "Motive, opportunity, and method, ladies and gentlemen. Method—well, Mr. Streck couldn't dispose of his murder weapons. He was born with them on the ends of his fingers. Opportunity, then. This creature was present at every single one of the crimes. And motivation. The accused, I guess you've probably noticed, is a mutant." Wydell paused for a wave of laughter to sweep the court. "The victims were members of a group, the Friends of Humanity, which has been fighting for the rights of ordinary folks against the so-called mutant menace. Some time ago, there was an incident involving the victims and Arthur Streck's sister. The victims were brought to trial—Streck claimed they'd assaulted her—but the jury thought otherwise and the case was dismissed."

There was a note in Wydell's voice that suggested this was a cause of some satisfaction to him. Logan wondered if he'd prosecuted that case too. And how fair the trial had been if he had. Shifting to a more comfortable position, Logan settled down for a long and depressing day. Justice seemed about the last thing Xavier had brought him here to witness.

Bobby pushed the remains of his lunch listlessly around his plate and sighed. It hardly seemed possible, but this was even worse than he'd imagined, what with the claustrophobic, clinical little room they'd shut the jury up in for their meal, the terrible quality of the meal itself, and the hushed antimutant conversations he could hear going on among his fellow jurors. But then, the prosecution case was so strong that even he thought Streck was guilty. The guy looked shifty, too, and this claim that he'd only been in the areas of the crimes because he'd signed up with a new agency specializing in mutants and he'd had job interviews near each crime was so obviously fraudulent that Bobby couldn't believe Streck was trying it.

So here he was, sitting in this miserable little room with a bunch of people he didn't dare speak to. And there she was: the gorgeous Rachel Mostel. He was sure there must be all sorts of laws against having an affair with another juror, but he just couldn't seem to keep his eyes off her. Most of the rest of the jury seemed to feel the same way. Trust him—unlucky at cards and unlucky in love.

He felt himself blushing fiercely as he realized that she had noticed him noticing her. Worse, she was walking toward him. He looked down at the unlovely remains of his fried eggplant, and hurriedly shovelled in another mouthful.

It was too late. His plate rattled as she sat down opposite him. "You're Bobby, aren't you?" God, her voice was as beautiful as the rest of her.

He began to answer, realized he still had a mouthful of food, flushed again, and swallowed. "Yes, but my friends call me Mr. Drake." She looked confused. "Joke," he said, waving his fork at her and, to his horror, splashing some eggplant juice on her cream-colored blouse.

She didn't seem to notice. She smiled, and leaned further toward him. He wondered if she could hear his heart pounding. "It's such a waste of time, isn't it?" she said softly.

Bobby frowned. "I'm not sure what you mean."

"This trial. I mean, everyone knows he did it."

"Do they?" Bobby said uncomfortably. "Do you really think we should be discussing it?"

"Why not?" said a gruff voice at his shoulder. Bobby twisted round to identify Joey, the jury's foreman—a squat bulldog of a man with a nicotine-stained moustache. "We all think the same." There were nods and grunts of assent from several of the other jury members who had begun to gather around. Most of them were staring at Rachel with something approaching awe in their eyes.

Rachel smiled at them. "He's a mutie," she said sweetly. "As far as I'm concerned, they're always guilty until proven innocent."

"Not much danger of that," another juror interjected. The grunts of agreement were more forceful.

Bobby felt about as out of place as a panda at a prayer meeting. "Don't you think we should wait till we see the evidence . . . ?" he began tentatively, trailing off as he felt Rachel's huge green eyes focus on him. He was still looking into them when the bailiff summoned the jury back to the courtroom. Even after he sat down, they remained in his memory.

The afternoon brought a parade of witnesses willing to testify that they'd seen Streck at the scenes of each crime. The forensic evidence, too, seemed pretty conclusive. Xavier projected a cautionary telepathic message—*They've only proved the murders* could *have been committed using Streck's claws, not that they were*—but Bobby thought he was grasping at straws. The pictures they showed the jury of the dismembered carcasses of the victims turned even his stomach, and he'd seen more death and pain in his lifetime than he cared to remember. He felt a shudder running through the jury, as if someone had just walked over all their graves.

Unable to stop himself, he turned his eyes to Rachel. She was looking at one of the photos with shock and horror. Bobby felt a wave of understanding sweep over him. So she didn't like mutants. So what? Would he like them if he didn't happen to be one himself?

The next photo they passed to the jury was of Streck's sister. It was taken shortly after her assault, and Bobby winced at the contusions on her fragile body. But when the photo was passed on he sensed it evoking an altogether different kind of horror inside him. He glanced across at the picture again as the next juror held it. She was pretty frightening, he supposed: scaled and tailed like her brother. Was it any wonder people didn't feel much sympathy for someone as freakish looking as she? And Bobby had seen— had fought—plenty of evil mutants in his time.

But what about his fellow X-Men? They were okay, weren't they? He'd had good times with them. They had helped him over problems in his life. They had saved his life too many times to count.

Except that Wolverine was dangerous—too close to the animal within him to trust completely. And nobody really knew where Gambit came from, with his glowing red eyes. His demonic glowing red eyes.

Bobby shook his head, telling himself this was an absurd

line of reasoning. But when the photo was passed back to him again, he couldn't feel anything except disgust.

Logan had chosen to wait in the narrow alley that ran beside the courtroom. The sun had sunk so low that its light didn't penetrate there, and water dripped down the dank walls in premature twilight. There was no reason not to wait out front; he just felt more at home here. His natural habitat. Charley was snug back at the mansion, chauffeured home by Cyke. But Logan had picked up the "meeting Bobby and sniffing around" detail. Just his luck.

There was Drake now, walking past the mouth of the alley. He was looking off to the left, so rapt he didn't notice Logan saunter up beside him. It was that woman he was watching, the good-looking juror. He was virtually drooling over her. Logan studied her: mile-long legs, healthy from working out rather than hard work. There was no denying, she was easy on the eye. Logan realized he was staring at her too, heart racing faster than his car, as she brushed past Bobby, flicking him a quick come-hither smile.

For a second, he didn't want anything in life more than her. And then it was gone, and she was just another well-groomed frail. And he had that feeling running through his blood, that I-was-real-ill-but-now-I'm-well buzz that told him his healing factor had done some work. Dammit, Drake went and fell for a *femme fatale*. Worse, a super-powered *femme fatale*.

He realized Bobby was about to walk off down the road after her. Sighing, he snaked out an arm and grabbed the scruff of his neck.

"What?" Bobby said irritably, halfheartedly trying to shake Logan off. His eyes never left the woman.

"Snap out of it, bub," Logan grated.

Bobby jerked his head round. His face briefly contorted into an alien mask of anger, like a pet that had unexpectedly turned rabid. Then it was just Bobby again. "Logan! And there I was just about to call a cab." As if he couldn't help it, he returned his gaze to the retreating woman. "She's something, isn't she?" he said softly.

Logan grunted. "I hear Hank says beauty's in the eye of the beholder. Maybe he oughtta change it to smell."

"Is that some kind of joke I'm not getting?"

"Depends how funny you think controlling folks' feelings is."

"What?" Bobby snapped. "Ground control calling Logan—what's the matter with you, buddy?" His lake-blue eyes looked into Logan's with genuine concern.

"Let me put it so you can understand. She walks past here, I feel drawn to her real strong, my healing factor kicks in, and I don't feel it no more. What does that sound like to you?"

Bobby frowned. "You think she's a mutant? Some kind of pheromone-control power like Spoor's?" He laughed suddenly. "You wouldn't say that if you'd heard the things she was saying about mutants!"

"Yeah?"

"All sorts of stuff in the courtroom. You know, the mutant menace spiel. She was mouthing off to all the other jurors. It was like some kind of Friends of Humanity meeting in there." His expression became more thoughtful. "She was saying all these things, and they were all agreeing, like they couldn't help themselves . . ." He looked after the retreating figure speculatively. A slight blush crept across his face. "I guess you think we should follow her, huh?"

An hour later, and they'd toured just about every street and downtown alley there was. The rain had strengthened, and after they'd slipped away to get into X-Men uniforms, Logan almost hadn't been able to pick up the trail again. It was dark now, too, dismal as only the fall could be. But they had found her, jittery and looking behind her every step, and now she seemed to have gotten wherever it was she was going.

They were in an old part of town: derelict warehouses, big and ugly, and not much else. She'd slipped into one of the most run-down buildings. It looked just as deserted as the rest, but Logan could see light creeping out the edges of the blacked-out windows, and he could smell people in there. Lots of them.

"She's definitely up to something," Bobby hissed.

"And they say a college education ain't worth anything," Logan said dryly. "We gotta get in there. How about you take guard duty and I sneak around?"

"No way!" Bobby said indignantly. "You might need me in there."

Logan looked him over. He seemed more businesslike and confident in his ice form. And he didn't look like he was going to change his mind. Logan sighed. "You keep control of yourself, boy. If it looks like you're falling under that frail's spell again, I'm taking you out."

Bobby nodded sharply. Logan pointed out a broken window, somewhere on the fifth floor, and they headed for it.

The night was very silent in that area, and Bobby's ice-laden footsteps echoed loudly in Logan's ears.

Logan shook his head. He scaled the decaying building with the ease of long practice and settled on a crumbling balcony beneath the window. Bobby looked up at him with some trepidation, his frozen hair gleaming silver in the rising moonlight. He looked so young: just a boy. Logan felt a sudden, choking sense of responsibility for him. Then Bobby grinned cheekily. He pointed at the wall in front of him and a knob of ice grew out of it. Pulling himself up it, he built another and then another. Mutant mountaineering.

Soon, they crouched together beneath the window. Muffled voices trickled through the shattered pane of glass. One voice, mainly, a deep confident one, and others joining in at intervals. It reminded Logan of something. A prayer meeting, he decided: the preacher leading the congregation.

Logan gestured Bobby to wait while he peered in through the window. Making sure he couldn't smell anyone nearby, he pushed his head carefully through the broken glass. An awkward shard gouged a deep cut in his cheek, but the familiar stinging of his accelerated healing factor knitting his skin back together, skin on muscle on bone, didn't distract him from what he saw. He let his breath out gently in a silent whistle of recognition.

There was a flag opposite. Flags all around the room, all showing the same thing: a flattened black cross on a red background, and three letters. *FoH*. Friends of Humanity. What kind of mutant would be meeting with a mutant-hating rabble like that?

While he'd been taking this in, Logan had been looking around—point man scouting the territory, he thought sourly. He was above a rusty-metal-and-rotting-wood platform. It circled the room, a giant, dark chamber that seemed to occupy most of the inside of the warehouse. The only illumination came from torches held by some of the hundred-odd congregation below. All looking at one man, the "preacher" on his stage, shouting out a sermon of hate against mutants. He finished some rousing phrase and they all cheered, lifting up their torches in an old salute. Logan remembered an SS meeting he'd broken into in a German castle, back in World War II. This was like that, only worse, because these people knew about that war and hadn't learned from it.

There was no danger of being seen. No one was paying any attention to much except the preacher. Turning back to the window, Logan released one of his six adamantium claws out of its housing and carefully cut off the shards of glass until the entrance was clear. Logan went in, then summoned Iceman in after him.

Bobby's eyes widened as he, too, took in the information that had intrigued Logan. He soon recovered himself and crouched down on the walkway beside him. "Gee, do you think we wore the right clothes for the party?" he whispered, smiling tensely. His expression became more serious. "But where's Rachel?"

Logan had all but forgotten the frail in the excitement of his discovery. Now he looked carefully around the room, his keener-than-human eyes searching her out. And there she was, in the darkness by the door, surrounded by men whose faces looked strangely distorted.

The preacher finished, and the congregation turned their attention to the woman. As she approached them, not with any enthusiasm, Logan thought, they, too, put something over their faces. Gas masks, he realized—more World War II imagery. They looked both macabre and absurdly comic, like postapocalyptic carnival masks, but it made sense if Logan was right about her. And he was always right.

Just then, Logan sensed a flicker of motion beside him. He felt himself shouldered aside as Bobby lunged forward. Logan grabbed at him, catching him around the waist before the young fool could throw himself off the walkway. "What the hell d'you think you're doing?" he hissed.

"I've got to help her!" Bobby returned, none too quietly. Cursing, Logan clapped his hand over Bobby's mouth and fought to hold the young man's squirming, cold body with his own. Below them, he saw two men in Friends of Humanity uniforms peering upward toward them. He held his breath, and tightened his grip on Bobby until he probably couldn't breathe either. For a taut stretch of time, the men continued looking up, muttering to each other. Then the darkness defeated them and they turned their attention back to the woman.

Logan felt Bobby's body relax beneath him, and he cautiously loosened his grip. "You got ahold of yourself, bub?"

Bobby nodded, and Logan took his hand from his mouth. "I'm sorry, Wolvie. I lost it for a moment. I felt her drawing me in. I knew she was calling out for help, but I couldn't stop myself." He shuddered as if he was cold—an odd sight in one covered in ice. "My God, no wonder they're scared of us."

They both looked down at Rachel, who now stood surrounded by a circle of Friends of Humanity soldiers. She didn't look at ease—Logan could hear the scrape of her high-heeled shoes as she shifted from foot to foot. And the men surrounding her were laughing and jeering, like boys who'd found a frog and were working themselves up to pulling its legs off.

"So, we're honored by the presence of the delightful Ms. Mostel." The speaker had emerged from the darkness at the back of the stage so quietly that even Logan hadn't noticed him. Although he wore nothing to distinguish him from the other men, Logan knew this was the leader of the pack.

Rachel's eyes were fixed on him, as if she sensed the same thing. "You know why I'm here," she said with a bravura that couldn't disguise the tremble in her voice.

"Indeed." The man looked at her a moment longer, his features hidden from her, as well as Logan, behind another gas mask. He seemed to enjoy whatever power it was he possessed over her, and they stood frozen for a moment in a tableau of domination. Then he made a sharp gesture at one of his men. "I guess it is time we paid the wages of sin," he said smoothly.

The thug moved to a large box that stood to one side of the group. He yanked back the black sheet covering it, revealing a metal cage. Imprisoned within it, grasping its thick bars, was a tiny, bedraggled girl. She was shivering convulsively, and with each shudder the cage rang like a cracked bell. This time, it was Bobby who had to hold Logan back as all his muscles tensed in outrage.

Rachel rushed up to the cage and awkwardly embraced

the child through its bars. Her child, Logan was sure. He felt a rage so strong, it nearly overpowered him.

After a few seconds, the leader stepped forward and said coolly, "That's very touching, but remember—it cost me a lot to get you appointed to that jury, and I need a conviction. If one is not forthcoming, well . . ." He tailed off, and Logan could sense that behind the gas mask, he was smiling. "You saw the photographs of what happened to Streck's sister. The same thing could easily happen to your daughter."

Rachel twisted around to face him, still embracing the little girl. "They're in the palm of my hand," she said bitterly. "They'll give any verdict I want." She lowered her eyes for a moment, then raised them again with a desperate challenge. "Why? So you'll get one more mutant sent to jail. Wouldn't you rather find the real person who killed your friends?"

There were snickers from the men around her. "How charmingly naïve," the leader murmured. "But you see, I know who was responsible for their deaths. And since I have no great desire to serve a prison sentence, I certainly don't want to bring him to justice."

Rachel looked at him with genuine shock. "You killed five of your own people just to get a mutant convicted of murder?"

The leader jumped down from the stage and moved rapidly toward her. She flinched away, but not fast enough to stop him viciously grasping her chin. "I killed them because they disobeyed my orders. They attacked Arthur Streck's sister, and worse, they allowed themselves to be caught for it. That court case was very damaging to our cause. It would have been even more so, if there'd been any chance of a conviction." There was loud, ugly laughter. Rachel struggled in his grip. Logan could see white indentations in her face where his fingers were biting into her. "When they disobeyed me, they wrote their own death sentences. And when that uppity mutant Streck caused me problems, he became the perfect murderer."

The FoH leader suddenly jerked his arm, flinging Rachel against the cage. "Now go and get some sleep. The prosecution case against Streck will be concluding tomorrow, and the defense will present their version of events. You'll need all your energy to stop the other jurors from being swayed."

Rachel reached through the bars to her hysterical daughter, but two thugs ran forward and dragged her from the room. The leader watched for a few moments, then turned and vanished back into the shadows at the back of the podium. The Friends of Humanity members were left standing around and looking vaguely unsatisfied. Bad stage management, Logan thought. Should've ended with a song.

He felt Bobby tense again under his hand, but he clamped down and extended his claws until they just nicked Bobby's ice sheath. "Not yet, bub."

"But—but they might be hurting her—"

"They ain't gonna harm their secret weapon, now, are they? She'll be all right 'til after the trial. So will the kid, but I wouldn't give a snowball's chance in hell of their surviving more'n five minutes afterwards."

Bobby relaxed. "You're right, of course." He thought for a moment. "We need to tell the judge what's going on. He can arrange for police protection."

"You're not thinkin' straight. You tell the judge what's goin' on and there'll be questions 'bout you an' how you know so all-fired much 'bout what's goin' on. At best you've lied durin' the empanelin' process. At worst you've interfered with the course of justice. We can't go ridin' roughshod over everythin'—we have to be subtle.''

Bobby turned and gave Logan a sarcastic look. "Subtlety being your speciality, of course. Any suggestions?''

Logan gazed down at the small girl huddled in the cage, her arms wrapped tight around her knees, her shoulders shaking. "Strikes me that the key to the whole thing is that kid down there. We get her out, then the FoH goons ain't got no hold over your lady friend, an' she can stop manipulatin' the jury. With a bit of luck, justice'll get done— well, as much justice as ever gets done in a courtroom.''

"Then let's go." Bobby rose to a crouch.

"No!" Logan snapped, but it was too late. The kid must've still been affected by Rachel's pheromone cry for help. He needed to do something chivalrous and heroic—or maybe just plain macho—and he wasn't going to wait and plan things carefully. With a sweeping gesture of his gloved hand he crystallized the water vapor in the warehouse. Logan watched as snow fell on the FoH thugs—not just in flakes, not even in flurries, but in bucket loads. Their guttering torches were extinguished within a moment, and they were left floundering in a two-foot-thick freezing blanket.

"I'll get the girl," Bobby yelled. "You cover my back!''

"Great," Logan growled as Bobby created an ice ramp from the platform down to the stage and slid down it, perfectly balanced.

Logan leaped down from the platform, his leg muscles

easily absorbing the impact as he hit the ground. Extending his claws, he gazed round at the assembled Friends of Humanity. "All right, gang," he snarled, "you wanna put your money where your mouths are?"

After a moment of astonishment, they came for him.

The first five jumped him, trying to bear him to the ground by force of numbers. They obviously didn't know with whom they were dealing. Logan crouched into a ball, then flung himself back to his feet. The five thugs went flying. Ten or twelve more hesitated, then piled in. Logan picked the first one off his feet and used him as a flail to beat the others away with. After a few moments the thug went limp, so Logan threw him up onto the platform and chose another one. "Strike one!" he yelled as he used the fresh club to knock another thug all the way across the room. "Strike two!" and another one went flying up onto the stage, trailing a ribbon of blood behind him.

Out of the corner of his eye, Logan spotted Bobby. He had frozen the lock of the cage and snapped it off, and he was pulling the terrified girl to safety. She was beating at his chest and generally making a nuisance of herself, and so Bobby was completely unaware of the thugs running up behind him.

"Iceman! Watch yer back!"

Bobby turned and extended his hand toward the running men. Icicles burst from his fingertips, slender spears that crossed the distance between him and them within a second. They ran onto the sharp points, then danced backward to free themselves amid a fairy-tale tinkle of breaking ice.

Something went *bang!* and Logan felt a hot stab of agony

in his shoulder. His nostrils burned with the acrid tang of cordite. He turned slowly, feeling the tissues knit together and the red-hot lead slug being pushed to the surface. One of the nearby thugs was holding a gun. In the time it took him to register that his victim was still standing, Logan had crossed the distance between them and slashed at his arm, claws fully extended. The man's hand went spinning away, still holding the gun, and the man sank to his knees. Logan could smell two more coming up behind him, so he whirled around, slicing parallel gashes across their faces. Blood sprayed into the air, its hot, coppery smell almost overpowering him. He took a deep breath and deliberately pulled himself back from the brink of berserker fury. This was no time to lose control.

"Hey, Frosty—time to make our apologies and leave."

Bobby weighed up the situation, then took a few paces toward the center of the room so that Logan was between him and the door. Somehow he had persuaded the girl that he was on her side, and she was clinging to his back like a pigtailed rucksack. Bobby extended both arms straight out, pointing past Logan and toward the door. A sudden *hisss!* made Logan flinch, and when he looked up he was in a tunnel of ice that ran from Bobby to the door. The Friends of Humanity were just blurred figures rushing around on the other side.

"Nice work," he said as Bobby ran toward him. "Ever considered goin' into the construction industry in Canada? There's plenty of Inuits I know'd be pleased to come to some kinda arrangement."

"Enough with the jokes," Bobby yelled, passing him. "We've got to get out of here."

"Oh, yeah," Logan said drily. "Thanks for remindin' me." Turning, he noticed that a few of the thugs nearest the cage had discovered the start of the frozen corridor and were beginning to advance along it toward him. His adamantium claws penetrated the ice on either side of him like knives through soft cheese. Taking a step back, he pulled. The ice crumbled in a wave extending back toward the cage, burying them in jagged blocks. Smiling at a job well done, he followed Bobby out of the warehouse.

As they ran across the neon-lit road and into an alley on the other side, Bobby looked back. The Friends of Humanity were spilling out of the warehouse like ants from a disturbed nest. He and Logan had barely even scratched the surface. There were hundreds of them and they had raided the armory. Most had handguns or rifles, a few were toting machine pistols, and at least one had a rocket launcher.

"What do they think this is," he said, aghast, "war?"

Logan glanced up at him. "Yeah," he said simply. "They do."

Bobby concentrated on the air above the road, pulling energy from the water molecules and condensing them onto the road surface, then absorbing even more energy, feeling it burn within him, as the water altered form again until it was a thin sheet of ice. The Friends of Humanity ran onto it unaware, and their arms flailed wildly as they tried to keep their balance. The girl clinging to his back giggled as they slipped, slid, and collided like something out of a Keystone Kops film. Some of them accidentally tightened their fingers on their triggers, and the night was shattered by gunfire.

"Here," Logan said, scooping the girl off Bobby's back, "let me take her. This might turn into a chase, an' I tire less easily than you, bub. 'Sides, you don't wanna give her frostbite."

Some of the Friends of Humanity had made it across the ice and were vanishing into the night. Others were talking on portable telephones. For the first time since he'd thrown himself down into the fray, Bobby stopped to think. "They'll be setting up roadblocks," he said. "This area of town is almost deserted, and they know we're on foot. If they can throw up a cordon fast enough they can search systematically. They're bound to find us."

"So, any bright ideas?" Logan asked. There was a distracted tone in his voice, and Bobby turned to look. The girl was riding high on his shoulders, pulling at the wisps of his sideburns that had escaped around the edges of his mask. The expression on the bottom half of Logan's face was a mixture of annoyance and amusement.

"How did they get here?" Bobby asked, indicating the thugs who were still lingering in the vicinity of the warehouse. "They don't all live here, I guess. They must have jobs, families, and lives."

"So they drove," Logan said. " 'Less they hired a bus."

"Which means they parked somewhere."

Logan nodded. "Let's go look, then." He twisted his neck so he could look up at the girl. She gazed down at him with wide, dark eyes: eyes just as beautiful as her mother's, Bobby reflected. "Hey, munchkin—you're gonna have to keep very quiet if you want to get out of here and see your momma again, and you do want to get out of here, don't you?"

She nodded solemnly.

"Good girl. What's your name, by the way?"

"I'm Sophie."

Logan grinned. "Good girl, Sophie."

The cars were parked in a deserted lot around the back of the warehouse, and guarded by three armed thugs. Some of the cars had been driven off to search for the escapees, but there were enough left to cover Logan and Bobby's approach. Logan had let Sophie scramble to the ground and was about to launch himself at the guards when Bobby put a restraining hand on his shoulder. Logan turned, a question in his eyes, but Bobby shook his head and pointed without even looking and froze the guards where they stood.

"Ain't that a little harsh, bub?" Logan said calmly as the guards toppled like statues to the ground.

"Don't worry—they'll thaw just fine."

Logan fixed him with a sardonic glance. "Hey—you don't have to prove anythin' to me," he said. "I ain't the one with the pheromones."

As Logan chose the car with the biggest engine, Bobby allowed himself a moment of doubt. He thought he had done what he had done in order to escape, but had he gone too far? Were Rachel's pheromones still buzzing around his system, affecting what he did, biasing his decisions? Anger flared through him. He'd been controlled by a woman before and he had almost gone mad as a result. The thought of having someone dictating his actions made his skin crawl. What did it say about him that he was so susceptible?

Logan waved to him from a tow truck that looked as if it had been made out of big sheets of iron soldered together. He had picked the lock with one of his claws. "It might hold us if we get into a firefight," he said as Bobby walked over with Sophie, "but I ain't bankin' on it. Some ice armor'd be a nice idea, don't'cha think?"

Bobby smiled, and nodded. "No problem."

Logan and Sophie climbed into the truck and shut the door. As Logan hot-wired the ignition, Bobby set to work swathing the bodywork in layer after layer of ice, leaving a tunnel for Logan to see through. By the time he had finished, the tow truck looked like a giant snowball on wheels. Walking up to the frozen surface, Bobby infiltrated his body into the ice, becoming part of it, surrendering himself to it and swimming through it until he came to the window on the passenger side. He pulled himself through like a localized avalanche and reconstituted himself into his ice-laden human form.

"Doesn't that hurt?" Sophie asked.

He smiled, ice in his heart. "Everything hurts," he said. "You learn to live with it."

Sophie stared at him uncertainly as Logan gunned the truck to life. Like a ghostly tank, the ice-armored vehicle rumbled toward the distant barricades.

Next morning, when Bobby Drake walked into the courthouse room where the jury was sequestered away before the day's business commenced, his eyes immediately went to Rachel Mostel. She was sitting alone, her head in her hands. It looked to Bobby like there was some kind of no-go area around her: none of the other jury members were sitting within ten feet of her, and nobody was even looking her way. Bobby felt his own eyes sliding away, trying to look anywhere else but at her, and he had to force them back in her direction. It was those damn pheromones again. Consciously or unconsciously, she was forcing people to ignore her. Perhaps the strain was getting to her.

He wished he could say something, tell her that her daughter was safe and the Friends of Humanity had no power over her anymore, but he didn't dare. She wouldn't believe him, and he would have blown his cover completely. No matter how much he wanted to comfort her, it wasn't a good move.

Within a few moments, the jury were escorted into the courtroom by the bailiff. Alan Wydell was sitting at the prosecution bench, thumbs hooked behind his lapels and a smile on his face. He looked the complete picture of confidence. Arthur Streck's counsel, by contrast, was already looking harassed.

Streck himself sat beside his counsel with his head bowed. His scales were dulled and his ears were flat against his head. He was beaten, and he knew it.

As they sat down in the jury box, Bobby shot a glance sideways at Rachel Mostel. She was looking at Arthur Streck and biting her lip. A pang of compassion shot though his heart, and he knew it wasn't just her pheromones. She didn't want to go through with it.

The bailiff announced the arrival of the judge, and everyone in the courtroom stood, apart from the wheelchair-bound Xavier, as she bustled in and made herself comfortable. The bailiff indicated that the court could sit and they did, apart from one person: Sophie Mostel, standing between Professor Xavier and Logan. She waved at her mother and grinned before Logan tugged her back to her seat.

Bobby watched Professor Xavier's face. His eyes were fixed on Rachel's, and when Bobby glanced back to her he saw that she was staring at Xavier with an expression of wonderment. A telepathic message telling her that everything was okay and her daughter was in safe hands? It seemed likely.

And a wave of happiness passed through the court. Bobby could track its progress as person after person grinned suddenly, then wondered why. Even Arthur Streck looked up and smiled.

After that, the trial proceeded normally—for the first time since it began, really. Alan Wydell, full of fire and brimstone, did his best to intimidate a series of defense witnesses, but Rachel wasn't cooperating. No longer influenced by her mutant powers, the jury shifted restlessly as they heard his words clearly for the first time. Wydell could tell something was wrong: his glance flickered across their faces disbelievingly as he realized the adulation and approval he was used to were missing.

And he kept looking at Rachel. Bobby filed that fact away for later consideration.

The judge called an hour's recess and the jury was sent back to its claustrophobic room. Bobby walked over to where Rachel was sitting, hoping that he could find out what Xavier had asked her to do, but she was busy writing a note. He took a step closer—or at least, he tried to—but something stopped him, like an invisible barrier hanging in midair. She didn't want to be bothered.

Back in the courtroom, the judge cleared her throat. "I

realize that you will be expecting the counsel for the defense to make his closing speech, but I'm afraid that I have a matter of some gravity to discuss."

Alan Wydell looked surprised. The counsel for the defense just looked relieved.

"The bailiff has handed me a note from one of the jurors," the judge continued. "This note alleges that there has been interference with the due process of the law. Whether or not this is true is a matter for the police to determine, and I am forced, therefore, to declare a mistrial—"

The rest of the judge's words were lost in the tumult of reporters trying to get to the door and of the rest of the public talking and shouting. Bobby wasn't sure who to look at—Arthur Streck, who looked as if he'd just been sandbagged from behind, or Rachel Mostel, who had much the same expression, or Streck's defense counsel, who looked like he was about to faint.

It was an hour before order was restored and the jury was dismissed. When Bobby finally got outside onto the courthouse steps, with the granite of the Westchester County Courthouse building glowing in the sunshine behind him, he felt happier than he had for days. The sky was blue, the trees were bowing slightly in the breeze, and the air smelled as if it had just been freshly made.

Logan and Professor Xavier were waiting for him at the bottom of the steps.

"So, you never got your moment of glory," Logan said, grinning. "I was expecting you to be foreman."

"I'll live," Bobby replied. He turned to the Professor. "What happens now?"

Xavier's face was as imperturbable as usual. "There will, of course, be an investigation into the tampering charge. Mr. Streck will not be retried until after that investigation, if at all. There has been so much negative publicity which, combined with the possible results of the investigation, would make a new indictment extremely difficult. Justice would, therefore, seem to have prevailed in this case, and we have dealt another blow to the Friends of Humanity. All in all, my friends, we have a positive result. Well done."

"An' it's my opinion," Logan added, "that the first thing the Friends of Humanity will do is lynch friend Streck from the nearest tree. If they can't get him one way, they'll get him another. So—did we do him a favor or not? I don't know."

"And Rachel?" Bobby asked, "What happens to her?"

Xavier looked pained. "As I made clear to her in a telepathic message, manipulation of a jury is illegal. She was coerced into it, and that will form the basis of a good defense, but in the interim she has been arrested. She understood what would happen, but she knew that it was the right thing to do. It is unfortunate, but . . ."

"And Sophie?" Bobby looked around wildly. "What about her?"

"I promised Ms. Mostel that we would look after young Sophie until she was released on bail," Xavier replied, "and that the Xavier Institute would fund her own defense. Warren has already driven her back to the mansion." Xavier smiled slightly as Logan pursed his lips and looked away. "I believe she is looking forward to playing with Uncle Wolverine."

Bobby was about to make a crack at Logan's expense

when a sudden commotion at the top of the steps attracted his attention. He turned, and his heart leaped within him. Rachel Mostel was being led away from the courthouse by two policemen, followed by a gaggle of reporters with flashing cameras and working tape recorders, all asking questions so loudly that they wouldn't have heard her even if she had answered. The policemen were wearing gas masks. Rachel was handcuffed, and she had been crying. Her eyes passed over Bobby and there was a flicker of recognition, but only as a fellow juror. She didn't know what he had done for her. She would probably never know, and he felt empty and hollow at the realization.

Alan Wydell emerged from the courtroom door. He stood nobly for a moment, the wind artfully disarranging his hair, until the press noticed him. They ran back up the steps, gabbling questions all the way.

"Yes," he boomed, "I am disappointed at the halting of the trial, but I am confident that the culprit—this mutant juror who has tried to influence the good people of the jury—will be prosecuted with the full force of the law. And—" he rode magisterially over the clamoured questions "—I am also confident that Arthur Streck will find himself in another court, a fairer court, a court that will deliver a true and just verdict of guilty!"

He strode off to a waiting car. Some cub reporters followed; the older, wiser ones knew that they had all they were going to get, and they left.

"And so it begins," Xavier murmured. "Already he is manipulating the facts: making it look like the jury was being influenced to find Mr. Streck innocent, rather than guilty. As Hiram Johnson once said, 'The first casualty when war comes is truth.' "

"Never mind that," Logan said. "Bobby, does somethin' strike you as familiar 'bout his little rabble-rousin' speech there?"

Bobby frowned, trying to remember. "Now you come to mention it, yeah. He sounded a lot like that Friends of Humanity guy."

Logan nodded. "Yup. An' besides—how did he know Rachel was a mutant? I didn't get a good whiff o' his scent in the warehouse, but the posture and tone match the guy behind the gas mask."

"I'll check to see whether the employment agency that sent Arthur Streck to those fake job interviews can be traced back to Mr. Wydell," the Professor said, "but I suspect I will find nothing. He strikes me as the sort of man who is very careful about not leaving traces."

They were all silent for a moment, staring after Rachel Mostel as the police car drove her away. How fair a trial would she get, Bobby wondered, if the ADA belonged to the Friends of Humanity? And was Logan right—would the FoH also be out to get Arthur Streck one way or another?

It looked as if they had won the battle, but the outcome of the war was still uncertain.

Together, the three of them moved off toward Bobby's car: Logan wheeling the Professor, Bobby walking alongside. Perhaps it was coincidence, perhaps Bobby's subconscious mind playing tricks, or perhaps just a freak effect of the weather but, as they reached the car, the first few flakes of snow began to fall from a cloudless blue sky.

ON THE AIR

Glenn Hauman

Illustration by Ron Lim

hank you for ordering this transcript of the May 20th episode of Viewpoints *starring Archer Finckley. This is Episode #0418 and features Warren Worthington III as Archer's guest. To order other transcripts of* Viewpoints, *send a check or money order to the address posted at the end of each episode.*

Finckley: Good evening! Welcome to *Viewpoints*, I'm your host, Archer Finckley. Tonight, we have a *very* special guest: he's young, he's handsome, he's rich, and he's got a pair of wings. I'm talking about the high-flying Warren Worthington III, the young head of Worthington Enterprises, better known to many as the Angel.

Warren was born to Warren Worthington II and his wife Kathryn, and was the heir to the Worthington Industries empire. While attending a private school as a teenager, he began to sprout wings from his back as he entered puberty. He used these wings to save the lives of many of his classmates during a dormitory fire, using a long nightshirt and a wig to disguise his identity, giving him an appearance which earned him the name the Avenging Angel.

At one point, he was a member of the infamous mutant group, the X-Men, under the simpler codename the Angel, but later left them to found the Champions, the first team of heroes to operate on the West Coast. Just prior to his time with the Champions, he revealed his secret identity, becoming the most visible mutant in public life. After the group disbanded, he later joined the Defenders, then reorganized under the leadership of the former Avenger Dr. Henry McCoy, also known as the Beast. He was also briefly associated with a team of mutants calling themselves "the X-Terminators."

Then tragedy struck when a crippling attack caused severe damage to his wings, and amputation was deemed necessary to prevent the spread of gangrene. Depressed, Worthington was seen taking off in his private plane, which then exploded in flight. He was believed dead, and with his death his financial empire began to disintegrate, aided by the discovery that he was funding the then-mutant-hunting organization, X-Factor. Then, months after his funeral services, he reappeared in the public eye, and we have him here tonight in his first extended interview since. We'll be taking your calls later in the show. But right now, it is my pleasure to introduce Warren Worthington.

Worthington: Thank you, Archer.

Finckley: Thank you very much for coming on the show tonight, Warren. You've been something of a recluse—

Worthington: Recluse? I wouldn't go that far.

Finckley: Well, this is the first interview you've given in the last couple of years, ever since your little, ah, accident.

Worthington: Accident isn't the term I would use. My disability happened as the result of a deliberate attack.

Finckley: No, I'm not referring to the injury to your wings, I'm referring to the plane explosion shortly thereafter.

Worthington: Oh, I'm sorry—that.

Finckley: Yes, that. Once and for all, would you care to set the record straight on what happened?

Worthington: As you said in your introduction, I'd been injured while fighting an organization dedicated to wiping out mutants, and had suffered severe damage to my wings.

Most doctors were, to put it mildly, stymied—they had no idea how to treat a body with wings attached. I felt the best thing I could do was get a long rest. However, I was very, very concerned that the same people who had injured me in the first place would take another shot at me, or someone else would take advantage. And I was incapable of defending myself, and any conventional form of protection would have been useless.

So we resorted to misdirection. Sleight of hand. We spread the story that my wings had been amputated, and I killed myself because I couldn't fly again. I was on a plane and wanted to die in the air. Actually, I hid myself away and waited for my wings to heal. And I broke off all outside contact, because that was the only way I felt I wouldn't be tracked and killed. Unfortunately, while I was in seclusion healing physically, one of my trusted associates decided this was a good time to wreck me financially, and since I was physically incapable and legally dead, there wasn't much I could do. When I was out of immediate physical danger and my wings were as healed as they were going to get, I came out of hiding and I started to rebuild my life.

Finckley: Since then, you haven't been anywhere near as public a figure as you were. After all, you are one of the most prominent "out" mutants.

Worthington: [laughs] Sorry, your choice of phrase— "out" mutants.

Finckley: There's something wrong with the phrase?

Worthington: It's an interesting crossover from the gay subculture. But unlike being gay, there are lots of mutants who can't hide who they are, regardless of whether or not they might want to.

Finckley: Yet you did for a long time. In fact, right now, I can't even tell there are wings underneath your suit.

Worthington: And don't think my tailor comes cheap. Look, such a nice blend of fabric—and these pleats! [laughs] My tailor is a miracle worker.

Finckley: Why don't you show your wings out more?

Worthington: The best answer—well, it's kind of embarassing to look at it this way, but try to imagine walking around with a hoop skirt strapped to your back, covered with a cape.

Finckley: I can imagine it must be very clumsy.

Worthington: You bend down and knock over a table. What a pain in the tailfeathers. Literally.

Finckley: So it's not embarassment or a publicity thing, or hiding your mutant ability?

Worthington: Now it's a bit of vanity—my wings are not pretty to behold anymore. But for the most part, it's just convenience for everybody else around me. I have nothing to hide, it's not like my face is unknown—God knows my face shows up in the paper enough, between the business section and the society pages, never mind the battles with Professor Power and the Secret Empire on the front page.

Finckley: How do you conceal your wings?

Worthington: I wear a special harness that keeps them flat against my back.

Finckley: Is it painful with your injured wings?

Worthington: I've learned to adjust.

Finckley: You were very publicly involved with two semi-prominent super-teams—the Champions and the Defenders—but both were quite brief. What led you to get involved in those endeavors? The world is, after all, full of super-teams.

Worthington: Well, the Champions was made up of a number of people who just had many different irons in the fire. I got involved with them because—well, to be blunt, I was there at the same time on the west coast. This was before the days of a West Coast branch of the Avengers. I like to think we were a viability test. As for the Defenders . . . again, it seemed like a good idea at the time.

Finckley: Considering how long the Champions lasted, I'd say they weren't terribly viable. Then again, the Avengers shut down their West Coast branch, too.

Worthington: The Champions served their need and function at the time. I don't know that it's a good thing or bad that they disbanded when they did; I'm sure that a lot of people benefitted from them being together. For any super hero group, you don't measure success by long-term cohesiveness or financial success, you measure it by the quality of the work they produced and the lives they touched. It's kind of like a musical group. Besides, it was nice to be in a group with people with bigger PR problems than me.

Finckley: And who would that be?

Worthington: Ghost Rider, clearly. When you hang out with someone with a flaming skull for a head, having a sixteen-foot wingspan sort of fades into the background. And of course Natasha [the Black Widow] was a Soviet defector, which brought its own special problems.

Finckley: Which leads me to my next question . . .

Worthington: Oh boy.

Finckley: You took quite a risk by publicly revealing your status as a mutant. What led to that decision?

Worthington: I was tired of hiding it, really . . . after all the entire issue of "protecting" my family seemed to be moot after my parents died.

Finckley: Weren't you worried about what it would do to your social status, not to mention your business?

Worthington: You have to consider the time and place. California is—or rather, was—more forgiving at the time of people different than themselves. Plus, having the name Angel and the appearance to go with it isn't what you might necessarily call a minus in certain circles.

Finckley: Still, Worthington Enterprises' stock *did* go down significantly after you spread your wings, so to speak.

Worthington: Ehh—it goes down, it goes up. I look at the long term, not the short. We've run ourselves into the ground as a country, as a people, thinking short term.

Finckley: Certainly that can't be the only reason you went public.

Worthington: No, it wasn't. A big reason was to bring home the fact that anybody could be a mutant, that it cuts across race and class. Even the bluebloods can have a mutant baby. It's not a "only gays, only Haitians, only poor white trash, only Jews, only blacks" sort of thing.

Finckley: Was that a big problem?

Worthington: Yes, it was and is. I found out that one of my oldest prep school friends, Cameron Hodge, a man I trusted with my finances and my life, hated mutants with a passion. He tried to destroy me and my friends numerous times—first from the inside of my own company, with embezzlement and spiteful PR while I was believed dead, although I found out he'd been doing it ever since I brought him into the company, then later by joining and leading rabid anti-mutant groups.

Finckley: Why would a man like that—from your comments, a man with the most pedigree of backgrounds—behave that way?

Worthington: I don't want to speculate on him in particular, but why does anybody do that who should know better? With some people if it's not the mutants, it's the moneylenders, it's the Masons, it's the Mormon Tabernacle Choir.

I've personally always been much more impressed with Hank McCoy's decision to go public. Hank has always been a courageous soul in that respect—there was no reason for him to reveal himself, he was unrecognizable.

Finckley: Ah, yes, you and Dr. McCoy served with the Defenders together. Of course, he is heavily involved in the current foofuraw over the so-called "Legacy Virus."

Worthington: Yes, he is.

Finckley: Now, as a mutant, you are suddenly at risk of contracting a deadly disease, in addition to any other problems being a mutant might cause.

Worthington: Believe me, catching a "mutant-killer" disease goes straight to the end of my list of problems. Being audited—*that* worries me.

Finckley: How do you feel about the fact that the existence of the virus was kept hidden from the general public for so long?

Worthington: I don't think "kept hidden from the general public" is an accurate phrase—it implies that there was a deliberate cover-up. Just as with AIDS, it took a long time to track down that such a disease was in operation—it took time to diagnose. The hysteria over making yourself known to be a mutant—indeed, many of the people who contracted it didn't know that they were mutants themselves until they became sick. Come to think of it, the first news stories about the virus came out after the first infection in the general population, when Dr. [Moira] MacTaggart caught it herself.

Finckley: Well, let's hope that your friend Dr. McCoy and his colleagues can find a cure. Moving on to more pleasant subjects, you were recently sighted at a Hellfire Club reception with a very attractive young woman on your arm. Might she be part of the reason why you've been less public lately?

Worthington: Yes? Which one? [laughs]

Finckley: I believe we have a photo here—Jim, can we get that up on screen? Yes, I believe that's her there.

Worthington: Oh, her! Betsy! [laughs] Boy, am I going to get in trouble for saying that.

Finckley: [chuckles] In that case, I assume we can take it as read that your social life has *not* suffered?

Worthington: Well, after the ordeal of putting my life back in order after the damage to my wings, it was more an issue of getting my head back together. But since then, I haven't lacked for a social life, no.

Finckley: Getting your head back together?

Worthington: For a while after the injuries to my wings, I was really, really morbid. Preoccupied with death—that and getting my wings back. If I couldn't fly again, I didn't want to live.

Finckley: How are your wings now? There were reports

at the time that your wings had been amputated, and you haven't shown them in public since, yet now you're claiming you still have them.

Worthington: Functional, but not much more than that. I can still fly, on occasion. But I really don't see myself getting involved in high-speed aerial combat as much as I used to, if ever.

Finckley: A career-ending injury?

Worthington: It was bound to end, sooner or later, just as with any athletic career. Well, any athletic career where people shoot at you on a regular basis.

Finckley: I imagine dealing with super-villains can be trying.

Worthington: Actually, I've never been comfortable with that phrase.

Finckley: Huh?

Worthington: "Super-villain." Dumb phrase. Simplistic mentality. Think about it. Nikita Khruschev stood on the floor of the UN and said he wanted Communism to encircle the globe. Did anybody ever call him a super-villain? Of course not. If somebody feels required to break a person's entire history and belief system into one word, I don't want to discuss politics with them.

By the same token, I'm not real thrilled with the abbreviation "mutant." What I am is a mutant human. The human part is very important. Just calling me a mutant, or calling anybody a mutant, obscures the fact that we're human at the core. Makes it easier to seperate us, deal with us as something from the outside.

Finckley: Since you brought up politics earlier, what are yours like?

Worthington: Libertarian, basically. The right to swing your fist ends where my nose begins. I don't believe the government should get in the way of my life, whether it's the IRS, the FTC, or the FAA. [laughs] In my public appearances, I always want to talk about the tax code and the business climate in this country, yet everybody always wants to hear me talk about, "Mutant rights! Mutant rights!"

Finckley: Okay, what's your opinion on mutant rights?

Worthington: A tough sell.

Finckley: Why is that?

Worthington: The problem with trying to rally behind "mutant rights" is that it's such an encompassing theme, and it's difficult to find a common theme to rally behind.

Finckley: I'm not sure I follow you.

Worthington: Well, let's say that every mutant had wings. If a hundred thousand people had them, there'd be a common thread among them. Somebody would start selling feather groomers, to add fluff and luster. People would join "Birds of a Feather" societies, and there would be a new variation on the Mile High Club.

But we don't all have wings. Some have tails, some have fur, some have glass skin. Other mutants have no unique exterior features at all, just an extra ability that marks them as different. But almost every mutation we've seen evidence of seems to be unique. So there isn't a common element to rally behind.

I'm in favor of equal rights and equal treatment under the law. Special treatment, I don't know if we need it.

Finckley: Are you implying that you can defend yourself by taking matters into your own hands?

Worthington: No, not at all. It's a personal belief. I don't see how beating a person with a tire chain because he's a mutant is better or worse than beating a person with a tire chain because he's human. Somebody's still being beaten.

Finckley: Do you believe that mutants are human and deserve protection under human law?

Worthington: I believe mutant humans are sentient and deserve protection under sentient law. Human, mutant human, mutated human, self-aware computers like the Vision, and resident aliens like Century should all be bound by the laws of the society they're in.

Finckley: Does being a mutant affect the way you conduct your business in any way? Do you find yourself shying away from any business deals, losing clients, things like that?

Worthington: Well, in our financial holdings, we've had to be very careful. In the eighties, we had some significant holdings in biotechnology stocks, just like every other large financial player in the market. Our problem was the impression started by some fundamentalist wackos that our investments in these companies were covers for secret research to turn out more mutants. Patently ridiculous, but we divested anyway.

Finckley: What else?

Worthington: Other than that—it's more the life I've led, it's led me to a wider variety of experiences than most people. I take advantage of the fact that I'm much more widely travelled, that I've seen so much more than most people. And of course, being shot at or kidnapped by demons makes the average business negotiation look easy.

Finckley: Do you know of cases where people don't do business in your companies because they're led by a mutant?

Worthington: A mutant boycott, you mean?

Finckley: In essence, yes.

Worthington: I know of a few, sure, they've been brought to my attention. And I know of people who won't do business with Japanese companies, or companies with South African holdings, or Jewish owned or Arab owned. I don't apologize for who I am or the life I lead; all someone who does a deal with me should care about is will I honor the deal? The smart ones do.

Finckley: Do you use your money to advance a mutant agenda?

Worthington: Didn't I just answer that?

Finckley: Not really.

Worthington: I use it to advance my agenda, and my clients and my stockholders. I believe that a more peaceful world is more successful, financially and otherwise, and anything that I can do to promote smoother running of the world is a plus. If that means donating to peace activities, I do it. If it means hiring a super-powered individual to do a job because he underbids everybody else and I can use the savings elsewhere, I do that too.

Finckley: Are you saying you support the Genoshan solution?

Worthington: Hell, no! I said hire, not enslave. Genoshans use slave labor, pure and simple. It's reprehensible whether it's blacks or mutants doing it. I can't even compare the two.

Finckley: What about X-Factor? Was that part of your agenda, to publicly hunt down mutants?

Worthington: X-Factor was intended to help deal with the sudden emergence of mutants, of people who suddenly developed mutant abilities. Take the example of Rusty Collins, a pyrokinetic. His abilities developed spontaneously and he had very little idea how to control them, and in that state he was a danger to himself and to anybody else around. We were able to subdue him without killing him, and later taught him how to control his abilities, effectively "neutralizing a mutant threat."

Finckley: You were later charged with fraud by a number of X-Factor's clients, who claimed that you bilked people out of exorbitnant amounts of money for putting on a dog-and-pony lightshow.

Worthington: I can't comment too deeply on that, as some of those lawsuits are still pending. But I can say that we have been vindicated in all of the cases that have been completed, and also that two of the lawsuits were thrown out because the opposing parties wanted a mutant corpse, and felt that we didn't do the job because there wasn't one.

Finckley: If it wasn't a secret agenda, why was your involvement and financial backing kept quiet?

Worthington: The main reason was that it was felt that if a mutant was shown to be doing this, it would be perceived as a consolidation, mutants banding together to get normal people. We wanted to avoid that.

Finckley: But isn't that what you did?

Worthington: We tried to defuse the tension between mutants and humans.

Finckley: By running inflammatory ads trumpeting the mutant menace?

Worthington: That was the work of the aforementioned embezzeller, backstabber, and all-around traitor to the human race—please, don't get me started on Cameron again.

Suffice it to say it got out of hand. Look, it had a solid reputation as doing good for human-mutant relations, or else the U.S. Government would never have acquired the rights to the X-Factor name for their own usage.

Finckley: The X-Factor debacle pretty much bankrupted you.

Worthington: Most of my personal holdings, yes. Between the costs of running X-Factor, the embezzlement, and my inability to be directly involved with the running of my holdings, combined with the death of my financial manager, my personal financial picture was a mess for a while. It didn't directly affect Worthington stock, except as a result of associations in people's minds with my problems.

Finckley: You've gotten a measure of that back, though, haven't you?

Worthington: I've rebuilt really rather nicely, although I'm not in the personal weight class I used to be. Lots of it is tied up in existing businesses, the occasional ongoing trust, things like that. The way I look at it is I now have to ask permission before I try to take over a company.

Finckley: Do you miss that level of wealth? Do you ever wish you had all that back?

Worthington: Hmmm . . . I like the quote, "Don't worry if you're rich or not, as long as you can live comfortably and have everything you want." And I guess it's hard to feel pity for someone who's lost so much, but he's still got a few million in assets.

Finckley: Have you learned anything from going from riches to rags to riches?

Worthington: I'd like to think I've stopped behaving like the money's never going to run out—it's happened once, and I'm little more aware of that. I always knew that application of money was a powerful ability, I guess I've just learned not to be so profligate with it. A little more judicious.

I also learned that living comfortably and having everything I want is not a function of having a million dollars any more than it is having a hundred dollars or a hundred million dollars. There are some things money can't buy, and the best way for me to find that out was to see what I could still get when I was broke, and what I really wanted. I wanted my wings so badly that I lost millions of dollars over them.

Finckley: So what are you doing with your money nowadays?

Worthington: The most important things I've done include starting up a venture capital firm, Worthington Enterprises—one devoted to causes I personally believe will improve the world, mainly focused in high-tech. What most people know as Worthington Industries is now on its own; although I still maintain a seat on the board, I'm no longer chairman and I'm no longer principal stockholder. The VC firm is a size I can control no matter what happens, and I want to keep it that way. I'm also keeping it closely held. The Worthington Foundation is still going strong, funding a number of worthy activities and super hero groups, as well as education activities, mutant anti-defamation, that sort of thing.

Finckley: How do you respond to charges that you're a dilletante super hero, only in it for the kicks?

Worthington: Sure, that's me. I stand in front of ray guns because I'm bored and looking for excitement. [laughs]

I used to be much more frivolous about my behavior in

general, but hey, I was young—don't forget, I was dodging bullets when most kids my age were dodging classes in high school. In my old age—

Finckley: Old age? You've only been doing this for a few years.

Worthington: Sometimes it seems like I've been at this for well over thirty years. Anyway, as I've gotten older, I've taken my responsibilities much more seriously—and I now realize I can make as much of an impact working within the existing structure.

Finckley: It sounds as if you've caved in and taken the easy way out.

Worthington: Not at all. I can do as much good by applying financial savvy and good will to the world's problems as I can by punching out a super-villain—often much more.

Finckley: Let's change the subject.

Worthington: Please.

Finckley: You mentioned the FAA earlier. Do you have a pilot's license?

Worthington: Why? I don't fly a plane. Well, not really well. They tend to explode. [laughs]

Finckley: Don't they give you grief about your flying around?

Worthington: Do they ever. I have an ongoing lawsuit pending stating that I should be allowed to fly wherever I want, and I'll win it, because the laws cover vehicular flight only, not unaided personal flight. Unfortunately, the injuries have limited that somewhat, and the plane explosion really ticked them off.

Finckley: They didn't take kindly to that, eh?

Worthington: Oh, no, not at all. So the battle continues.

Finckley: At least you don't have to worry about being pulled over while you're flying.

Worthington: True. This may be the penultimate case of, "The law's on the books, but they lack the means to enforce it."

Finckley: Let's take some calls. We have Audrey on the line from Long Island, New York.

Audrey: Didn't I hear a few years ago about a paternity suit against you?

Finckley: The boy born with wings, right?

Audrey: Yes, him. Was he your son?

Worthington: Absolutely not. A DNA test proved that. The argument that because he was born with wings he was my son didn't hold up. I mean, my father didn't have wings, does that mean the stork had an even bigger hand in delivering me?

Finckley: Thank you, Audrey. Crystal from Alabama, you're on the air.

Crystal: Mr. Worthington, I just really want to know what is it like to fly?

Worthington: You know, everybody asks that question, and I've never really been able to put it into words. I've talked it over with lots of other fliers—pilots and super-heroes—and I've never found anybody who quite gets it.

Finckley: Surely there's a common language of flight between you and, say, Iron Man?

Worthington: Not really. Iron Man isn't flying under his own power, he's got little boot jets that push him around. I'm the only person I know who flies under his own muscle power, pushing against gravity by flapping my own wings.

Finckley: Is it anything like deep-sea diving?

Worthington: Darned if I know, I can't do it.

Finckley: You can't swim?

Worthington: Not well, no. Even as a child, I could never go underwater—I found out later that my body was adapting itself to flight, and I've got things like hollow bones, just like a bird has. I just floated. And once my wings grew out, it became next to impossible to navigate on water.

Let me ask you, Crystal, what is it like to swim underwater?

Crystal: Gee, I don't know, I never thought about putting it in words before.

Worthington: You see my problem.

Finckley: What about hang gliding?

Worthington: Never tried it, couldn't see the point, really—I'll strap my own wings flat against my back so they don't get in the way and I'll glide on canvas instead. No thanks, sounds dangerous. [snaps fingers] You know what it's a little like? Roller coasters!

Finckley: You're kidding.

Worthington: No, really! A slow steady buildup to a high altitude, then off you go, up, down side to side, hard bank, maybe a loop, wind rushing through your hair—it's not that far off.

Finckley: Thanks for your call, Crystal.

Worthington: Good night, Crystal.

Finckley: I'm curious. As a super hero yourself, who are your heroes?

Worthington: Oooh, tough question. Captain America, certainly. He was willing to take a chance on two mutants who wanted to do good when nobody else would, Quicksilver and the Scarlet Witch, and they went on to save the world time and again. Hercules once told me that on Olympus the gods measured wisdom against Athena, speed against Hermes, and power against Zeus—but they measured courage against Captain America.

Finckley: Goodness.

Worthington: Great quote, isn't it? I marked the way he'd said that, it's always stuck in my mind.

Finckley: Who else?

Worthington: Charles Xavier, for constantly espousing a view of a world where mutants and nonmutants can live together with a minimum of conflict, despite great personal inconvenience, cost, and threats.

Finckley: Let's go back to the phones. Hallie from California, you're on.

Hallie: Yes, just a silly question . . . you're so beautiful.

Worthington: Why, thank you, I'm flattered.

Hallie: Your eyes are so piercing . . . do you wear tinted contacts?

Worthington: Nope, this is my natural eye color. Baby blue all over.

Finckley: Thanks for your call, Hallie.

Worthington: [laughs]

Finckley: What, did I miss something?

Worthington: Never mind—private joke.

Finckley: Care to explain it?

Worthington: Not on this show!

Finckley: Fine, be that way! Next caller, Rudy from Oregon, hello.

Rudy: Archer, I want to ask you a question.

Finckley: Go ahead.

Rudy: Are you familiar with the book of Jude?

Finckley: Nope, can't say that I am.

Worthington: I don't have it memorized cold.

Rudy: "And the angels which kept not their first estate, but left their own habitiation, he hath reserved in everlasting chains under darkness unto the judgment of the great day.

"Even as Sodom and Gomorrah, and the cities about them in like manner, giving themselves over to fornication, and going after strange flesh, are set forth for an example, suffering the vengeance of eternal fire.

"Likewise also these filthy dreamers defile the flesh, despise dominion, and speak evil of dignities."

Worthington: I believe that's followed by "Yet Michael the Archangel, when contending with the devil he disputed about the body of Moses, durst not bring against him a railing accusation, but said 'The Lord rebuke thee'."

Rudy: What about Isaiah? "But your iniquities have separated between you and your God, and your sins have hid his face from you, that he will not hear."

Finckley: Do you have a question, Rudy?

Rudy: Yes, why do you have this inhuman blasphemer on your show, this fr—

[LINE DISCONNECTED]

Finckley: I'm terribly sorry about this, Warren.

Worthington: It's all right, I knew it might happen.

Finckley: Still, it an unconscionable thing to have to endure.

Worthington: "Out of the mouths of babes and sucklings." Psalms, chapter 8, verse 2. Remember earlier in the show when I said there wasn't anything universal to mutants? Actually, I take that back. Mutants do have a common element—bozos like that.

Finckley: In light of the last caller, and with the *nom-de-guerre* Angel, I have to ask: are you religious? Do you follow a particular faith?

Worthington: [pause] I've known women who believed they were goddesses, beings who have been called gods for centuries, and creatures who might as well be demons because I can't think of anything else to explain them. But as for actually knowing God—[pause] the best answer I have is that I believe that the closer you get to understanding God, the farther away He slips from you. My belief is that the mind of God is perpetually unknowable, and forever changing. Change is God, probably.

Finckley: But do you follow a particular faith or religion?

Worthington: My religious beliefs have been hard thought out and are constantly under revision. I suspect that every holy person has gotten a chunk of it and passed on what he could; I think every religious belief has a hunk of truth, and/or every religion is true for the one who believes in it.

But I'll tell you this much—I used to be a hell of a lot more tolerant of organized religion before I heard of William Stryker.

Finckley: Obviously. Reverend Stryker tried to wipe out every mutant in the world.

Worthington: When a man takes out a loaded gun in the middle of Madison Square Garden on public television and gets ready to shoot it at friends of mine, I get disgusted. And more, I get scared.

Finckley: Scared?

Worthington: Are you kidding? The people who scare me the most, at least on the domestic political front, are the people who think nothing about doing exactly that, shooting us down to win an argument, and their various banner-carriers, including Stryker and his ilk. They scare me because they want to make Christianity the national religion, and my experience with monotheocracies is that they are intolerant, hypocritical, and often violent. The founding fathers, I think it was specifically Jefferson, said that the reason the first thing in the Bill of Rights was that Congress shall make no law respecting an establishment of religion was "in order to avoid the very tensions that have kept Europe awash in blood for centuries." Awash in blood.

Finckley: Powerful phrase.

Worthington: I know that Stryker doesn't represent a majority of Americans, or a majority of Republicans, or a majority of Christians, or a majority of anybody. Still, I wish more people who are marginally on his side would take him to task for being a bigot.

Finckley: What about the argument that superhuman powers are on loan from God, and only God is the source of all power?

Worthington: Okay, let's take that point of view for a second, in fact, let's take it a step further. I, Warren Worthington III, am blessed by the Lord God Almighty, and further have been given the appearance of a cherubim to help spread the Lord's word as foretold in Exodus 23:20, "I send an Angel before thee, to keep thee in the way." Luke 2:10, "And the angel said unto them, Fear not: for, behold, I bring to you great tidings of joy, which shall be to all people." And I preach tolerance from Malachi 2:10,

"Have we not all one father? Hath not one God created us?"

Man, it sure doesn't seem to be working, does it?

Finckley: Guess not.

Worthington: Granted, I'm not pushing the metaphor hard—you wouldn't believe how many quotes there are regarding angels in Revelations. I wish we hadn't lost the connection with the last caller, I would have loved to match him on scripture. I think the next verse in Jude is, "But these speak evil of those things which they know not: but what they know naturally, as brute beasts, in those things they corrupt themselves."

Finckley: One more call for the night—Ethan from Minneapolis, hello.

Ethan: Hey, Warren, dude!

Worthington: Hello, Ethan.

Ethan: I gotta know, dude—do you molt?

Worthington: Oh, man! [laughs] You know, when somebody asked the President on live TV whether he wore boxers or briefs, I wondered what was going to be my boxers or briefs question tonight.

Finckley: I think we have the winner.

Worthington: No, I use Prell to keep my feathers soft and managable. Do I molt—sheesh.

Finckley: On that note, I guess we should start to wrap up.

Worthington: Yeah, I'd like to go out on a somewhat higher note.

Finckley: What haven't we touched on? What do you think is the most pressing issue facing mutants today?

Worthington: To my mind, the most pressing issue facing anybody, mutant or otherwise, is that the world has gotten to the point where everything matters, and yet we as a people totter somewhere between apathy and anarchy. We have now reached a point in our evolution as a society where anybody, any one individual, can wreak havoc on dozens, hundreds, even millions of people. If somebody feels that they've been wronged, because they were beaten as a child or their people are being persecuted or their nation lost the last war or they hear voices from aliens, they will lash out—and it doesn't matter whether it's *homo superior* using power blasts or *homo sapiens* using a sniper rifle. And they're all motivated by fear, fear, fear—fear that a town is going to stone a mutant to death, fear that one mutant is going to destroy a town. But it doesn't even have to be a mutant—a computer hacker with a grudge can destroy the world by cracking the Pentagon and setting off nukes.

This is the most urgent message I can make to everybody listening tonight, male or female, white, brown, black, or blue. Every decade is a scientific and social milestone, which means that every year counts as well, and every month, every week, every day. You, yes you, are needed, right now, to make a difference. Large quantities of plutonium, the most explosive element known to humanity, the critical ingredient in nuclear bombs, are unaccounted for, and not a government on earth can tell you where all of it is. A cheerful organization calling itself Mere Humans Plotting To Overthrow The World Next Tuesday After Lunch is distributing plans describing how to build your very own thirty-megaton bomb. Terrorism proliferates, from people of all races, color, and nationalities, whatever, against anyone and everyone. And so many people are so filled with pain and fear, that some can't help but bubble over and cause tragedies. Nobody is safe anymore, remember Patty Hearst getting kidnapped or Tony Stark being shot. Society can no longer afford to let people be abused, persecuted, or ignored, or even feel that they are; the stakes, the consequences are way too high. We all need every available hand we can get—you, if you're not busy and give a damn about your world—and we need you *immediately*. Every act of our lives is either a step toward the achievevment of all our hopes and dreams or a step back toward the stupidity and self-pity that can destroy us. Any single act of love and hope may be the grain that tips the scale toward survival, and any single act of cruelty or injustice may be the scale that tips the balance the other way. We need to start working together to prevent those tragedies and make the world a better place, a happier place, one where no one feels jealous or slighted because somebody else is rich and I'm not, someone else has a home and I don't, someone hurt my friend so I'll kill him. Utopia or oblivion is the only choice we have left. We have to take responsibility for our own actions, instead of blaming it on the other guy.

We were talking about religion before and how mutations fit into all of it. Kurt Vonnegut said, "A great swindle of our time is the assumption that science has made religion obsolete." I really believe that. There is nothing in science that contradicts the works of mercy recommended by St. Thomas Aquinas—teaching the ignorant, consoling the sad, bearing with the oppresive and troublesome, feeding the hungry, sheltering the homeless, visiting prisoners and the sick, and praying for us all. We all need you—on the side of the angels.

Finckley: On the side of the angels?

Worthington: Precisely. On the side of the angels.

Finckley: I can't think of a better note to go out on. Thank you for coming on the show tonight, Warren.

Worthington: Thank you for having me here, I really enjoyed myself.

Finckley: Join us here tomorrow night, when our guest on the show will be New York District Attorney Blake Tower. Does the high-profile DA plan on throwing his hat in the ring for Mayor of New York? Tune in tomorrow and find out. See you then. Thank you for watching, good night.

SUMMER BREEZE

Jenn Saint-John & Tammy Lynne Dunn

Illustration by James W. Fry

D r. Jerome Watkins took a deep breath in a vain attempt to calm his racing heart. The pipette in his hand held the latest strain of the bacteria he'd spent his entire professional life developing, ready for its greatest and final test.

Maybe I really have it this time, he thought. *All those years of research and study, all those compromises I made, and it comes down to this moment.*

He carefully transferred the contents of the pipette into a petri dish containing a small plastic block, and took a deliberate step backward to observe the effects. Arms crossed, he nervously sucked his lower lip into his mouth and began chewing on it absentmindedly, waiting.

He didn't wait long. In less than a minute, the square began to dissolve. Tiny streams of fluorescent green plastic goop became miniature rivers, and within two minutes, the block was gone. Were it not for the half ounce or so of green liquid the consistency of milk, one would never have known the block had been there.

Suppressing his desire to cheer and dance, Dr. Watkins allowed himself only a brief smile of joy and relief before turning to the computer to enter the test data and begin the modeling for the next stage of the experiment.

"I knew it could work," he told himself. "And no matter what else may happen, these bacteria will solve so many landfill problems. The ecological benefits are well worth risking the other outcome. And the other won't happen. No sane person would let it happen. They won't. They couldn't."

Without warning, the laboratory door burst open and

two strangers stormed into the room. Startled, Watkins jumped out of his chair and moved protectively toward the experimental area.

"Who are you? What do you want here?" he cried.

Baring his teeth in a feral grin, the one who resembled an olive-furred baboon replied, "Not much. Just your life's work, flatscan."

The creature had to be a mutant, since he used the derogatory term many mutants used for "normal" humans. He moved slowly and steadily towards Watkins, the dank scent of rotting mushrooms intensifying the nearer he came. Watkins moaned softly as the world around him began to swim. Erratic, brightly colored circles of light rotated around his head, making him dizzy. He felt a wave of nausea crash over him, and he clutched the edge of the lab counter, desperately fighting to stay upright.

He lost the battle and sank to his knees, retching helplessly. The nausea completely enveloped him, making him unable to think or speak. He vaguely saw the other mutant, the one who looked like a bedwarfed giant with mechanical arms, working the computer and transferring disk after disk of files. He fought for speech, forcing out each word between waves of nausea.

"You . . . can't . . . do . . . this. Mustn't. The . . . danger." His voice trailed off again as he emptied the contents of his stomach onto the floor.

"Too late, flatscan," the mutant at the computer sneered as he gathered up the disks he'd copied.

The last thing Watkins saw before he finally succumbed to blessed unconsciousness was a small cyclone of papers from his desk formed as the cool summer breeze blew in from the lab door left open in the haste of the mutants' exit.

Dr. Hank McCoy muttered to himself in frustration as he looked at the latest column of figures from his test data. The member of the X-Men team known as the Beast would seem so close to finding a cure for the Legacy Virus, only to see his hopes turn to despair. Stryfe, the villain who had originally engineered the virus, had anticipated all the major routes a scientist would take in trying to construct a cure. He sighed heavily.

"Discouraged, Hank?" Storm asked as she quietly entered the room.

"Indeed, I'm afraid that I am, Ororo. It's times like this that I know exactly what Keats meant when he said, 'There is not a fiercer hell than the failure in a great object.'"

"I have another problem for you, my friend. Turn on the TV, Channel 7. There's something you need to see."

When the image settled, Beast saw a mutant of obvious Slavic origin, large boned, but squat. The arms with which he was gesticulating emphatically were mechanical, and he had the wild-eyed fanatical expression Hank had come to associate with the Acolytes, the fanatic followers of Magneto, who shared that villain's desire for mutant conquest of the world.

"That's Katu, isn't it?" he asked.

Storm nodded. "Turn it up. You need to hear what he's saying to understand our newest problem."

Once the volume was up, they could hear Katu in mid-sentence. ". . . you flatscans have no choice but to give in to our demands if you wish your society to remain intact.

We have obtained and duplicated one of your biological weapons, a bacterium that consumes plastic. We've placed the bacterium, in sufficient quantity to destroy your so-called civilization, in a bomb located for ideal worldwide dispersal. The bomb will be detonated within three days if our demands are not met.

"First, all mutants currently held against their will are to be released immediately to the Acolytes. We will no longer permit you to torture and experiment with our brothers and sisters.

"Secondly, all human occupants of the northwestern states of Washington, Oregon, Idaho, and Montana in the United States of America are to be evacuated and relocated. The states will be turned over to the Acolytes for the formation of a mutant nation."

Katu looked up from his notes and faced the cameras directly. "We know you will not submit to these demands. We also know you will underestimate the amount of destruction these bacteria can cause. Your financial structures will crumble as your computer disks and tapes are destroyed. Your vehicles and construction equipment will be inoperable. Your factories will require complete overhauls before they will be able to produce again. Millions will fall ill or die because crucial medical supplies are stored in plastic containers. Once the bacteria have contaminated your water supplies, those humans with plastic in their bodies—such as pacemakers—will flood and overwhelm your hospitals. How many millions will be killed or injured in the inevitable riots and panic, do you think? There is no aspect of your lives that will remain as it was."

Katu smiled. That the smile was genuine neither Beast

nor Storm doubted for a moment. It was an unscripted, sincere expression of enjoyment, and it sent chills down the spines of both X-Men.

"We will laugh and celebrate as your society falls. Then we shall build *our* society—a mutant society—out of your ashes. It's been well over a century since Darwin first described to you the process of evolution, and you still have failed to grasp even its simplest principles. Now you'll see it in action."

Bishop strode into the room as Katu's final words cast a deeper pall over the two X-Men. "It's being continually broadcast via satellite all over the world. I see no reason to believe he's lying to us, although we've found no record of such a bacterium."

Beast breathed out a deep sigh and spoke slowly. "Oh, my stars and garters. He's not lying."

Startled, Bishop stared at Beast. "What? How do you know?"

Beast made his way over to the conference table, sat down, and gestured to the others to join him. "About two years ago, a Dr. Jerome Watkins consulted with me on the production of just this type of bacteria. I wasn't able to commit to working with him full-time on the project, but I have helped him with a few problems he's encountered here and there. The bacterium was being created to reduce plastic waste materials."

"Is it possible that Watkins was secretly working for the Acolytes on this project?" Storm queried.

"I don't think so, Ororo. First, Watkins has been working for the U.S. government for the past decade doing environmental research. I checked his credentials most thoroughly before I agreed to do any consulting work for him. He's a good man. Secondly, I don't think the Acolytes would ever consider working with a human," Beast turned to Bishop, who nodded.

"Such an alliance would be most uncharacteristic of the Acolytes," Bishop agreed. "It's much more likely that they got wind of the project somehow and decided to turn it to their own ends."

"No matter how the situation has developed, though," Beast stated, "we must find a way to stop it."

Storm looked thoughtful for a moment. "Then the question is how the Acolytes obtained the bacterium, assuming it is the same one, and if it is the same, where is Dr. Watkins now, and does he know how to stop it?"

Beast walked over to the communications console and had it dial Watkins's home and lab. There was no response at either location. "Jerome worked out of a lab in Dallas. I'll fly down there and see if I can locate him. Maybe he has some answers for us."

Storm nodded and glanced over at Bishop. "Good. In the meantime, Bishop and I can try to trace the Acolytes to their newest base of operations. If our deadline is only three days away, we don't have much time."

In just a few hours, Beast stood outside the open door to Watkins's laboratory. Alert, not knowing what to expect, he cautiously made his way toward the observation window of the main room, where he saw what appeared to be the wreckage of an experiment. He was mentally taking notes on the extent of the destruction when a faint, low moan sent him toward the storage cabinets.

"Dr. Watkins? Jerome? Is that you?"

Hearing another moan, McCoy used his superhuman strength to pull the storage cabinet out of the way. There, in a space he would have thought too small to hide anyone, sat Watkins. Curled up in a fetal position, he shook with convulsions, occasionally giving voice to the pitiful moans that had led Beast to him. He turned his face toward Beast, who had extended a hand to him, and instantly recoiled.

"No! No! Just leave me alone!" he begged. "You already got what you came for."

"Jerome, it's me," McCoy said kindly. "Hank McCoy. You know me. I'm here to help you."

"H-H-Hank?" Watkins asked, and blinked several times, as if trying to clear his vision. This time when Beast extended his hand, it was accepted. Watkins tried to stay upright, but leaned heavily on Beast as he launched into an explanation of what had happened.

"I was entering the final data on the bacterium when two mutants burst into the room. They took everything . . . the research data, the samples . . . everything." He looked at Beast, his eyes clouded and anguished. "I tried to stop them, Hank. But one of them . . . he . . . he . . ." Watkins broke off his sentence and began sobbing softly. "I thought you were another one of them."

Beast laid a comforting hand on Watkins's shoulder and pressed it gently. "I know this is hard for you, Jerome, but you have to tell me everything. What did he do?"

"He used some kind of hallucinogenic power on me. I've never felt such a thing in my life. Pain, nausea, dizziness . . . I couldn't move. I couldn't do anything as they stole my life's work!'' Watkins began sobbing again. "They took everything.''

Beast gripped Watkins's arm and helped him into a chair. "Jerome, let me dress your wound, and then you must come back with me to the Xavier Institute. Right away.''

When Watkins started to protest, Beast held up a hand to silence him. "Hear me out before you decline, if you please. The men who stole your research are members of a group called the Acolytes. They have taken the materials and research stolen from you and have somehow modified it into a bomb.'' He saw Watkins blanche but did not stop. "The Acolytes have taken the bomb and have placed it in an unknown location where it will disperse the bacterium around the entire globe. They have threatened to detonate the device should their demands not be met within seventy-two hours.'' Briefly, he recounted the Acolyte demands.

"Oh, Lord,'' Watkins groaned. "No government would ever agree to those conditions.'' His voice became resigned. "And that mutant, Katu, could well be right. The destructive power of this organism . . . human society will be hardest hit by the damage. Mutants will be able to use their abilities to work around the more obvious difficulties.''

"And no doubt they've been planning this for some time,'' Beast added drily, "and so are prepared for the devastation they intend to wreak upon humanity. The only chance we have is to develop a counteragent and find the device before it is detonated. My teammates are working on that end even as we speak.''

"They took all my notes on the bacterium, but I should

be able to reconstruct it from memory; I've been working with the same agent for months now."

Beast helped Watkins to stand. "We'll use the Institute lab. My friends will be waiting for us. Besides, you won't get better health care in any hospital, and I'm afraid you really need it."

Thousands of miles away, Storm and Bishop had tracked down the last known location of Katu and the Earth-stationed Acolytes, deep in the Great Sandy Desert of Australia. Although the buildings appeared deserted, Bishop took no chances as he entered the main building. Plasma rifle at the ready, he entered quietly, Storm close behind him. The room was empty except for some furniture and a few pieces of scrap paper, left behind when the Acolytes closed down shop. Storm picked up a loosely wadded piece of paper from one corner and spread it open on one of the desks.

"Bishop, look at this. An aviation weather report. If I'm reading this correctly, the Acolytes were getting weather conditions and information on the area surrounding the Bahamas." She pointed to a faint penciled circle on the sheet. "It appears that they were especially interested in the conditions around Cat Island."

"Good. That's somewhere for us to start. And look at this." He held out a sheet of paper he'd recovered from one of the other desks. "Evidence that the Acolytes have the bacterium Hank told us about. It's a printout of some test results. Look at the header: Project XFS1147, Chief Researcher, Dr. Jerome Watkins."

"We've found what we came for," Storm said. "Let's go back and see if Hank was able to locate Watkins."

When Bishop and Storm arrived back at the Institute, they found Beast and Watkins hard at work in the laboratory.

"Who is this person?" Bishop demanded as he eyed Watkins with obvious mistrust.

"Storm, Bishop, may I present to you Dr. Jerome Watkins, the researcher I told you about earlier," Beast replied.

Bishop's eyes narrowed dangerously. "The doctor responsible for creating the bacterium the Acolytes are going to use to try and destroy us all?"

Before Beast could confirm the query, Bishop crossed the room, taking Watkins by the lapels and shoving his back against a wall. "How much did the Acolytes pay you?" he demanded.

Watkins struggled ineffectually against Bishop's iron grip. "Nothing. I wasn't working for them, I swear it!" His voice came out high, with a note of panic, and he looked pleadingly at Beast. "Get him off of me, Hank, please!"

Storm laid her hand over one of Bishop's. "Let him go, Bishop. I believe he's telling the truth."

Beast nodded his agreement. "He came here of his own free will to help me try to find a containing agent."

Bishop let go of Watkins and stepped back a few paces but still glared at the small man in suspicion. "I don't like his being in the mansion. How do you know he isn't just *pretending* to help you—that he's not really leading you in the wrong direction? How are we to know that we can trust him?" He crossed his arms in front of him as if daring Watkins to prove him wrong.

Ever practical, Beast replied, "How are we to know that we can't? I think I would know if I were being led down the proverbial primrose path, Bishop. Besides, this is the best place for us to work. Surely you are aware of that."

Bishop relaxed his stance somewhat and moved a few steps farther away from Watkins. He reached into his pocket and pulled out the papers he and Storm had taken from the deserted Acolyte hideout, handing them to Beast. "From all indications, we believe them to be heading to the Bahamas with the bacterial bomb."

Beast scanned the papers quickly. "We know they have the bacterium, we think we know where they're taking it. Now Jerome and I must work hard to find a neutralizing agent before they decide to detonate the bomb."

Storm moved toward the door. "You and Dr. Watkins keep working, Hank. Bishop and I will fly to the Caribbean and check out Cat Island."

Beast nodded as he turned to continue his lab work. "That would seem the most logical way to proceed. We'll keep you informed as to our progress."

Beast and Watkins had little success. When their latest experiment failed, Watkins pounded the table in frustration. "We've tried everything I know to do, Hank. I'm all out of ideas." Watkins removed his glasses and rubbed the bridge of his nose. "I should never have gotten involved in this project in the first place. I knew what could happen. No matter what they said, or how much money they gave me for research, I should have known better. It's not worth the consequences." He paused and closed his eyes for a moment. "Nothing could be worth that price."

Beast's furry blue brow wrinkled in confusion. "What consequences are you talking about, Jerome?"

Watkins blinked rapidly and nervously cleared his throat several times before answering. "The bacterium can do more damage than I've told you, Hank."

"How? Tell me, Jerome. You need to tell me everything." McCoy's voice was low, almost soothing, as he sensed Watkins's fear.

"When the government found out, on its completion, how successful the bacterium was going to be, they commissioned me to make certain 'improvements' on it. Purely hypothetical, they said. Just in case. They told me to turn it into a biological weapon—one never to be used, but available for possible use against cybernetic soldiers. That's a definite concern in this day and age." Watkins took a deep breath before continuing, and when he spoke, his voice was shaky. "The reproductive rate is phenomenal. It's highly resistant to conventional antibacterial agents. It maintains integrity when absorbed through the skin or by consumption of contaminated food or water. Frankly, it would be virtually impossible for a society to contain it if released."

Beast made a soft, strangled sound of protest. "Jerome, did you stop to think what the consequences of the use of an agent like that would be? Of the millions of innocent lives that would be lost in the panic as their society was destroyed? Noncombatant lives?"

"I didn't let myself think about it, Hank. I told myself that it would never come to that, that no sane government would ever unleash such a monstrosity. I told myself that the benefits of the bacterium—the ecological benefits—outweighed all other considerations. With modifications, it can still be used as I originally designed it. I *told* myself that it was all in the name of research." Watkins covered his face with his hands, letting self-pity overwhelm him. "I suppose the truth of the matter was that I didn't want to know what they were going to do with it. I was going to take the additional research funds they promised to give me when this project was finished and go away someplace where I wouldn't have to deal with the consequences of my creation."

Both men were silent for several minutes before resuming their work.

To all appearances, Cat Island was picture-postcard perfect. "This is the last place I'd suspect of having a devastating biological weapon on it. It's almost annoyingly beautiful," Bishop said sternly.

Storm extended her hands and felt the warm summer tropical breeze flow through her fingers as a wind current gently first lifted, then deposited her on the ground next to Bishop. "The air circulation pattern is unique here. Should the bacteria be released, the wind currents would quickly carry it to all corners of the globe. I seriously doubt any area would remain unaffected for long."

Bishop started walking up the beach from where they'd landed the *Blackbird*. "I say we start searching for the Acolyte base. It won't take long, considering how small this island is."

"I agree," Storm replied, "but I caution you not to take any action until we hear from Hank and Dr. Watkins. We cannot risk the Acolytes releasing the bacterium until we have an antidote. The danger is too great."

For a moment it looked as if Bishop was going to argue the point, but eventually he nodded his agreement and they set off together in search of the enemy. Within a short time they came upon a small bungalow about a mile inland from the X-Men's landing point on the beach. Storm and Bishop ducked into the cover of the pine wood forest as the Acolytes Katu and Spoor emerged from the bungalow and sprawled out on the sand just outside the door.

"Let's take them," Bishop hissed to Storm. "Then we can make them tell us where the bomb is."

Storm shook her head. "That is too risky. Even if they told us the location of the bomb, it may have a failsafe or dead-man switch on it that they could activate before we could reach it. We cannot risk detonation. I will stay here and watch these two while you search for the bomb."

After a moment's silence, Bishop nodded his agreement and headed farther inland, while Storm sat and patiently kept watch over the two Acolytes.

Back at the Institute, Beast and Watkins had re-created the plastic-devouring bacterium, but were having little luck producing a counteragent. Watkins piped a dab of liquid onto a slide treated with the bacterium and looked into the microscope. He shouted and gestured excitedly to Beast, motioning for him to come take a look. "I think we've finally hit something here, Hank!"

Seconds later, Beast pulled back and shook his head. "We're closer, but the agent only slowed the bacteria down. It became active again."

"We were so close," Watkins sighed, and cursed under his breath. "But slowing it down isn't enough. I gave it a high reproductive rate, so we need to slow it down, yes, but then we need something to move in for the kill."

"Two different agents," Beast mused. "Maybe we should try to engineer a virus within these growth-slowing bacteria. As the plastic-converting bacteria consume the slowing agent, the virus would be released."

Hours later, Watkins watched, bleary eyed, as Beast performed the final test on their latest offering. Both scientists held their breath as they waited to see what would happen. Thirty seconds . . . one minute . . . two minutes . . . five minutes . . . there was still no sign of activity from the plastic-consuming bacteria after the initial introduction of the counteragent. Then they saw the color change that marked the deterioration of the plastic consumer, and began to breathe again.

Beast extended his hand, and Watkins took it. As they shook hands on their victory, Beast was already turning to the next phase of the job—creating a large enough quantity to counter the bomb. "We've got just under a day. Even with accelerants, it will be difficult to produce sufficient counteragent and get it to Cat Island. Let us hope we will have enough time."

"Hank, I want to ask a favor."

Beast glanced toward Watkins, mildly surprised. "What is it, Jerome?"

"I want to go with you to the island." He held up a hand as Beast began to protest. "I have to see this thing through to the finish, Hank. I'm responsible for this situation; I started it with my research. I have to be there, to make sure that the bacteria is truly destroyed." He looked ready to plead his case and was slightly surprised when Beast did no more than nod his head in agreement. Not knowing what to say, Watkins started gathering the materials they needed to begin creating the new batch of counteragent.

"The United States government, and the goverments of the world, will not give in to demands made by terrorist groups. I'm here to assure you all that the country's best scientists are now close to a breakthrough which will enable us to counteract any bacteria that the Acolytes might unleash. It is just a matter of time before—"

From behind the bushes screening the path in front of the bungalow, Storm watched as Katu reached over and switched off the portable radio on the patio table in front of him.

"Fools!" Katu shouted. "Do they really think they have a chance of stopping the destruction this will unleash? These are the last whimpers of humanity." He stood up and began to pace back and forth along the path, pausing just a few feet from Storm without noticing her presence.

"Let them whine," Spoor replied. "Their days are numbered, and they know it."

Storm started slightly as she felt a hand on her shoulder. She turned to see Bishop directly behind her. A few feet behind him were Beast and Dr. Watkins. Watkins held a large vial in his hands. They retreated out of hearing distance of the bungalow.

"We managed to produce a counteragent for the bacterium, but we had no time for testing on a large scale," Beast told Storm and Bishop. "I can't promise that it will work."

"Now," Storm said quietly, "all we have to do is find

the bomb and disarm it. If everything goes well, we won't need the counteragent. Good work, Beast. You, too, Doctor."

"I've searched over the entire island, and there's no sign of the bomb," Bishop pointed out. "It's possible the device is inside the bungalow, but to get to it, we'll have to go through those two." Bishop nodded in Katu and Spoor's direction.

"I have noticed that either Spoor or Katu is with the radio at all times. They have not left it alone for a moment. Now, that could be because they want to keep listening in case their demands are met, but I wonder..." Storm mused.

"An intriguing possibility, Storm," Beast said.

"We'll check out the radio as well as the bungalow," Bishop decided.

"Jerome, you are not equipped or trained to battle with these two," Beast said not unkindly. "For your own safety, please stay hidden here until we have secured the area. Your part is done."

"Since our powers share some similarities, I will deal with Katu," Storm decided. "Spoor and the bomb are up to you two. Are we ready?"

After receiving the nods of agreement, Storm launched herself into the air, propelled by the island winds that were hers to command. Pushed by the gathering winds, the clouds gathered behind her and began to darken.

As soon as he caught sight of Storm, Katu spat out an oath and gathered his powers in opposition. Where Storm controlled specific elements of nature, Katu produced atmospheric anomalies that countered them. Within seconds, the winds around the island raged, and sand from the nearby beach flayed their skin, while the heavens opened up to pelt them with freezing rains. When Storm called forth thunderstorms, Katu countered with a change in the pressure system to push the storm back. The two were so evenly matched that it was obvious that the victory would go to the one who held off exhaustion the longer.

Taking advantage of his distraction as he watched the battle, Bishop stepped into the clearing in front of Spoor, planting his feet and levelling his plasma rifle at his enemy. "Where is the bomb, Acolyte?" he demanded.

A sly smile came to Spoor's face. "Ah, X-Man. Come to save the human race, have you?" He cackled. "It's too late. They have only minutes left before the bomb detonates and puts an end to their tyranny over mutants."

"Using violence to end violence, are you?" Beast leapt into the clearing in front of the bungalow. "Rarely have those tactics succeeded, and never without tremendous cost to all the parties involved."

Spoor looked from one to another and backed away a few steps. "We gave them their chance. They chose not to take it. On their heads be it." Without warning, he rushed toward Beast, releasing his hallucinogenic pheromones at full strength.

Even the Beast's phenomenal agility did not enable him to dodge the pheremones, and he crashed to the ground, holding first his head, then his stomach, as waves of sharp pain cascaded over him. Knife after hallucinatory knife stabbed him, and each slice felt as real as if it had been made with cold steel. He lay there, helpless, but struggling to get up and fight back.

When he saw that Beast had fallen to the pheromones, Bishop ran to the pair and stepped between them. Bishop's own involuntary powers reflected the Acolyte's pheromones back upon himself, with quick results. The Acolyte fell to the ground, screaming, the visions in his head taking control of him, immobilizing him as effectively as he had Beast.

Bishop picked up the now-helpless Spoor and looked at his fellow X-Man. "I can handle him. You help Storm." He strained to be heard above the roaring winds of Storm and Katu's battle.

Beast rose to his feet, the effects of the pheromones quickly wearing off. A few quick hops brought him behind Katu. The Acolyte was completely focused on his intense battle with Storm and didn't even notice the Beast until the X-Man delivered a quick blow to the back of the head. The Inuit mutant fell unconscious and the Beast carried him into the bungalow.

Exhausted, Storm drifted back to the ground, landed, and trailed Beast into the building, followed in turn by Watkins. Bishop deposited Spoor in the room off the main entrance and stepped aside to let Beast enter with Katu. Both Acolytes were unconscious and likely to remain that way for some time.

Leaving their foes in the cottage, they walked back out onto the patio. The radio was still on the table.

It was Storm who first noticed the clock on the stereo. "Look! That's not the time! It's counting down."

Watkins handed Beast the vial of counteragent. "We have to be ready to release this should the need arise."

Bishop turned to Watkins. "You can stand over there in

the doorway and keep an eye on those two while we try to defuse the bomb.''

Watkins was surprised. "Stand guard over them? Me?"

Bishop nodded. "Just watch them carefully and let us know when they start to wake up."

Beast moved into place to dispense the counteragent should that be required. Still weakened from her stalemate with Katu, Storm steeled herself to contain the expelled bacteria should the bomb accidentally detonate during the disarming process. Watkins could feel the tension in the air as Bishop removed the radio casing, carefully placing it to one side.

Uncovered, the bomb proved to be an intricate series of multicolored wires in elaborate and confusing combinations. Slowly, Bishop snipped one wire after another. Wire cutters poised over the final series of connections, he stopped and whistled softly. "Tricky little fiends. Thorough too," he muttered under his breath. "They almost fooled me. They've connected a second trigger mechanism, but it's very subtle."

"Should we be worrying?" Beast asked.

Bishop shook his head. "Not yet. It's just going to take a little longer for me to disarm."

Distracted from his watch by Bishop's difficulties, Watkins failed to notice Spoor's stirring in the room behind him. Without warning, he felt a flood of heat surround him and smelled smoke. He felt the flames charring his skin, and in a blind panic to escape the blaze, ran full speed toward the ocean—straight at Bishop, who was engrossed in the delicate process of disarming the second trigger.

"Jerome, what are you doing?" Beast cried out. He leapt

forward in a desperate attempt to intercept Watkins, but was too late.

With one sweep of his arm as he tried to force his way to perceived safety, Watkins brushed the wire cutters in Bishop's hand against the trigger mechanism. In the brief seconds before the explosion, Spoor lost consciousness again, and Watkins and Bishop were face to face, eye to eye.

Bishop stared in horror at the man before him, then saw something he didn't expect. He saw true sorrow reflected in Watkins's eyes. The shame of being responsible for the bacterium's creation plain on his face, Watkins turned away in the last moments and threw himself over the bomb.

The explosion threw Watkins in one direction and Bishop in another. Storm reacted immediately, gathering the bacteria in a funnel of wind and fighting to contain them. "Quickly, Hank! Release the counteragent!" she yelled over the force of the wind.

Beast released the stopper on the vial and fed it into the wind funnel, watching its light color mix with the darker shades of the consumer bacteria. He turned and saw Bishop rise, slightly shaken, but unharmed. Not that the bomb would have harmed him in any case; Bishop's power allowed him to absorb any energy he was hit with. But Watkins had no way of knowing that.

The Beast ran to Watkins then, who lay still on the ground.

"H-h-help me, Hank," the scientist managed to cough out. Gently, Beast helped Watkins to sit up.

They all watched anxiously as Storm fought to contain the mixture of destruction and hope, her limbs drooping slightly as her strength began to flag. Fearing the worst, they watched the plastic-consuming bacteria begin to make their mark on the patio furniture, which, as the umbrella and table began to dissolve and small puddles of goo filled the seats of the chairs, began to resemble a Dali painting.

Storm's strength completely depleted, she collapsed on the ground, releasing the swirling cloud of bacteria. No longer artificially contained, the cloud dispersed out into the island's natural wind pattern. Bishop went to Storm's side, raising her to her feet and letting her lean on him as they walked toward the Acolytes' transport. Beast picked up the injured Watkins, cradling him as a child, and followed the other X-Men down the path to learn if the world as they knew it would continue.

The Acolyte plane was on the far side of the bungalow, and as they watched, the wings began to droop towards the ground as the compound dissolved. Soon half the wing was melting, hanging limply in the air. They held their breath and waited.

Seconds passed, and then minutes, the silence broken only by Watkins' strangled breathing, but there was no further deterioration of the plane.

"It worked, Hank." Watkins's voice came out garbled, his breathing heavy and labored. "We were able to stop it."

Beast looked down at the man in his arms. "That we did, friend."

Watkins grasped Beast's furred hand, squeezing it tightly. "We made a good team."

Beast nodded once and watched as Watkins' eyes slowly closed and his breathing slowed. "Jerome?"

Then the sounds of breathing stopped. Dr. Jerome Watkins was still and silent, his goal accomplished and his conscience, if not cleared, then relieved, as he let himself slip away.

Beast took a deep breath and lifted the body of his friend and colleague, preparing to carry him out to the beach to the *Blackbird*.

"You ruined our best chance for a mutant society this day, X-Men," Katu's voiced boomed out from behind them, more sorrow than anger in his words. "You could have let the bacteria do its job. It would have given us freedom!"

Beast looked back only once. He stared at Katu for a moment, then down at Watkins's body in his arms. "I would not pay this price for your 'freedom.' It would bring no peace, only violence, hatred, sorrow, and regret. There will be no true freedom until we can work together."

With that, the X-Men moved toward the beach.

"What about the Acolytes?" Bishop asked. "What shall we do with them?"

"Leave them," said Beast. "They have to live with themselves. And they have 'nothing to look backward to with pride, and nothing to look forward to with hope.' "

"Shakespeare?" Storm asked.

"Robert Frost," Beast replied as they walked away.

Three days later, Beast sat alone in his laboratory, reading over a new medical journal when he glanced up at the video monitor. On the screen Graydon Creed, the leader of the mutant-hating Friends of Humanity, pounded a small wooden podium like a crazed evangelist. His mouth worked furiously, and out of a sense of morbid curiosity, Beast turned up the volume.

"I tell you people, without mutants and their kind we would not be subjected to threats like the one we had last week. We would not need to live in fear of one of their plagues robbing us of our future, like a thief in the night. We would not have to constantly guard ourselves against this evil if the government would put them into forced labor isolation centers, as we have repeatedly advocated. If I am elected to office, I will write a bill that places all mutants in a controlled environment, so as to keep our country safe for the American people—for *humans*."

Beast shut off the monitor, unable to listen to any more of the venomous speech. For a moment he felt a pang of sorrow that so many humans saw things in the same light as Creed. Then he remembered Jerome Watkins and his sacrifice. Until the fresh summer breeze of change did come, Watkins's sacrifice would give him hope and faith that change was possible.

LIFE IS BUT A DREAM

Stan Timmons

Illustration by Rick Leonardi & Terry Austin

ll of this happened, give or take.

The sun was shining and a brisk wind blew marshmallow clouds across its face, painting the suburbs in light/shadow/light, giving everything a shutterbox effect.

There were the hypnotic drones of electric lawn-mowers, and the smell of freshly cut grass and timothy hung sweetly on the air. A radio in the dash of a '65 Mustang that a shade-tree mechanic was restoring proclaimed the good news that the Cincinnati Reds were winning the first game of a scheduled double-header against the Pirates.

A bird perched on the rim of a stone birdbath in the Beckers' front yard; he dipped his bill into the cool, clear water and tipped his head back, allowing the water to trickle down his throat. Afterward, refreshed, he trilled an unbroken string of notes. Somewhere down the neatly manicured block, in a tree in a yard bordered by just-cropped shrubbery and a newly painted white picket fence, another bird answered.

There was a steady whip and whir of a lawn sprinkler, and, in someone's backyard, on an orderly red brick patio, hamburgers and hot dogs cooked over an open grill.

The sun broke from behind the last of the clouds and its light on the water of the backyard pond looked like scattered coins.

It was one of those rare and perfect days, thought Rogue, that couldn't go any farther toward proving God's existence than if He had left His fingerprints all over everything.

Rogue looked away from the window set above the kitchen sink and adjusted the flow of water from the faucet.

She was scrubbing and peeling potatoes, starting to get things ready for tonight's dinner. She had already put the rack of lamb in the Dutch oven and basted it once with a mint sauce she had made, but she would need Remy's help if she was going to have supper ready, the table set, and have a hot, relaxing bath before the guests arrived.

Behind her, the Frigidaire clunked as it proudly made another ice cube and started cheerily on making another, not content to rest too long upon its laurels.

At the thought of Remy, she glanced at the drain board of the double sink and the simple gold ring sitting there, where she had put it when she started supper. Apart from these rare times, she had not taken it from her hand since that day when, for better or worse, for richer or poorer, Remy had placed it there.

"We've had the worse and we've had the poorer," she spoke to the sun-washed, airy kitchens, "now we have the better and richer to look forward to."

She was pulled from her reverie by the crack of a softball against a bat and the cheers of children. She looked out the window just in time to see Remy waving the runner on to second. He was always involved with the neighborhood kids in some fashion, refereeing them in a game of touch football or coaching them in a game of softball. He was surprisingly at home with children—the kid in him, Rogue supposed. She didn't mind him spending his Saturday afternoons with them, since it seemed most of the other parents were too busy for them, but she absolutely drew the line at his trying to teach them to gamble.

"Life's a big gamble," he had said trying to sweet-talk his way around her when she put her foot down. "Don' think so? Then how come half of 'life' is made up of 'if'? Hey, why you t'ink life is but a dream?"

Rogue had laughed and responded, "I can play that one, too, swamp rat. 'God is love, love is blind, Ray Charles is blind, therefore, Ray Charles is God.'"

"He *is* God!" Remy replied then. "Ray an' Charlie Parker."

"Head for home! Head for home!" Remy now shouted at the runner. The boy crossed the plate to the sound of cheers, just a split second ahead of the ball.

"Remy!" Rogue called from the opened back door. "Time f'you t'head home too, lover."

Remy smiled and waved at her across the vacant lot.

"Right dere, *petite fille!*" He said something else to the children and started jogging for the house. The sun, sailing toward the west where clouds waited to devour it, threw Remy's shadow out long behind him, like a small, frightened child racing to catch up.

"Forks on de left or de right?"

But Rogue didn't hear him. She was too busy checking the last of the arrangements. For the hundredth time.

"Sweet—forks—left or right?"

"That's fine," she answered distractedly.

"We havin' red wine or white wit' de elephant?"

"Now y'bein' silly; y'know we ate the last of the elephant weeks ago."

"Ah, so you are in dere somewhere!"

"Sorry, sugar. I just want everything to go all right tonight."

Remy set the silverware aside and stepped around the

dining room table to where Rogue stood, rearranging the fresh-cut flowers in the centerpiece. For the hundredth time.

"Everyt'ing be fine, *chère*. We've had plenty o' parties."

She smiled crookedly and corrected him. "We've *been* to plenty of parties, Remy. This is the first one we ever gave."

"Every day a party in de Big Easy," he said, taking her hand, feeling the warmth of her flesh next to his. "Every day a party if you live to de fullest." And he nestled his cheek to hers, closing his eyes and slow-dancing to a music only he could hear. God, perhaps, or Bird. Or Mingus. "Po' darlin'. Want so bad for us to fit in. Want so bad for us to be normal."

"Is that so wrong?"

He looked at her and she could feel it then, building between them: a spark, an ember, slowly building, rising, threatening to catch their whole world ablaze.

"You already fit in, *chère*, where it matters most. In LeBeau's eternal heart."

He kissed her then and was still kissing her when the doorbell rang. Their guests had to wait a few minutes on the porch, and dinner was slightly dry, but Rogue found she somehow didn't mind.

Scott and Jean Summers owned the mock-Tudor style house next door to Rogue and Remy; they had lived in the neighborhood for quite awhile before the LeBeaus, and naturally took them under their wing. It turned out they had all attended, at various times, the same exclusive school for gifted individuals, and that only helped to cement the blocks of their friendship. Jean once asked Rogue how she had gotten that name, and Rogue replied, "M'mom's like that." That offhanded comment had sealed their fate and they were inseparable companions thereafter. Scott and Remy, two men unaccustomed to expressing their emotions, maintained a guarded but solid acquaintanceship, partly based on their mutual love of cooking. Remy had to admire a man who could go back for seconds on his four-alarm crawfish bisque. "Dat about de bravest t'ing Remy ever seen anyone ever do, *mon ami*," LeBeau had said, only half-jokingly, and Scott had nearly smiled.

The Summerses often entertained, inviting Remy and Rogue over when they did, and they knew a wide assortment of people: Bobby Drake, a CPA frozen in the past, with a glacial heart that couldn't be moved or warmed by all the lights of Christmas, it seemed; Henry McCoy, an obsessively brilliant but apish biophysicist who hid his insecurities behind a constant barrage of big words; Warren Worthington III, a foppish millionaire who tried to show the world he deserved his enormous wealth by giving vast fortunes away to charity and who tried to show he deserved love by being with a different girl every week.

All of them, it seemed to Rogue, were the walking wounded, all suffering some ancient, buried tragedy with an impossible grace and nobility.

But tonight, ah, tonight the Summerses had brought with them Logan, an odd, bestial, frightening, earthy, hugely lusty man who ate his meal ravenously, attacking it with his bare hands and issuing barely human grunts as he gnawed and tore the meat from the bone.

"Dat a man who know how t'grab life by de t'roat!"

Remy exclaimed admiringly. "You grab 'im one for Remy, eh?"

"Grab 'im yourself, bub," Logan replied around a mouthful of food, grease, and blood running down his chin. "I got some throat-wringin' o' my own t'do."

Rogue started to laugh, needed to laugh very badly—he reminded her of the Tasmanian Devil from the old Bugs Bunny cartoons, all teeth and claws and appetite—but then their eyes met—locked like magnets slamming together—and Rogue felt herself deflate like a pricked balloon. He smiled, a smile that never quite reached the eyes, and she had the feeling that it was her throat he had grabbed, and he was grinding her to bone and blood and paste.

"Where on earth did y'ever find him?"

"Who? Logan?" Jean asked. She was helping Rogue clear the decimated table. "Friend of Scott's. Met him in the Canadian woods. Don't really know much about him." She shrugged dismissively. "I think he might have been in some sort of intelligence outfit—maybe part of some top-secret experiment. He's odd, but he's harmless—if you're on his good side."

"Where's that? Couple hundred miles away?"

Jean laughed and saw then that Rogue was serious; she was deeply disturbed by Logan.

"Sweetheart, I wouldn't let him come around my house if he wasn't harmless. We wouldn't have brought him here. You know me; I've always been good at reading people."

Rogue touched Logan's plate, littered with picked bones like a miniature desert, and shuddered. She quickly dropped the plate into the pile, as if touching it too long would cause an empathy to form, somehow contaminate her, taint her, make her like him.

"And I can read you too," Jean said, tipping Rogue's chin up with her finger, forcing Rogue to look at her, look her in the eyes. "There's something else at work here, something more than just feeling uncomfortable around Logan. Is it anything you want to talk to me about?"

"It's nothin', it's . . . When you find the man you love, how come the honeymoon doesn't last f'rever?"

Jean traced her finger along the contours of Rogue's high cheekbones, a sister comforting her sibling, a mother soothing her child. "Welcome to marriage, phase two," she said.

"Does it have t'be that way?" Rogue asked, and there was something like terror in her voice.

And now it was Jean's turn to look away. "You wouldn't be normal if it weren't," she said. "This wouldn't be real life."

"Well, like th'man says, 'reality bites.' "

"It can," Jean agreed, with her words at least, but not her voice. "It cuts and bites and tears, this life, but take heart. It only gets better."

"You and Scott—y'all seem so happy . . . what's y' secret?"

Jean considered this for a long moment before answering. "Well, Scott's my world—but he's not my *whole* world, you understand? That's too big a burden to put on him— or anyone."

Rogue thought about that while Jean finished busing the table. There were greasy, bloody fingerprints on the tablecloth where Logan had sat. He would never take the place of a strolling violinist at dinner, that was for sure.

"I'll help you with dessert," Jean offered.

"What about kids?"

"I guess—but, if it's all the same to you, I think I'd rather have cake and coffee."

Rogue looked puzzled, then exploded with laughter, the first honest laugh Jean had heard from her all night.

In the den, lushly paneled and appointed with built-in bookcases containing many folios and first editions, and one wall comprised of a giant screen television, the latest stereo equipment and shelves bowed in the middle from the weight of jazz, blues, R&B, and rock CDs and vinyl, a room largely given over to the intellectual and emotional, Logan was holding court over Sazerac and cigars (Scott had neither), regaling the other men with his bawdy jokes and impossible exploits.

He had told them of hunting leopards with the Maharaja of Mysore and his subsequent dalliance with the emperor's harem and barely escaping detection by the guards, of his time in Japan, and sailing from Nice to Morocco through a freak storm that nearly sank his small ship, and of owning a bar in Madripoor.

As Rogue and Jean entered the den bearing a tray of *satsuma* cake and coffee, Logan was in the middle of his tale of running with the bulls in Pamplona. He had been doing well, he said, until the man in front of him slipped on the wet cobblestones and Logan fell over him. The first of the bulls rolled over them both like a wave of hooves and horns. To save himself, Logan said, he grabbed on to the bull's underside and held on for a mad, miles-long run through the streets of Spain. "It was that, or get trampled by Spain's supply o' *toros.*"

"That sounds like a lot o' bull," commented Rogue, a wry smile creasing the corners of her mouth, and everyone, even Scott, laughed.

"Good one, gal," Logan said, puffing deeply on his smelly cigar. He took the dessert plate Rogue offered, surreptitiously stroking her finger with his. She withdrew as if she had just thrust her hand into a sack of squirming snakes and maggots. "You got a funny girl there, Gumbo. You better watch somebody doesn't take 'er away from you."

"How 'bout it, *chère?* Was it worth it?"

Rogue paused in the brushing of her hair, watching Remy in the mirror of the vanity. "Yeah, I think so."

Remy laughed. "Dat Logan, he a character, don' you t'ink? De stories he tell, *chère*, you wouldn't believe. He stop jus' shy o' claimin' credit for advisin' God on dat sun in da mornin', moon at night t'ing. He want Scott an' Remy t'go huntin' wit' him sometime, get in touch wit' our 'hairy *homme.*' "

Irrational fear squeezed her heart with icy, skeletal fingers. "I don't want you to go," she said hurriedly, breathlessly.

"*Quoi?*"

"I don't like him, Remy. There's somethin' about him, he makes me feel so—" (*alive*) "—afraid. Please . . . promise me . . . stay away from him."

"You serious?"

He saw she was.

"Okay. I promise."

She seemed to relax, visibly, and returned to brushing her hair. Remy stood behind her, watching her silently, like a ghost. "Is dat all? All dat's bothering you, I mean?"

That was a good question, the only one. Was that all that was bothering her? Really?

No. No, she couldn't honestly say it was. But how could she tell him that, although she loved him more than ever, more than anyone or anything, something had begun to feel wrong between them? Something she herself would be hard pressed to name, other than to say he wasn't the man she had met and fallen in love with. Some vital, elemental spark had seemingly gone out of him and somehow ended up in Logan.

And could she honestly say it was only Logan whom she didn't trust?

Was there any reason the honeymoon couldn't last forever?

But that wouldn't be normal. Jean had told her so. It wouldn't be real life, and, in real life, things change. People change.

"*Chère?* Somet'in' else botherin' you?"

The look on his face, so like a lost little boy, and she felt love for him well up from the bottom of her heart and soul and spread out and engulf the both of them.

"Nothin' as bad as all that, sugar," she said with a barely contained enthusiasm. "I just wanted to wait till the right time t'tell you—I'm pregnant!"

Remy's jaw dropped and his mouth worked without forming words. He tried again and did marginally better this time.

"Remy a daddy? How? When? How long you known, gal?"

"I just found out m'self."

Remy moved to her, where she sat on the seat before the vanity, took the golden brush from her hand and set it aside.

"A baby, *chère*," he said softly, wonderingly, in awe of this oldest everyday miracle of all. "Remy a daddy." This time it was not a question, but joyful declaration. He held Rogue to him and she thought she felt the warm salt of a tear on her exposed neck and shoulder.

"It best be a girl, *fille*, so it get her mama's beauty. Double Remy's joy."

"Double or nothin', huh?"

"Remy bet on worse odds," he said, and something else occurred to him then. "Hey, but what you ain't tol' LeBeau is when? When de baby due?"

"Well . . ." She smiled enigmatically, and when he looked at her again, he wondered how he had not noticed her enormous girth before. Was he *that* blind? "As a matter of fact . . ." she said.

"Push harder! Push!"

"I *am* pushin'!"

"You squeezin' Remy's hand kind o' hard, *chère*—"

"As bad as this hurts—y'lucky—y'hand is *all* I'm squeezin'!"

"There's the head! Doctor Xavier, there's—"

"Remy can see the head, *chère*! It . . . it . . . oh!"

"Somebody revive that man and get him out of the way."

* * *

"I tell you, it was Remy's low blood sugar . . ."

But nobody was paying any attention to the proud father; all eyes were on the mother and the small tenant who had just been evicted from his tiny amniotic apartment, reclining in their hospital bed. Through the unrolling of the day, Rogue had had several visitors, her own mother, Raven Darkhölme, first among them. She had given her pronouncement that the baby—a boy—was "good—he doesn't look a thing like his father and, mercifully, nothing like his uncle." After her visit, Rogue assured Remy that was simply her mother's way of expressing her approval.

"What she say 'bout Remy when you marry him, den?"

"Oh she *really* expressed her approval then," Rogue answered, and they both laughed.

There had been others, and Scott and Jean had been by twice. On their second visit, Rogue and Remy asked them to be the baby's godparents.

The day nurse, Ororo, brought Charlie (they had decided to name the baby Charles because he looked like Xavier—bald and serious) in for his afternoon feeding. Ororo was Rogue's favorite of the nurses because she was like a grace note in the discordance of the hospital.

"He's such a good baby," Ororo said, smiling. "So perfect. He never cries, even when he's hungry or wet. What's your secret?"

"No secret," offered Remy. "He got perfect parents. Don' you know we ain't human?"

Rogue shivered, then. The baby was perfect. Remy was almost giddy. Her mother was pleased. Even the nurse admired their happiness. So why wasn't she content?

A shaft of late-afternoon sunlight angled through the window and fell on the family tree, painting everything in the room the color of fool's gold.

She returned home with the baby. Her crusades were little ones, waged against grass and chocolate stains, dingy floors, and balancing the checkbook. Day after meaningless day blew past with the bland uniformity of sand.

She was dusting the gilt-framed portrait of Remy, Charlie, and herself when the doorbell rang. She returned the photograph to its place on the piano and answered the door. She was expecting it to be Jean, dropping by with the new Crichton book she'd promised to lend her, but her heart gave a wild, surging leap, banging against her ribs like a wild bird in a cage when she saw her caller was—

"Logan?"

He was wearing a black tank top, exposing his hirsute arms and shoulders, his back and chest. He was leaning easily against the door frame, never taking his eyes from Rogue.

"Remy—" she started, and had to back up and try again. "Remy, he ain't here."

"I didn't come t'see Gumbo boy," he answered. "I came t'see you. T'give you whatcha need."

She told herself that she should slam the door in his face, but she didn't move a muscle.

"I can smell it on you, darlin'. Smell the disappointment an' frustration an'—"

Whispering, she finished, "Yearnin'."

"Got it in one," he answered with a feral grin. "You're yearnin' for the wild side. For a *man*."

"I—I already got a man."

"You," he said, lighting a cigar, "got a watered down copy of a man."

He stepped closer and she could smell the beer on his breath, the stale cigars the stink of sweat: the smell of life. She could feel these scents enfolding her and at the same time, felt her senses expanding outward like ripples in a pond. She became aware of the sound of her own excited breathing, the sound of the blood drums pounding out a Charlie Watts solo in her ears; she could feel the weight of the air on her skin, the bead of sweat behind her left ear; she could see the slow dance of the dust motes in the late afternoon sun and the lazy flight of the honeybee in her front yard, and the individual leaves of grass, all part of some great, cosmic puzzle.

Logan moved closer to kiss her.

"Don't worry, darlin'. I'm the best there is that at what I do."

Again she told herself she should do something. Again she didn't move a muscle, but allowed him to move close enough to kiss her.

"Dat's not what Remy hear!" the Cajun said, striking Logan a staggering blow from behind with his softball bat. Logan spun around in one fluid motion, swinging with his claws at the same time Remy brought his bat up. The blades buried themselves deep in the soft ash and Remy wrenched the staff away, declawing Logan in the same movement.

Unluckily, Logan didn't need the claws to be an animal, and his blocky right fist looped in and landed solidly on Remy's nose, mashing it flat against his face. Remy used the move to trap Logan's arm under his left arm, and simultaneously brought up his leg to strike Logan repeatedly in the side of the head and neck.

By this point, both men were snarling, growling, wordless creatures, rolling on the floor, punching, kicking, biting. Remy slammed Logan's head into the piano leg, over and over, making the keyboard issue a crazy, jangling chord than hung in the air forever. The family portrait slipped down the side of the Steinway and smashed on the floor.

Rogue had, in some secret room of her heart, wanted to have two men fight over her, but not like this. It was impossible to tell where one man began and the other left off with the cutting and growling and biting, and so Rogue did the only sane and sensible thing she could—she laughed.

She laughed so hard that tears streamed down her cheeks and prismed her vision, and she had to force herself to stop laughing long enough to say, "End program."

And at her command, the walls and furniture of the home dissolved around her, replaced by the bulwarks of the mansion's Danger Room, cold and gray and uniform. Nothing comforting there, other than its familiarity.

"Who writes y'dialogue?" Rogue asked the men, as fragile and translucent as figures carved from soap bubbles. "Some love-starved little girl?" They didn't answer as they vanished with a cold, hard snap, but then, there was no need. She wrote their dialogue, their life-scripts, with the help of the incredible alien computer of the Xavier Institute, a gift from the empress of a society whose technology far outstripped Earth's. She had been trying to pretend to have a normal life through the holographic images of the Danger Room, had been hoping to lose herself, if only for

221

a moment, in the fantasy, to achieve some manner of epiphany. She had the computer program images of her teammates, but without powers, extrapolate how they might have been if they weren't all mutants—if they were normal.

But neither she nor the alien computer had a true idea of what normal *was*. As a result, whenever the program got too tricky to navigate—too real or humdrum—she simply fast-forwarded over that particular glitch into a new scene or situation.

She had hoped for a chance to realize her dream of being able to touch and hold and love Remy, something she could not do with anyone thanks to her mutant power that forced her to absorb the powers and memories of anyone she made flesh-to-flesh contact with. But she felt only the more empty and cheated for her efforts. What good were dreams if you could only hold them in your sleep?

Although the Danger Room could replicate perfectly feel and texture, even though it could create images that looked and sounded and behaved like the originals, it couldn't capture the little things, the burning passions and buried hurts that made the people real and unique and alive. The memories were real; it was just that the events never happened, and the fire and humor she loved about Remy simply couldn't be captured by a holographic construct.

Even if she couldn't touch the man she loved in this reality, in this imperfect world, at least it was Remy.

It was impossible to guess whether she would ever get her powers under control to the point of having a normal life, but it was worth hoping she would.

After all, half of "life" is made up of "if," and some-times, in the end, hope is all we really have.

"And all we need," she said with a firm voice to that quiet room. "If life was perfect, if life was easy, we'd never dream, an' it was a dream that built this mansion."

She set a smile on her face, squared her shoulders, and left the room without a backward glance.

ORDER FROM CHAOS

Evan Skolnick

Illustration by Dave Cockrum & John Nyberg

Tawfiq Badr's expression as he tumbled through the hot Egyptian air told the whole story. Yes, he'd been a pickpocket for a very long time. Yes, he'd honed the surreptitious art to an exacting science, here in the controlled mayhem of Cairo's bustling open-air market. Yes, he'd had his fair share of close scrapes and run-ins with the local authorities.

And, no, he'd never had a victim literally blow him off his feet.

But that's exactly what was happening. To Tawfiq, the two American women had looked like easy prey—or at least the younger one had: a pale, spoiled, overdressed, and complaining teenager lugging far too many suitcases through the tightly packed bazaar. Her companion—a tall, serene and confident-looking white-haired black woman wearing a sensible khaki outfit—seemed much more at home in this pungent sea of human motion. But even if the African Amazon saw him snatch the girl's wallet, what could she do against a wily, seasoned professional like Tawfiq?

The answer, apparently, was that she could cause motion in the very air, summoning a hot desert wind of such force that it lifted and tumbled Tawfiq as if he were a feather caught in a sirocco. The wallet he had just purloined from the girl's garish yellow overcoat dropped from his own pocket and onto the dusty ground—as did four other wallets he had lifted earlier that afternoon.

"Freakin' animals!" the pale girl snapped, dropping her suitcases and rushing over to retrieve her wallet, as Tawfiq landed in a dusty heap about ten feet away. "I hate this place already, Storm!" she complained to her companion, who was already striding purposefully toward the shaken pickpocket.

With scores of slack-jawed Egyptian dealers and international tourists looking on in disbelief, "Storm" grabbed the man by the coat and easily lifted him to his feet. Tawfiq looked into her eyes, and saw that her blue irises had completely disappeared, forcing him to stare at an eerie, all-white gaze that chilled his soul. "Who do you work for?" she asked him in perfect Egyptian Arabic. "El-Gibar?"

"N-no," Tawfiq stammered in his native language, feeling the hackles on his neck involuntarily rise—almost as if electricity were being pumped into him by the very touch of the woman. "Don't work for anyone, not for a long time—"

"Well, if you see Achmed," she interrupted Tawfiq, inexplicably smiling now, "tell him I said hello. He'll know who you mean," she added, releasing her grip on the pickpocket's collar. Dazed, Tawfiq instinctively backed away from her, his eyeballs darting around the immediate area for signs of police—then he fled, expertly disappearing into the crowd of flesh within seconds.

Storm sighed as she walked back toward her companion, who was now standing there, with five wallets in her hands. "I'd forgotten how much I miss this place, Jubilee," Storm told her in English, with an ironic smirk.

"Yeah, cool home turf, Storm," Jubilation Lee answered with a snort, pocketing her own wallet and eyeing the other four. "Makes Sarajevo look like Disney World, y'know? Maybe if we're lucky, the local Mickey Mouse'll stop by and beat the crap out of us."

Smiling, Storm retrieved their luggage. "I know this isn't the easiest or safest route to our hotel from the airport," she admitted, "but I couldn't pass up the chance to take a walk through my old stomping grounds."

"You mean 'old *stealing* grounds,'" Jubilee grumbled, buttoning her wallet pocket shut. "I know you grew up around here, used to be a pickpocket yourself—heck, *I* used to be a packrat hangin' out in Hollywood Mall, I know what it's like—but this place is just nasty!"

"You get used to it, Jubilee—people are remarkably adaptable creatures," Storm answered, taking the four extra wallets from her dark-haired companion and swapping them for a couple of suitcases. "We'll return these wallets to the authorities when we get to the hotel."

"What about the smell?" Jubilee asked, wrinkling her nose as she and Storm moved farther into the bazaar. "Do you get used to that? And how about the flies? And the sweat? And the camels spitting? Yeccch! And every guy lookin' at you like you're on sale? And what about . . ."

Jubilee's ceaseless complaining faded into the recesses of Storm's consciousness, as feelings of nostalgia once again overwhelmed her. It didn't seem like very long ago that five-year-old Ororo Munroe, the Manhattan-born daughter of an American photojournalist and a Kenyan princess, had found herself orphaned on these rough streets of Cairo.

She remembered being taken in by Egyptian master thief Achmed el-Gibar, who had a whole troop of children who stole for him. Ororo quickly became his prize pupil, and within a year, she was considered by el-Gibar (and, more importantly, by the police) to be the most accomplished juvenile thief and pickpocket in all of Cairo.

Seven years of Ororo's life—nearly her entire child-hood—were spent this way, in this place. Lifting wallets, darting into and out of crowds, picking locks, duping tour-ists—it wasn't a bad life for a child who had known little else. But when she was twelve years old, Ororo suddenly felt a strong desire to go south, to seek out her African ances-tors.

Leaving Cairo and her life of petty crime behind, young Ororo trekked across the Sahara on foot. It took her nearly a year to reach the Serengeti Plain, home of her mother's tribe. And during that long journey, Ororo's womanhood blossomed—as did her uncanny ability to control the weather.

Upon rejoining the tribes of her mother's youth near the base of Mount Kilimanjaro, Ororo learned that she and her mother, N'Daré, were descended from a line of African witch-priestesses that could be traced back to the dawn of humanity. All the women in this line of descent had white hair, blue eyes, and the potential for magical abilities.

Ororo's newfound power to control the weather, how-ever, was neither magical nor mystical. Rather, it was the by-product of a random mutation of her DNA. Like so many others, Ororo was a mutant, a member, not of *homo sapiens*, but of the newly emerging subgenus *homo superior*.

Ororo used her weather-altering abilities to help several local Kenyan tribes in times of need. In return, they wor-shipped her as a goddess. Money, theft, conflict, fear—all these things became little more than fading memories to her. More contented than she had ever been, Ororo spent much of her young adulthood fully enjoying the life of a deity. Indeed, who wouldn't?

Then came the day Professor Charles Xavier came to Ororo's African home and persuaded her to use her mutant powers to benefit all humanity. Xavier, a mutant himself, had used his telepathic abilities, technological expertise, and diplomatic skills to found the X-Men—a group of mutant heroes whose mission was to find and protect emerging young mutants from prejudiced humans, and to educate the mutants in the proper control and use of their powers, so that they would be a danger neither to themselves nor anyone else.

Ororo agreed to accompany Xavier back to her native New York. There she was given the code name "Storm" and enlisted in the X-Men. Over the years, she and her teammates had many adventures, and saved the lives of countless humans and mutants. Eventually, the X-Men lineup grew, changed, and split into subteams. The latest spin-off team was called Generation X, a group of younger mutants under the tutelage of Sean Cassidy and Emma Frost. It was to this latest X-team that the mutant firecracker Jubilation Lee was assigned.

". . . not like I exactly *asked* to come along, y'know," Jubilee's still-whining voice penetrated Storm's reminiscenses, as the two women emerged from the far side of the bazaar and turned toward the Corniche, Cairo's traffic-clogged main avenue. " 'It'll be good for you to get away for a few days,' " Jubilee quoted Emma Frost, while doing a passable impersonation of the blonde leader's icy tone.

" 'Aye, 't'will at that, darlin', good experience f'r ya,' " Jubilee continued her solo conversation, now imitating Cassidy's thick Irish brogue. Then, switching to her own Valley Girl singsong accent: "Yeah, like I can't figure out that you and the rest of Gen X just want this spaz out of your hair for a few days. Not *too* obvious . . ."

"Jubilee, stop acting like Oliver Stone," Storm chided her gently. "There's no conspiracy here."

Jubilee's eyebrows shot up in mock surprise. "Whoa, reality check—was that a semihip pop-culture reference? From *you?*"

"See? I *have* been in America too long." Storm smiled. She could see their hotel in the distance, not more than ten blocks away. "Almost there now, Jubilation."

"Jubilation is *right,*" Jubilee grumbled, hoisting her bags to a more comfortable position, blowing sweat-drenched hair out of her eyes, and pressing on. "Can't believe we didn't get a taxi, had to hoof it right through Body Odor Central, get my wallet picked, you showin' off your powers, swear I never should've let myself get talked into . . ."

Storm found herself tuning Jubilee out again, as the sights of the Corniche evoked other, more recent—and more disturbing—memories. The previous week, Storm had received a letter from her childhood pickpocket friend Alia Taymur. Years earlier, the two girls had been semiregular partners in crime; one would cause a distraction, while the other picked the tourists' pockets clean. Both had escaped the life of crime before it consumed them. Storm had graduated first to goddess, then to full-fledged heroine. Alia had gone back to school and become a prominent Egyptian mathematician.

But the letter Storm had received via Federal Express wasn't from a dignified, reserved mathematician, it was from the frightened little girl Ororo remembered from her childhood. *Ororo, please come back to Cairo. Meet me at our old secret*

cache, next Friday at 9 p.m. I need your help. I can't do this alone.
—Alia

The thirty-story Cairo International Hotel loomed large above Storm and Jubilee as they approached its revolving doors. "You see, Jubilee?" Ororo said. "We survived."

"Aces," Jubilee moaned, limping up the steps while stubbornly refusing to let the bellboy help her with her luggage. "Now, if we can only find a toilet I don't have to hover over . . ."

It would be wrong to say he saw them enter the city, check into the hotel, unpack their bags. Or that he saw them at all.

No, he simply sensed two new variables entering the equation; strange attractors invisibly pulling the data in a new direction. He felt the numbers changing, the future shifting. Everything is numbers, *he reminded himself.* Reality is math. Nothing is random. There are no accidents.

Damian Sharpe breathed shallowly, blinked sweat from his eyes, and tried to stay focused on his meditation. But standard perception of reality kept penetrating. It was too small in here, not at all comfortable.

Of course it's uncomfortable, *he nearly blurted to himself.* It's a damn tomb!

He blinked again, found himself coming out of the trance. The candles had burned about halfway down, and outside the sunlight was fading fast. Staying in his cross-legged yoga position, Sharpe looked down at the ancient Egyptian tomb's stone floor. Carefully arranged around him were the nine artifacts he'd worked so long and hard to gather. Six years of scamming university research grants, tracking down talismans, translating ancient glyphs, learning incantations, studying chaos theory . . .

He stood at the brink of impossibility itself, grasping at science so advanced it seemed like magic, and effectively was magic. Practicing ancient spells that bridged the gap between science and the supernatural. Decrypting the work of mathematicians who used chaos theory over two thousand years before Western science even noticed or named it.

What it came down to was simply this: all things are predictable, if you know the initial conditions and understand physics to an infinite degree. Everything that seems random is just the interaction of so many variables that we can't keep track of them, so we write them off as being random. But they're not. And he who can keep track of all the variables can predict the future with one hundred percent accuracy.

Predict the future—and control it.

Sharpe sighed and began meditating again, trying to achieve affinity with the nine chaos talismans. Their power, though hobbled by the lack of the tenth and final artifact, was still great. And soon, very soon, he would use the combined power of the nine to locate and retrieve the tenth.

Once the two new variables were factored out of the equation, of course . . .

"Thank God the concept of a bath is universal," Jubilee sighed from the hotel bathroom.

"Glad you're enjoying it," Storm called back while finishing her unpacking.

"Totally," Jubilee replied, blowing bubbles across the bathwater's gently undulating surface. Then, realizing she might not be the only person feeling the need for cleanliness after their midafternoon trek, she added, "Hey, you waiting for the tub?"

"No, you relax," Storm told Jubilee almost absentmindedly, as she closed her bureau drawer, then looked out their tenth-floor window at the darkening Egyptian sky. Cairo, the Jewel of the Nile, was starting to glisten as, one by one, city lights were turned on. "I want to feel like a native right now," Storm continued, as much to Jubilee as to herself.

"Well, you're sure gonna smell like one," Jubes whispered, but Storm's acute hearing picked up on it. She was too distracted to chide the youth on her manners, however; Jubilee was deep in the throes of culture shock, and Ororo knew she was secretly loving every minute.

Besides, Ororo's mind was otherwise occupied. The original note from Alia was disturbing enough, and the message left at the hotel's front desk—in which Alia had mysteriously changed tonight's meeting time and place—only added to Storm's uneasiness.

But there was something else too. Something *wrong* out there. Waiting. Watching. And, most of all, calculating.

Ororo knew she wouldn't get any answers sitting around the hotel room for the next three hours, waiting for the rendezvous with Alia. And she wanted more information before she walked right into what might turn out to be some kind of trap.

"Jubilation, I'm going to go out and get some air," she called out. "I'll bring something back for dinner, and then we can meet up with Alia."

"Fine by me," Jubilee called back as Storm headed for the door. "Don't drink the water."

Storm chuckled, then left Jubilation to relax in the tub.

* * *

Ororo walked out into the rapidly cooling Egyptian air, watching the sky turn a hundred shades of red, orange, blue, and purple as the sun mercifully withdrew, giving the desert city some respite from the day's searing heat.

She wished she could fully appreciate the sunset's beauty, but that strange feeling of wrongness was growing more intense, almost as if it were watching her. There was a coldness to it, the kind of razor-sharp logic and order you feel when confronted by a dizzying mathematical equation you can't solve.

Mathematics—was it Alia herself who was the threat? That hadn't even occurred to Storm until she arrived at the hotel, and felt the bizarre oppressiveness of the city. She'd never experienced anything like it before, and barely even understood why she associated these feelings with numbers.

But Cairo had changed little since she last called it home, at least in the important ways. Ororo still knew where to go to get the word on the street, without getting her throat slit. She had been more than capable of taking care of herself as a gawky street urchin; now, returned as a virtual goddess, Storm knew the city's secrets would soon reveal themselves to her probing eyes, one way or another.

She ducked into a dark alley. . . .

Towels aren't too shabby, either, Jubilee silently admitted to herself as she pulled a comfortable oversized sweatshirt over her black tights and hung the fluffy white hotel towel up to dry. *This place is starting to look up.*

She flopped onto one of the queen-sized beds, fearing the worst—and finding herself once again pleasantly surprised by the mattress's enveloping softness. "This'll be murder on my back," she muttered to herself, her face half-buried in a pillow. "But that's what vacation's all about, right?"

It was starting to feel like a proper vacation, too, instead of the hellish obligatory field trip Jubilee had thought it was going to be. She almost wished the rest of Generation X were here so they could all do a way-cool night on the town. . . . But she knew was too tired for that, anyway.

Noticing the old-fashioned-looking television remote control on the bed table, Jubilee rolled over lazily and grabbed it, turning on the small TV across the room. "Foreign TV—cool," she told herself, until she realized that there were only five channels, and they were all in Arabic. "My best friend in the whole wide world, turned against me," she sighed, turning the TV off and rolling again onto her back. "Maybe I'll see if there're any cute guys . . . down . . . stairs. . . ." Her voice trailed off as the long day's journey and jet lag caught up with her, and she dropped off to sleep.

At first Jubilee thought the buzzing was her alarm clock. Through a fog of half-sleep, she reached over to the night table, and began her usual ritual of flopping her hand around until the offending noise stopped. She knocked the TV remote onto the floor, smacked the phone, and banged her hand into the bedside lamp. But the buzzing was coming from the other direction.

Then Jubilee remembered that her alarm clock was over five thousand miles away.

Her sticky eyelids blinked reluctantly open as she turned to see what was making the buzzing, crackling noise. It seemed to be coming from outside, or from near the window. But she didn't see anything there. Jubilee wondered if maybe there were an electrical short-circuit in one of the walls, or—

Her eyes caught movement. Sitting up, she kept her gaze focused on the window. The air was undulating, crackling, *moving*. Like the heat distortion she'd seen in the desert from the jet, or like the kind of fluid distortion you might observe underwater.

It was moving toward her.

Flowing through the cracks in the multipaned window, the boundaries of its amorphous form were now becoming clearer to Jubilee. It was like the thing from that old *Blob* movie, except that it was nearly invisible and hovering in the air. The crackling noise it made was definitely getting closer. Tendrils of the thing reached toward Jubilee, who scrambled to get off the bed while grabbing for the phone.

She suddenly felt a sharp stinging sensation on her lower right leg, and yelped as she instinctively pulled away and fell onto the floor, with the phone falling on top of her. "Help!" Jubilee screamed into the phone receiver, not waiting for the front desk to pick up. She saw that the skin on her leg where the tendril had touched her had exploded outward, as if a microscopic firecracker had been implanted under her skin and detonated.

"Firecrackers, huh?" she asked herself as she watched the thing still pulling itself through the spaces between the window panes, still reaching for her. "Two can play at that game, Sparky," she answered herself, pointing at the bizarre phantom and letting her mutant ability handle the rest.

Bursts of brightly colored energy shot from her outstretched hand and exploded in and around the faceless thing. Jubilee was used to seeing the bright flashes of her infamous "energy plasmoids"—they'd saved her skin on more than one occasion—but right now the dazzling display was making it hard to see what (if any) effect her attack had had on the creature.

"Hello?" the front desk clerk's voice came through on the phone, in heavily accented English. "What is going on up there?"

"Your freakin' see-through curtains are tryin' to eat me, dude!" Jubilee yelled back into the mouthpiece, ceasing fire and trying to see if the phantom was still there. "If you've got cops in this town, you better send for 'em, pronto!"

The confused clerk started asking more questions, but Jubilee had stopped listening as she let the receiver drop to the carpeted floor. The barely discernible phantom had been blown into several chunks by her onslaught of "fireworks"—and now they were all converging on her!

To the chaos spirit, Jubilation Lee was nothing more than a stream of data that was to be moved to another section of the master equation. From the spirit's purely mathematical point of view, she was a virus in the program of reality itself. The chaos spirit had only one goal—to rewrite the code of Jubilation Lee so that she would function, not as a living, breathing, active variable, but as a dead, cold zero.

"Comin' through!" Jubilee's voice pierced the early-evening bustle in the hotel lobby. "Heads up!"

Heads obligingly turned as Jubilee, still clad in her over-sized sweatshirt and firing barrage after barrage of fireworks behind her, blew into the main lobby, still pursued by the indistinct, globulous thing. The tourists and native Egyptians, seeing explosions and fearing terrorist gunplay, screamed and scattered or dropped down behind furniture.

Jubilee's eyes had started to adjust to the thing's energy signature; she could see it more easily now. She knew that it always coalesced back into its original single form no matter how many times she tried to blow it apart. And she knew that it was moving a lot faster, here in the open air, than it had been when trying to sift itself through the hotel room window.

It was faster than Jubilee, and she knew that too.

Her only chance was to somehow find Storm. Once Jubilee got outside, she could send up a fireworks flare as high as possible, and hope that Ororo saw it from wherever she was.

The thing touched Jubilee again, and the back of her neck erupted in pain—she could feel blood trickling down her neck and back. She instinctively threw herself forward onto the marble floor, rolled once, and fired back with her maximum-force fireworks. The detonation was deafening, like a small bomb. The thing was shredded—along with most of the front lobby. Jubilee herself was blown backwards along the floor, toward the front doors. More screams from terrified tourists followed the still-echoing reverberations of the blast.

Jubilee, holding the back of her neck and applying pressure to stop the bleeding, staggered out through one of the hotel's revolving front doors. Once outside, she risked a glance behind her, and saw that the thing was *again* reforming itself. She had perhaps ten seconds before it would be back on her.

Gathering her strength, Jubilee raised both arms skyward and fired off one huge fireball toward the sky. She mentally willed it to keep rising as high as possible before detonating in a dazzling burst of color about two hundred feet in the air.

She looked back toward the hotel, and saw that the whatever-it-was had already reassembled itself, and was oozing through the cracks in a revolving door.

She staggered across the Corniche, dimly aware of the cars honking and steering crazily to avoid hitting her. She ducked into an alley, hoping it wasn't a dead end.

The alley led onto a quiet side-street, but Jubilee knew she was running out of time. She didn't even risk looking behind her, for fear it would slow her down. Instead, she left a trail of exploding fireworks behind her as she ran, hoping it would slow the pursuit, but knowing that the thing was recovering from the blasts at an ever-increasing rate.

"Storm!" Jubilee called hoarsely, dodging into another alley, emerging onto another road. "Storrrrm!" she screamed, not wanting to die alone on these unfamiliar streets, so far from home. Hearing no response, she risked a quick look over her shoulder, and noted with some satisfaction that it was still a good thirty feet behind her.

Jubilee suddenly cried out in pain as her shin smashed into a garbage can and she went sprawling onto the cobblestone sidewalk. The early evening sky whirled crazily above her as she rolled painfully onto her back. She tried to scrabble to her feet, already knowing that it was over, she was dead—

—and then she noticed the hooded figure in white desert robes standing right next to her. But rather than run away from her as everyone else on the street had been doing, this person stepped between Jubilee and the rapidly approaching energy, as if to intervene.

"Wait, you don't know what you're doing—" Jubilee started to warn.

"Yes, I do, child," a woman's voice answered sternly from under the hood, in English laced with a slight Egyptian accent. "Now, stay down!"

Dumbfounded, Jubilee complied—not that she was in any shape to do much else—as the thing moved ever closer to them. The robed woman raised her right arm toward it, and Jubilee thought she might've been holding something in her hand.

As her pursuer approached within five feet, a series of bright white lines began forming in the air, all seemingly emanating from the woman's right palm. More and more straight lines burned themselves into the air, forming a geometrically perfect spiderweblike pattern between the women and the indistinct energy form, which stopped its forward movement and hovered in the air before the growing web of light.

The lines continued to appear, now reaching up and around the thing to form a more three-dimensional pattern—like old-style computer graphics, Jubilee thought numbly. There were dozens of lines, then scores, then hundreds, creating a delicate-looking cage of light around the now-motionless phantom.

A tendril of energy extended from the creature between the "bars" of its rapidly forming cage, almost experimentally—and was abruptly recoiled. The light-cage continued to form around it. Then, finally complete in breathtakingly perfect symmetry, the cage began to shrink.

Jubilee slowly got to her feet, awed by the clashing of forces she did not comprehend. The cage's rate of implosion seemed to increase exponentially, until it winked out of existence in a pinpoint of light, apparently taking its prisoner with it.

"Wicked," Jubilee muttered, looking at the mysterious woman as she pulled back her hood to reveal a beautiful Egyptian with pitch-black eyes and matching long hair. "Thanks, I don't know how you knew about—"

"I'm Ororo's friend, Alia Taymur," the woman answered solemnly. "You *must* be Jubilee. I had hoped we wouldn't meet this way."

"Hey, better this way than at the funeral parlor," Jubilee answered ruefully, holding out her right hand to Alia, then pulling it back on finding that it was covered in her own blood. "Geez."

Alia held out in her right palm the object with which she had subdued the energy thing. Jubilee could now see that it was a flat stone disc, an ancient artifact of some kind inscribed with Egyptian hieroglyphics. It had four hooklike extensions that fit between the fingers of Alia's hand, allowing her to hold on to it even when her palm was open.

Alia held the artifact close to Jubilee, who assumed the woman was simply showing it to her. But then Alia whispered something in a language Jubilee hadn't heard before, not even in the cacophony of the bazaar. Jubilee pulled back slightly as the enigmatic symbols on the disc's face glowed with the same bright white intensity that the cage had emitted earlier—then faded back to ordinary stone.

Jubilee looked at her right hand again. It was clean. She felt the back of her neck, and found no trace of the wound that had been stinging only moments before. Her leg, too, had been miraculously healed, and her black tights had been repaired.

"What the—" Jubilee marveled. "How'd you do that? What's goin' on here?"

"The fractal disc can be used to retroactively alter very small, simple variables in the equation of reality—especially those that were artificially manipulated in the first place," Alia answered. "Because the chaos spirit was unable to alter any major variables, I can cancel most of the minor ones out."

"Right, should've known," Jubilee said with mild sarcasm. "And as for what's going on . . . ?"

"We'll go to the rendezvous point first," Alia answered, taking Jubilee by the arm and leading her into a dark alley. "Once Ororo's joined us, I'll be able to tell you both why I need your help."

"Why *you* need *our* help, huh?" Jubilee asked ironically, rubbing the back of her neck again.

Jubilee pulled her hands into the long sleeves of her sweatshirt and shivered a little, sitting cross-legged on the dock and looking out onto the Nile. She couldn't believe how a city that was so hot by day could be so chilly by night; in this respect, Cairo was even worse than the Australian outback, where she had lived alongside the X-Men for a while.

It was about ten-thirty at night, and Storm and Alia

were just ending their trip down Memory Lane, and none too soon for Jubilee. She had listened at first to the street-urchin tales of wonder and woe, but talking over old times and old friends quickly loses its appeal if you weren't actually there in the first place.

According to Storm, she had returned to the hotel and found no evidence of the damage caused by Jubilee's encounter with the thing that Alia called a "chaos spirit"— just a missing Jubilee. Alia had apparently used that disc of hers to undo most of the aftereffects of the chase, and had also left a phone message at the front desk letting Storm know that Jubilee was safe.

Alia's stern manner was replaced by childlike giddiness when Storm showed up at the preappointed meeting place on the docks of the river. Storm, too, let a good portion of her guard down upon seeing her childhood friend. They had written each other a few letters over the years, but that didn't mean there wasn't a lot of catching up to be done. And that's what the two old pickpocket partners had been doing for the past half hour, talking and laughing while Jubilee pretended to listen and stared out at the dark surface of the river.

She wished she had had such a girlfriend when she had been younger—or even now, for that matter. It seemed like such a special kind of friendship, but female bonding was something that Jubilee's childhood as a homeless mutant orphan in Beverly Hills hadn't lent itself to. Even now, the only person who seemed to really understand Jubilee was Logan, the berserker mutant who called himself Wolverine. And what did that say about Jubilee?

"All right, enough old stories, Alia," Storm decided, noticing Jubilee's uncharacteristically quiet demeanor. "We need to talk about why you asked me out here."

"You're right," Alia admitted, the smile fading from her face and her big dark eyes looking down almost in shame. "It's just—I've been facing this alone for so long, it's so nice to have someone to talk to."

Jubilee looked over at Alia again. Maybe they were more alike than Jubes had realized.

"It's all right, Alia," Storm comforted her. "But I don't want to wait for another of those so-called 'chaos spirits' to come looking for us."

"There are far worse things that could come looking, believe me," Alia answered, meeting her friend's eyes again with her own. "Over the past three months, I've fought off a bizarre array of these 'mathemagical' creatures, as I call them. In fact, I had to delay our meeting tonight in order to deal with one of them. And they're all after this," she added, holding out the fractal disc she had used to save Jubilee.

"Can you tell us what that thing is, now?" Jubilee asked, not unkindly but a little impatiently. She didn't want to wait for another creature to show up, either.

"I've had this artifact for nearly twenty years," Alia told them while running her fingers over the disc's engraved hieroglyphics. "I lifted it off a man who must've been an archaeologist. When I first saw it, I figured it was just some kind of souvenir. I knew el-Gibar would have no use for it, and I thought it might come in handy as a concealed weapon," she said, palming the disc and swinging her open hand in the air to demonstrate its damage potential.

"Sensible," Ororo commented, to Jubilee's surprise.

She still wasn't used to seeing this side of Storm. "Almost invisible until it's being used."

"Exactly," Alia agreed. "It was only later, when I was studying the physics of chaotic systems, that I saw an article theorizing that the ancient Egyptians had dabbled in some kind of supernatural approach to chaos theory."

"I've heard of that, but I never really got it," Jubilee broke in. "Fractals and stuff like that, right? What is chaos theory, anyway?"

"It's a new kind of science that helps us understand the properties of irregular fluctuations in nature," Alia told her, as if reading from a mathematics texts. "A chaotic system is simply one that's sensitive to initial conditions. For example, the Earth's weather systems are chaotic—that's why they're so hard to predict."

"Because there are so many variables?" Storm asked, also curious.

"That, and the fact that even the slightest miscalculation at the outset will lead to results that diverge farther and farther from what you predicted," Alia explained. "For example, a butterfly flapping its wings on the United States' west coast might have what appears to be an infinitesimally small effect on the weather system there, correct?"

"A butterfly?" Jubilee asked, chuckling despite herself. "Yeah, I think you could pretty much count that effect as being zero."

"Ah, but you can't," Alia told her with a smile. "The effect might be *almost* zero, and totally negligible for all intents and purposes right there and then. But the slight breeze from its wings would affect the air molecules around it, which would in turn slightly alter the courses of the air molecules next to them, and so on. By the time a month had passed and the weather system had made its way around the world and back, that slight change in initial conditions could've helped cause a thunderstorm that would otherwise never have happened.''

"Whoa," Jubilee said. "Heaviness."

"That's why, despite all our recent advances with satellites and radar technologies, weather prediction beyond a day or two will never be one hundred percent accurate, nor even come close. It's impossible to know all the starting variables to an infinite degree—and even the slightest miscalculation on Monday can grow to a huge miscalculation by Friday.''

"So it is just a theory," Storm concluded, "with little practical basis in reality.''

"Scientists are still exploring the ways chaos theory can be applied to help our understanding of turbulent systems like the weather, electrical currents, heart arrythmia, epileptic seizures, the movement of the planets. . . .'' Alia answered, trailing off.

"But what does that have to do with this disc, and with that thing that came after me?" Jubilee asked impatiently. She had never been much of a math whiz.

"Like I was saying, I did some research and found that the ancient Egyptians were apparently dabbling in this area over two thousand years ago," Alia told them. "They had more of a supernatural approach, of course, but I believe it all comes down to the ability to comprehend and actually rewrite the mathematical code that we call reality.''

"Mathematical code?" Storm asked. "I don't understand.''

"If you accept that all matter in the entire universe is composed of atoms and subatomic structures that follow very strict physical laws," Alia continued, "then it's possible to see those atoms as being numbers in a huge cosmic equation, which all fit together to form what we perceive as reality. Now, if it were possible to read those numbers, to see the equation, to understand the mathematics of it—"

"You could change some of the numbers and alter reality?" Jubilee finished. "Wow."

"Don't be too sure," Alia contended. "Both you and Ororo display mutant powers that may very well be tapping into this 'mathemagical' sphere of influence. Especially you, Ororo—your ability to affect a chaotic system like the weather may involve your mutant x-factor helping you retroactively change initial conditions on a truly cosmic scale."

"Intriguing," Storm admitted, "but you still haven't told us who—or what—is sending these creatures after you and that artifact."

"I believe it's an American archaeologist named Damian Sharpe," Alia answered.

"Damian? Ooh, that's a bad *Omen*," Jubilee joked halfheartedly.

"There are a total of ten fractal talismans listed in the historical records," Alia continued. "Over the past decade, Sharpe has been involved in the recovery of the other nine. It's said that the talismans can't be destroyed by conventional means—that if you try to do so, they'll simply reappear someplace else. That's why I haven't just thrown this disc away or smashed it—it'd show up somewhere else, and he'd find it. He only lacks this one. And he's willing to do almost anything to get it."

"Why?" Storm pressed. "What will he do?"

"If he's able to bring all ten talismans together?" Alia asked ruefully. "Anything he wants, Ororo."

He was just about to call it a night, when they silently beckoned to him.

His candles were extinguished and packed, the nine talismans were safely stored in his beaten-up leather backpack, and Damian Sharpe had concluded that the numbers favored a morning attempt to rework the variables. He was just opening the door to his dirt-encrusted Jeep, knowing that tonight's failure to eliminate one of the strange attractors would make tomorrow's efforts doubly challenging.

But the talismans called to him in a way they never had before. Something was happening, the numbers were changing, *right now.*

He looked up at the stars, and for a moment just stood there in the deep desert, dumbfounded. It appeared as though some cosmic prankster had decided to draw lines between the stars—as if to give official weight to the ancient astrological signs that had been founded so close to this very site, in ancient Babylon, thousands of years before.

Then he realized the lines were not in fact connecting the stars, but were coalescing into a geometically perfect pattern, which was growing and moving directly toward him.

The tenth talisman, he realized in awe, dropping his backpack and fumbling to get it open. *She's bringing it right to me!*

He yanked the bag open, and was surprised to see that the stone artifacts were glowing with an eerie green light. He reached for the largest of them, the fractal breastplate—

—and was smashed backward as the glowing flat stone flew out of the backpack and into his chest!

Burning, screaming, Sharpe was only dimly aware of the other talismans also impossibly leaping toward him *nothing is impossible* painfully grafting themselves to his knees, elbows, waist *pain is mere perception* feeling his conventional grasp of reality fade *an illusion no more real than a picture on TV* overwhelmed by his dream-state image of the master equation.

The numbers continued to change.

"There he is!" Jubilee yelled to Storm and Alia as the three women floated high above the craggy desert. "Gotta be, right?"

Storm concentrated on keeping her compatriots and herself afloat on mutant-controlled desert winds as they followed the geometric light pattern emitted by Alia's fractal disc. The talisman was building a bridge of light across the sky, a fiery white latticework that was leading them toward a glowing green figure writhing on the ground, next to a Jeep parked near the entrance to some kind of archaeological dig.

"It looks like he is in pain," Storm observed as they descended on Damian Sharpe's twitching body. Nine glowing stone talismans were attached—no, *fused* to him: a helmet, a breastplate, a backplate, shin-and thigh-guards, a medallion at his throat, and a fractal disc identical to Alia's in his left palm. "Alia . . . ?" Storm started to ask.

But Alia was screaming, her right palm crisping as her fractal disc began to glow with the same green energy that was emanating from Sharpe's adornments. "Their energy is building," Alia managed to choke out as the women landed and Storm caught Alia before she fell to the ground. "Can't hold out long before they're drawn together."

Sharpe stopped twitching. He leapt to his feet with unnatural speed and agility, turning to face the newcomers. His body seethed and crackled with green energy, and the talismans on his body now resembled the ancient Egyptian battle armor after which they had obviously been patterned.

"It's sucked him in," Alia explained, fighting the green energy creeping up her right arm. "He's lost all sense of reality—all he sees is the equation! And if he gets the last talisman, he'll be able to change it in any way he wants!"

"Then he shall not have it," Storm declared. She raised an arm toward Sharpe and, like Zeus himself, fired off a lightning bolt. But the jagged arc of electricity somehow raced around Sharpe's body, as if purposely avoiding him.

Or as if its trajectory had been recalculated at the last millisecond.

"That can't be good," Jubilee said, trying to blitz Sharpe with a barrage of fireworks—but they exploded almost immediately after Jubilee created them, blowing the surprised teen off her feet and temporarily blinding her.

(Sharpe laughed maniacally, watching the numbers change and shift right before him. It was within his grasp, he could almost taste full comprehension of the equation—if he could just remove those annoying extra variables. . . .)

Raising the fractal disc in his left hand, Sharpe aimed it at Storm and Alia and released a cone-shaped beam of energy with the same liquid-air consistency of the chaos spirit that had chased Jubilee earlier. Alia quickly countered with a spiderweb shield, which seemed to absorb the assault. But

Alia screamed in pain as the talisman's green energy continued to flow up her arm. She was losing the ability to hang on to reality.

Storm floated up into the air again, and summoned a gale-force wind to blow Sharpe back. But he seemed totally unaffected by it, as if the air itself were moving around him, not into him. Jubilee risked another volley of fireworks, with no discernible effect on their opponent. Seemingly oblivious to the mutant heroines and their desperate attacks, he started walking toward Alia.

He fired another energy beam at her, and she blocked it with another spider-web shield—but just barely. Though her knowledge of mathematics served her well, Alia still possessed only one of the talismans, against the combined power of Sharpe's nine. And she somehow sensed that the artifacts *wanted* to come together—they hungered to rewrite the equation of reality, over and over, forever.

In a last-ditch effort, Storm used her control over the wind to lift Sharpe's Jeep into the air, then brought it crashing down on him. "Now, Jubilee!" Storm called, and the teen launched a maximum-power fireburst into the twisted wreckage, detonating it from within. The vehicle's gas tank ignited, answering Jubilee's controlled explosion with an even louder one.

Ororo bent the winds, protecting Alia, Jubilee, and herself from the flying metal shrapnel. The wind also served to blow away the smoke that enshrouded the remains of the Jeep.

And, glowing more brightly than ever, Damian Sharpe emerged smiling from the wreck, reaching for Alia with his left hand. A tendril of bright green energy started to form in the air between his fractal disc and Alia's. Still fighting the energy of the talisman in her right hand, Alia started reluctantly to stagger toward him.

"We've got to get you out of here!" Storm realized, swooping down on Alia to lift her away. "Come on!"

"No!" Alia protested, grabbing hold of Storm's arm and forcing her hand down to touch the fractal disc. Storm screamed, as much from the intense supernatural heat as from the thought that one of her oldest friends was betraying her to chaos itself!

Storm gasped, unable to remove her hand from the blinding disc. Reality started to warp, twist, become a strange mass of color. She felt sick as her perceptions lurched and shifted to another plane.

She felt light. Saw silence. Heard coldness. Sensed nothing but variables, numbers, possibilities. They would drown her before she could comprehend them.

She tried to focus on the familiar. The sun. The rain. The wind.

Just more numbers.

She cried out in despair, unable to accept a universe laid bare to its pure mathematical core. No beauty, no grace, no justice. Just numbers. Her very soul rebelled, withdrew, surrendered, inverted.

Sun. Rain. Wind. Nothing but numbers.

She was drowning.

But she would *not* die like this! She would not be cancelled, rounded down, written off. The world may have been nothing more than a massive equation on God's pocket calculator—but she was more than that. She was alive!

She shifted the numbers then, feeling the rush she knew so well, the rush of wind through her hair. She was Storm. Chaos knew enough to arrange itself to her liking.

Now she saw the nine offending points of light. They had possessed a man, driven him to madness, used his body as a conduit through which they could infect reality.

He wasn't the target. They were.

She reached for their numbers, too, and told them where to go.

They hissed in protest.

"Hey, I think she's waking up," Jubilee noted with a smile. "Looks like we get our lift home, after all."

"Ororo?" Alia called gently to her, as she lifted her head slowly from the sandy rock. "Praise Allah."

"Yeah, all'a that," Jubilee said, bending over Storm. "You okay, chief?"

"I—I believe I am," Storm ventured, never more pleased to see Jubilee's mischievously smiling face. She sat up, trying to figure out just what had happened.

"You used Alia's disc to eighty-six all of Sharpe's little toys," Jubilee answered Ororo's unspoken query. "Don't know how you did it, Storm, but it was rad."

"I'm not sure how I did it, either," Storm admitted, allowing Alia and Jubilee to help her to her feet. Alia's right arm was back to normal, and the fractal disc—no longer glowing—lay on the ground, looking much like the innocent desert souvenir for which Alia Taymur had first mistaken it.

Storm looked around for Sharpe, but there was nothing. Not even a body. "What happened to him?" Storm asked.

"We were hoping you could tell us that," Alia admitted. "With your natural ability to affect chaotic systems, Ororo, I suspected you would have greater control over the fractal talismans than either Sharpe or I ever could. You'd only been touching the disc for a second when a flash of light shot out from my disc and into Sharpe. Then he was gone with the talismans, and you were unconscious."

Storm struggled to piece her memory together. Here in the world of flesh, form, and feeling, it was already hard to shift her perceptions back to the nightmarish digital world that had almost swallowed her soul. "I—I believe I used the fractal disc to retroactively eliminate the other nine artifacts from ever having been constructed," she said. "It couldn't affect or unmake itself, but at least the threat is largely diminished."

"What about Sharpe?" Jubilee wanted to know. "Is he toast, or—?"

"I think I simply 'reset' him, Jubilee," Storm recalled. "He's alive, out there somewhere. None of this ever happened to him. He's never heard of the chaos talismans, because the only one that ever existed is that one." She pointed at the stone disc on the ground.

Alia picked it up and studied its encrypted surface, as she had done a thousand times before. "So there's no way to eliminate this last one," she ventured. "I guess I'm stuck with the last fractal artifact in the world."

"The only one," Storm corrected. "Most people would have a hard time using it to predict or control the lottery numbers, let alone alter reality to their liking," she said. "But in the wrong hands, its power could still be more than a little dangerous."

"Then I'll have to protect it vigorously, and use it wisely, eh?" Alia smiled at the two mutants. "Maybe that break-through in accurate weather prediction is just around the corner."

Storm laughed, sweeping her arm in the air and sum-moning a wind gust that lifted the three women into the cool night air, back toward Cairo.

HOSTAGES

J. Steven York

Illustration by Ralph Reese

T*he hunt.* Logan paused at the edge of a snow-covered meadow, his body motionless yet tensed. All his senses were sharp, hyperaware. The golden light of morning filtered through the last remains of the clouds that had deposited the snow late the previous night, traces of tiny footprints left by birds and other small animals, and a well-worn scar of a game trail, where a herd of deer must have recently passed. He sniffed, breathing their lingering musk, the sweetness of spruce and evergreen, and the cool, fresh smell of the snow itself.

He sniffed again. *There.* He sorted though the scents: rabbit, field mouse, the overpowering musk of deer, and there, nearly lost in the riot of nature—a hint of herbal shampoo, a floral perfume, and human sweat. *Prey.*

He quickened his pace, cold air burning in his lungs, snow crunching softly under his boots, hands out and ready, the corded muscles in his arms—the ones that would pop his razor claws out through the backs of his hands—flexing unconsciously, teasing just short of the release point.

The hunt. This was when he felt truly alive, when he could shed the tangled life of the man called Logan like an ill-fitted coat and earn his other name: Wolverine.

The trail followed the deer path, and even his keen senses were able to follow it only in spots, like an invisible dotted line across the snow-covered fields. Then, the dots came closer, stronger, not just perfume and sweat, but the new leather of her shoes, the worn denim of her jeans.

He climbed the tree quickly, quietly, careful not to disturb the snow-laden branches. The woman was there, crouched in a clearing, throwing out handfuls of seed to hungry birds. She was beautiful, long red hair spilling over the fleece collar of her coat. Though a few flakes of snow had begun falling, none of it seemed to touch her, as though nature itself stood in awe of the woman.

Wolverine was not immune to her charms. He watched, transfixed, and took a deep breath, softly releasing it, before popping his claws. The sting of the blades piercing his skin brought his instincts back to razor clarity. He judged the distance to the woman, and tensed to leap.

Just then, the woman smiled without turning, and he felt a familiar touch inside his mind. *You really didn't think you could sneak up on a telepath, did you, Logan?*

He relaxed and sheathed his claws. "Least you could have done, Jean darlin', was to let me tag off and say, 'You're it.' Some things, the Danger Room just ain't no good for practicing. Did you follow that deer trail on purpose? If so, I give you credit for good instincts."

Jean turned toward him and laughed softly, her eyes twinkling with inner light. *Come down so we can talk.*

An invisible force tingled around Logan, and he felt himself lifted from the tree, to float softly down next to Jean.

"I'll confess, you did surprise me, at least in that I didn't expect to see you, or anyone, out here. How did you find me?"

"I got back from Muir Island and the mansion was empty, but I found your note and figured I'd just missed you."

"But I just said I was going out for a few hours. I didn't say where, and we're miles from the mansion."

"Charley's Rolls was missing, so I figured you took it. I

called the cell phone in the car, and back-traced the signal. A little spy trick I picked up from Nick Fury." He looked down at the birds. Frightened by his presence, they hopped skittishly away from the bounty of seed on the snow. "You come here often?"

She brushed her hair back around her right ear and gazed off at the horizon. "Sometimes, when the Institute becomes too familiar, and the din of telepathic voices in my head unbearable, I come out here to be alone, to escape, and to think. Our lives—" the words seemed to catch in her throat "—our lives are so full of chaos and horror. There's so little time to think and reflect. I need this time alone."

Logan suddenly felt like an intruder. He still had feelings for Jean, feelings that had led him to her on the chance they could spend some time alone together. Now it seemed that he'd invaded something important and private. "Hey, I didn't know. I got stuff to do back at the ranch."

He started to turn, but she reached out to touch his arm. "No, stay. This is a wild place, as much yours as mine." She smiled. "I'd be glad to share it with a friend."

Logan hesitated. What could he read into that touch? Had there been something in her eyes, something in her voice? Jean was married to Scott now, but he knew their attraction had once been mutual. There was a dark aspect to Jean not unlike his own. Had he only imagined this new spark between them? For all his hypersenses, he couldn't read minds.

"Walk with me," she said.

They were silent for a while. The hunt was over for now, the hunter's sensibilities submerged. Now he could see the forest through Jean's eyes, the white blanketed hills, the snow-draped trees, the soft sound of the wind. It relaxed him, and heightened his awareness of Jean. Her sidelong glances created an uncomfortable tension. "We really are alone out here," he said.

She glanced around casually, her eyes focused on infinity, and he knew that she was telepathically scanning their surroundings. "There's only one person within three miles of us—a hiker." Her smile flashed and boiled over into a laugh. "It's just so *quiet*. I can hear myself think, Logan. I wonder if you can even know what I'm feeling."

But he did, or thought he did, the way he felt sometimes when he escaped the cacophony of human civilization for the wild places.

"I can relax for once," she went on, "let down my psychic shields and . . ."

Logan wasn't looking at her the precise instant she screamed, his gaze having drifted to the trail ahead. His reaction was instant and automatic, his claws out and up, flashing in the sun as he spun, seeking the threat. But there was nothing, only Jean on her knees in the snow, sobbing in horror, and staring at her empty hands.

"No," she said, "no." Abruptly, she seemed to remember herself. "We're too late!"

She reached up and clutched his forearm. Whether it was to calm him, for comfort, or to help pull herself back to her feet, he couldn't be sure. She stood, wobbling for a moment, then she began to run, unsteadily at first, then faster. "This way!"

Logan followed, more out of concern for her than anything else. They were running toward nothing as far as he could tell, a section of tree line like any other, about a quarter mile distant. They'd covered perhaps a dozen yards when Logan felt the familiar tingling around him, and the snow fell away under his feet. Whatever had happened to Jean, she was recovering. They soared over the tree line and a ridge beyond. He could see the highway curving ahead where he'd left his Jeep.

They dropped down near a junction between two hiking paths, both well marked with fresh prints and the tracks of cross-country skis. But Logan's attention was drawn immediately to a dark heap just visible in the shadow of a trail marker, half under the low limbs of an evergreen. It looked like nothing, perhaps a pile of rags, but it was the *smell*. He signaled Jean to stay back as he crouched by the body. It was a young woman in her twenties, small build, red hair only a shade or two darker than Jean's. Someone, something, had gutted her like a fish. She'd been dead only a few minutes.

There was no helping her. He could only find the killer. Now that he knew what to look for, the trail should be easy. The killer would be covered in fresh blood, a strong smell, easy to track. It took only a moment to pick it up and follow it up the trail toward the highway. He zigzagged up the trail like a bloodhound on the scent, moving rapidly because there were few places where the killer could part from the trail without leaving obvious tracks.

Then Logan stopped, puzzled, and doubled back for a few yards. He sniffed deeply. The blood trail was fading, almost gone. But that was impossible. Blood is not easily washed off. It should remain in the clothes, the hair, the skin, under the nails. Nevertheless it was fading, and what remained under it was strange and difficult to follow, a faint tang of human sweat, adrenaline, ozone, and an undeniable *something else.*

Logan knew he was losing time. Ignoring caution, he charged ahead, checking the scent only when there was a very obvious possibility the killer could have left the trail. Better to risk a chance of losing him than the certainty of falling hopelessly behind.

He went on for several minutes until the trees thinned ahead, and he heard the sound of a truck downshifting on the highway. It was then he knew he was too late. The trail ended in a roadside turnout, at fresh tire tracks and a fading cloud of exhaust fumes. "Damn," he said, the word swallowed in a sudden gust of frigid wind.

He was worried that Jean hadn't contacted him telepathically, and it was some relief when he found her kneeling quietly by the body.

She looked up at him, the tear streaks already drying on her cheeks, a burning anger in her eyes. "Her name was Petra. I was in her mind when she died." She swallowed, struggling for control. "It isn't the first time, but you can't imagine anything more terrible. I saw her killer, a big man, silver hair, with—" her brow furrowed, as though she were trying to remember the image "—knives of green fire."

Logan knelt next to her. "I lost him. He took a car. No way to track him on the highway. You sure about those knives?" The look in her eyes said she was very sure. He nodded. "It would fit. This ain't no ordinary killer, that's for sure."

"I couldn't read him, Logan, not at all. I didn't even know he was here until the moment he struck. Then it was as if a cloak were thrown aside for a moment, just for a moment."

"You get anything?"

She frowned. "It was confusing, not like one person, but several voices, three or four, talking at once, some to me, some among themselves. It was all a jumble, so difficult to sort out. One of them is a killer, a serial killer, and he'll kill again. One of them, well, I think our killer may have a hostage, Logan. And this was the really strange thing. I'd swear that one of them, *only* one of them, was a mutant."

They returned to Logan's Jeep and called the state police from his cell phone. Jean knew someone in the department, a woman whose brother was a low-level mutant, to whom she could tell their whole story with some expectation of being believed.

She clicked off the phone and looked at Logan. "Drive," she said. "We can't leave this to the police."

He looked up and down the empty highway. "Which way?"

"There are only two to choose from." She hesitated only a moment before glancing back over her shoulder. "That way."

He was already turning. "You know something, darlin'?"

"I'm just guessing, Logan. Fifty-fifty chance, and God forgive me if I'm wrong."

Logan drove as fast as he dared on the slick road. The Jeep was surefooted but top heavy like most four-by-fours. He knew its limitations, and pushed every one. What he didn't know was where they were going, or what they were looking for. He glanced over at Jean, uncertain if she was scanning, or just watching the scenery.

"My friend on the state police said there were three other killings in this part of the state last year, all outdoors, all around the time of the first heavy snow. Not as brutal as what we just saw, and no evidence of anything supernatural or superhuman, but . . . these crimes often escalate as the killer gains confidence. The police considered the idea that there was a new serial killer operating, but they found no solid evidence to link them, and the files are still open." The sun flashed through the trees into her eyes, making her blink and turn away. "The code name on the file is 'Snowman.' "

"Well, when we meet the devil, at least we know what to call him." Logan tapped an index finger against his temple. "You gettin' anything?"

She shook her head. "I can't read him, Logan. Maybe he was distracted by bloodlust and lowered his defenses for a moment."

"Great. So all we gotta do is wait for someone else to get killed." He saw the hurt in her eyes, and regretted his words immediately. "Sorry, darlin'. I know you're doing the best you can."

She put her fingertips over her mouth. "Unless," she said. "Unless. I said there were several voices. One was a killer, one was a hostage, the others, I'm not sure about. It's like one of them might be trying to help us."

Logan shook his head. "None of this makes sense. I followed one trail back to the highway. He didn't have a flamin' entourage with him."

She looked at him, raising an eyebrow. "Are *you* sure, Logan?"

And of course, he wasn't. The scent had been strange, unlike anything he'd encountered before. There had been that extra something he'd detected, but still only one trail of scent. "If there was more than one, they must have been ridin' piggyback."

"I have another idea, too, about how the Snowman picks his victims. Some killers go for a particular physical type—children, or women with long, straight hair—but there was nothing like that in the first three killings. Different sexes, different ages, but I do see something now they may have missed. All of them could be seen as weak or infirm in some way. The last victim was a small woman. One of the earlier ones was in a wheelchair, another an old man with a cane, and so on. For all his apparent power, he preys on the weakest . . ." Just then she glanced up.

"*Logan, stop!*"

He slammed on the brakes, and the Jeep went into a four-wheel skid. He turned with it, powering it through a full circle. For a moment he thought they'd get to try out the roll bar, then they were stopped, right in the middle of a five-way intersection. He spun his head from side to side, looking both for cross traffic and less conventional threats. "What?"

Jean already had the door open, and had dropped to the icy pavement. "I know this. I've seen it before through someone else's eyes. No, not seen; remembered, or maybe thought. That jumble of images I saw—this was one of them, not a memory, but a plan. He came this way and turned." She turned in a complete circle, looking down each road. "But which way?"

A metallic glint caught Logan's eye, and he climbed out of the Jeep to investigate. At the far right of the intersection the metal support for a stop sign had been bent flat by some impact. "We didn't do that." He knelt to examine the post where it has been scraped down to shiny metal, sniffing the exposed surface. "Fresh. Done in the last hour." He inspected a lone tire track, far enough onto the shoulder not to be lost among the hundreds of others. "It matches what I saw at the turnout."

He stepped back to the fallen sign, popped the two outer claws on his right hand, and brought it down *hard*. Jean flinched at the sound of shearing metal, but the post sliced like butter. He tossed her a three-inch section of metal.

She looked at it, puzzled.

"Now we know something else," he explained, pointing a claw at a smear of pale green paint. "We know what color his wheels are."

Back in the car, Jean glanced down at the piece of metal resting on the dash. "Not very stylish, is it?"

"Good for us. Easier to spot. Besides, this isn't a new car. No catalytic converter. I could smell that much back at the turnout. Look for a beater. This is getting better. Half an hour back I didn't think we had a prayer."

"You aren't smiling."

"This business is too serious for smilin', but you're right. Stupid mistake clipping that sign. No reason for it. Good light, not much traffic, and we weren't right on his tail.

Stupid move with us after him, but probably useless if anyone else were doing it. You got something from him during your contact—you think he knows about us too? Him, or our invisible 'helper'?" That part still didn't make sense to Logan. Were they talking about one person? Two? Four? A busload? And just who was siding with who?

Jean seemed confused too. She shook her head. "Maybe, I don't know. I keep moving the pieces around in my head, and I keep coming back to one result. It doesn't make sense, but I think the *hostage* is the mutant."

Logan gripped the wheel tighter. A nonmutant killer with super powers, a nonexistent hostage who was a mutant, and a mystery cast of equally nonexistent supporting characters. They were coming into a village, and Jean was looking around anxiously.

"This could be it," she said. "Slow down."

"I don't see any cars the right color."

"There," she pointed at a directional sign, "that way."

Logan read the sign as they turned: COMMUNITY SENIOR CENTER ¼ MILE. "Another guess?"

She shook her head. "Logic."

The center was a converted school building, two stories of brick and marble blackened with age. Though the sign out front advertised a potluck lunch to have been held only a few hours before, the place was nearly deserted now. There was no sign of the green beater they were looking for.

"Go around the block," Jean suggested.

Still no sign of the car. They were cruising slowly through a tree-lined residential street when Jean's face went ashen. "I can read them, Logan, like someone opening a door. He's stalking his victim now!"

She directed him through several turns toward a block several streets east.

"It's an elderly woman walking home from the potluck. I'm going to try and warn her telepathically. I only hope I don't frighten her into inaction." Jean's eyes closed and she frowned with concentration. "She understands. She's trying to get to safety, Logan, but she's too slow! The Snowman is moving toward her!"

"She only needs ta buy us a couple seconds, darlin'." He wrenched the wheel to the right, sliding into the empty driveway of a brick rambler, into the backyard, and straight through a picket fence. They hit a snowbank and cleared a frozen drainage ditch by at least six feet.

Logan's head hit the roll-bar as they landed, but he hardly noticed. Ahead he could see the old woman trying to run across a stretch of park meadow, an overturned two-wheel cart abandoned behind her. And he could see the killer, the Snowman, only a few yards behind. He threw the door open and jumped out while the Jeep was still slowing.

The Snowman stopped his advance when he spotted Wolverine, but he didn't withdraw. Instead, he reached into his belt, cross-armed, with both hands, and drew a pair of ordinary looking hunting knives.

So much for "knives of green fire," Logan thought. He unsheathed his claws, anticipating his strike. He thought of the gutted young woman, the terrified old lady, the three bodies from last year, and mercy was not foremost on his mind.

Logan leapt, claws out. He hit, and hit hard. His claws

raked off something invisible, millimeters from the Snow-man's skin, leaving behind streaks of green electricity.

His momentum carried him past the killer; he landed off-balance and tumbled twice before coming up in a crouch.

He spun. The killer stood his ground, sheets of green lightning dancing around his body. In the background, he could see Jean helping the woman to safety. He had to keep the Snowman's attention distracted. Logan growled deep in his throat, and charged for another attack. He moved in close, slashing with what should have been killing strokes. They skittered off harmlessly, stirring up the lightning, which flowed up the Snowman's arms and into his knives.

The Snowman laughed and brought down his left arm.

The thick leather of Logan's jacket sliced like tissue pa-per, and he felt the knife bite deep and jam between two of his ribs. He grunted as the knife pulled free, and tried to return a blow of his own. Ineffective. The Snowman's other knife fell. Logan tried to stop it, and the blade sliced his forearm to the bone. He staggered. Before he could recover, the first blade stabbed completely through Logan's left thigh.

Logan fell, rolling clear of his attacker. The green fire went with him, burning deep in his wounds, fighting his healing factor. The effort of the struggle dropped him to his knees, near unconsciousness.

He looked up, and through his blurry vision, the Snow-man seemed to be running away. Logan could hear laugh-ing. "Did he get her?" he hissed through clenched teeth.

She's safe, Jean's thoughts reached him as a note of bell-like clarity in a pool of pain and confusion. *I'm going to try to stop him telekinetically if I can, and probe him at close range if I can't.*

"Don't," Logan managed to whisper. Then the screaming began again.

Logan leaned against the fender of the Jeep, trying to clear his head.

Next to him, the elderly woman was beaming at Jean, seemingly unfazed by the attack. "She's my guardian angel," the woman kept saying, "I saw her in a vision."

Whatever gave comfort, Logan supposed, though right then her "guardian angel" looked like she'd been dragged through the deep end of the pool. Jean sat in the Jeep's passenger seat, dazed and bedraggled, her hair wet with melting snow. He'd found her fallen in a snowbank and carried her back to the rig.

Jean shook her head slowly, stringy ringlets of hair tumbling over her face. Speaking telepathically, so as not to let the old woman know more than she needed to, she said, *Got to stop them, Logan. They'll kill again unless we can stop them.*

He reached out and brushed the hair back from her eyes. *You sure you're okay, Red? You're talking "them" and "they" again.*

She looked up, and met his eyes with a tired, but lucid, stare. *I understand now, Logan, what we're dealing with in the Snowman. The true horror of it nearly flattened me. The killer, the hostage, the mutant, and two others, the little boy and the old woman, all in one body.*

Logan raised an eyebrow. *Multiple personalities? No way. Mutant isn't personality, it's genes. I don't have to be the Professor to know that.*

I didn't understand it at first either. But the mutant isn't an aspect of the killer's shattered personality; he's the killer's third victim. She sighed, and wiped the moisture from her eyes. *Imagine a young mutant, his power not yet expressed, a very unusual power. He was a symbiont, capable of surviving the death of his physical body by bonding with another being at the moment of death. Now imagine he becomes the victim of a serial killer, and at the moment of his death . . .*

Logan's thoughts went grim. *He jumps straight into the body of his own killer.*

He can't control the host body, and his power makes him a true symbiont, not a parasite. His power "pays the rent" somehow. Maybe by making the host better at what he does. In this case, he certainly made the Snowman into a better killer, maybe a perfect one.

So, the victim, the mutant, he's the "hostage"? He's the one that's been helping us?

Yes, he's the hostage, and it makes sense that he's the one helping us. Maybe he can control the body, but only when the host is sufficiently distracted. She hesitated. *During a killing, for instance.*

Logan just grunted.

I'm also worried, Jean continued, *about what will happen if the symbiont draws too much attention to himself.*

What do you mean?

I mean, if you already have three personalities, what's the big deal if another one shows up? But if you learn that one of those personalities is an alien from outside? He might be able to kill the boy, or wipe his personality and take his powers. We just don't know.

Logan looked down at his shredded and bloodied

clothes. His wounds were completely healed. The effects of the green fire had burned themselves out in a few minutes. Still, it made the Snowman one of the more formidable opponents he'd ever faced. He sighed, and climbed into the driver's seat of the Jeep. "Ma'am," he said to the smiling woman, who probably had no idea why the two of them had been so quiet for the last few minutes, "you head home now." She nodded, and watched as they drove off across the park.

They had picked up one other useful piece of information: Logan had recovered soon enough to catch a glimpse of the Snowman's vehicle as it drove away across the park, a vintage green Corvair van, ancient and spotted with rust. They were building the clues to run the Snowman down, but could they find him before he killed again, and what would they do with him when they had him?

Logan stopped at the main road and looked both ways. "I need some help, Red. Which way?"

She shook her head. "You know I can't track him, Logan."

"We know somebody in there is tryin' to help you, and you've already been inside his mind now. Give it a try."

She closed her eyes and concentrated, teeth gritted, breath held, her face lined with the strain. This continued for thirty seconds or so. Then her eyes snapped open. She blinked. "I saw something, just a flash, it could have been another victim. I couldn't tell anything except—it was a man walking a dog."

Logan unfolded a map and scanned the surrounding area. A small notation caught his eye. "A dog? Like a seein'-eye dog?"

She nodded. "It would fit the killer's pattern."

"There's a training academy for 'em in the next town east of here, 'bout six miles." He tossed her the map without folding it and punched the accelerator. They skidded onto the highway.

Jean threw the map in the back, and drew herself up in her seat. She was finally recovering from their battle. "We still don't know what to do with the Snowman when we find him. My TK seems to be as useless against him as your claws, and even if we could harm him, we don't know what it would do to the innocent mutant trapped inside his body."

"Could be," suggested Logan, "that he'd just jump to a new host."

"We don't know that. It could be he can make the transfer only once. Our best bet is to find a way to contain him and take him back to the Institute—maybe the Professor can help him."

"Whatever," Logan said as he skidded the Jeep around an especially sharp corner, but he remained unconvinced. While he wasn't thrilled with the idea of the symbiont setting up housekeeping in Jean's or his body, there were worse alternatives.

They soon found the Oltion Dog Training Academy, but no sign of the killer's van or a man walking with a dog. Logan had another idea. "That man you saw must have left here not long ago with a dog. We don't have to find the hunter if we can track the prey."

They left the Jeep in front of the academy while Logan attempted to pick up the trail. He'd circled only a part of the building before finding it. The nice thing about dogs was that they were very easy to track by smell, especially when they were wet.

The trail led away from the road, through the academy grounds, and into the back country. They were headed up a steep grade paralleling a stream when Jean glanced back over her shoulder and pointed. Visible through the trees, parked next to a side road, was the light green van.

Logan picked up his pace, and trusted that Jean would keep time. As they rounded the next bend, the trail crossed from one side of the ravine to the other, via an arched concrete bridge that soared high over the rocky stream.

"It's happening," Jean cried.

On the center of the bridge Logan could see three figures: two human and one canine. As they came closer, it became apparent that the dog was trying to defend its fallen master from the Snowman. It was a battle as brave as it was hopeless. Only the dog's speed kept it from being cut to ribbons. That was a lesson Wolverine took careful note of as he broke into a full sprint.

Logan, he heard her in his thoughts, *while you attack on the physical plane, I'm going to attempt to contact the mutant by deep probe. There may be a way we can help you from inside, or at least learn something useful.*

He didn't even think, *Be careful.* The time for care was past. This was war.

Logan ran onto the bridge just in time. The dog was withdrawing in defeat, bleeding from several seemingly minor cuts. The dog hunched down near the railing where his master had fallen. The man seemed disoriented, if unhurt. Logan placed himself between the killer and his intended victim, but kept his distance.

They danced a dance of death for a moment, then the Snowman struck. Logan stepped just outside the knife's arc, then replied with a thrust of his own, aiming not for the vitals or limbs, but for the eyes. As always, the Snowman's bioelectric field protected him from the blow, but he still instinctively pulled back, trying to protect his face.

Made you jump, thought Logan. It was a small victory, but he'd settle for anything at this point. The strike also had an unanticipated secondary effect. The green fire lingered over the Snowman's face, interfering with his vision.

While he's confused, Logan, I'm going in . . .

Then things went terribly wrong. Jean's psyche was suddenly sucked inside the Snowman, and, through their contact, a part of Logan as well.

It was a strange sensation, to see his physical self still doing battle with the Snowman, to still be a part of that, and yet to exist on this inner plane as well.

He and Jean were falling, though he had no fear of it. They were falling down a long shaft, like the vent of a deep volcano. He could see a shrinking circle of blue sky, wispy with cloud, far above, dwindling to only a spot as they reached the bottom. He had no memory of stopping, and yet they were there.

As he looked around the dark, fog shrouded plane, he saw four others besides Jean and himself standing there. One of them, a thin teenage boy with dishwater-blond hair, stepped forward. The symbiont, Logan knew.

"You came," the symbiont said, his eyes wide with wonder. "Tommy said you'd come, but I didn't believe him."

A flash of pain pulled Logan back into the part of his consciousness existing in the physical plane. The battle had gotten close and bloody while his attention was elsewhere, and, from his current perspective, seemed to move in slow motion. Fury and confusion marked the Snowman's face as he slashed at Logan, flashes of green fire illuminating his face in stark shadows.

A spray of blood arched through the air, his own, Logan realized. *Got to pull back, get room to move.* As he did, he saw Jean standing at the end of the bridge, frozen in midstride, the blind man still propped against the railing, and the Snowman, moving toward him. Logan moved to protect the helpless man.

Snap. He was back on the astral plane. Jean emerged from the shadows, holding the hand of a young black boy of about nine. "This is Tommy," she said. "He wants to help us end the killing."

The boy's eyes were large and gentle, and it was hard to believe that he was part of the Snowman. He looked up at Logan and nodded sadly. "We done some bad things, mister. Got to make it stop. That's why I brought your lady friend to help our friend Roger," he pointed at the symbiont, "and you, Mr. Wolverine, to help fight our Snowbeast."

The nameless old woman glanced at Logan contemptuously, then turned her back on him. Three aspects of the Snowman, Jean had said. Tommy was one, this woman another, and the third . . . Something roared behind him. He turned to face a child's nightmare: a buffalo sized lion made of soiled velvet drapery fabric and old buttons, held together with crude hand stitchery, its back crusted with fallen snow, as though it had just shambled out of a snowbank. Despite its bulk, it moved with easy grace, its eyes glowed with green fire, and when it roared, it revealed a maw studded with very real teeth.

This was it, the killer's dark soul, the inner beast. Logan knew it well, knew what could happen if it were set loose.

Tommy stepped forward, challenging the beast. "Got to stop it! Got to stop the killing, Snowbeast! Got to make it end!"

"*Nooooo*," the Snowbeast roared, brushing the boy aside with his paw. "*Kill the weak! Kill the weak!*" He turned toward Roger, the symbiont. "*Kill—the outsider?*"

More pain, as his claws locked with the killer's knives and the blades slid down to bite into his knuckles. *Too close. Too close again.* He shoved the Snowman backward, stepping back himself.

He was bleeding from a dozen places, none too serious, but the green energy was sapping his strength, and impeding his healing. He needed the breather.

The Snowman leaned back against the bridge rail, casually wiping a little saliva from the corner of his mouth. He looked at Logan and laughed. Then, too quickly for Logan to act, he grabbed the terrified blind man by his collar, pulled him up onto the bridge railing, and climbed up after him.

The concrete railing was only four or five inches wide and covered with snow. Using strength that could only have been granted by his symbiosis, the Snowman held the struggling man out over the drop.

"*No!*" cried Tommy. The Snowbeast lumbered toward the young mutant. Logan popped his claws, relieved that they worked here as well as the real world, plunging his right claws into the Snowbeast's side, ripping down in a long stroke. But there was no blood, just more of the green fire, spewing out, burning where it touched.

"Tommy," urged Jean, "you have to help us."

The boy just sat watching the battle, arms curled around his knees. "Can't do nothing without Auntie." He gestured at the old woman. "Her and me could outvote the Snow-beast, but she won't vote. She don't care. It's always that way."

Logan leapt and rolled beyond the Snowbeast's claws. "We need help, Red, or the man's gonna die. What about Blondie there?" He nodded toward the young symbiont be-fore having to fend off another of the Snowbeast's attacks.

Roger shook his head. "I can't control his powers. I've tried, but I *can't.*"

"Then," said Jean, "control *yours.* I'll help you see your true nature." She waved her hand toward the three aspects of the Snowman. "You have the ability to enhance your host, compensate for his shortcomings, to make him better at what he is. But you didn't understand that when you were suddenly cast into this poor shattered creature. You made him a better killer, and that's all, but Roger, you can make him whole."

The Snowbeast stopped for a moment, looking up in response to the words, then redoubled his attack on Logan.

"No," said Roger, "I don't know how."

"I'll help you," said Jean.

Some part of Logan could see the Snowman's fingers loosening from the man's collar, even as the Snowbeast landed on top of his chest, huge jaws snapping shut just short of his throat.

"Now would be a good time," he growled, freeing an arm to fend off another bite.

Then the Snowbeast was screaming, joining the chorus of Tommy and the old woman, with Jean, and with the mutant teenager, and finally with Logan himself, an animal howl rising from deep in his throat.

The weight lifted from Logan's body as the Snowbeast and his other aspects were drawn together into a boiling ball of green anger and rage. Then the color warmed, to yellow, and then orange, and the ball coalesced into a single figure, the silver-haired man they had called the Snowman.

Suddenly, Logan was back in the real world. The Snowman still stood on the railing, a look of growing realization and horror on his face. In the corner of his vision, Logan saw Jean stagger from the psychic backlash of returning to her own body.

"Help me," the blind man croaked, and the Snowman seemed to notice for the first time the helpless victim dangling from his hand. He placed the man's feet back on the railing, but did not release him.

"What have we done?" asked the Snowman. "What have *I* done?" The Snowman turned his face toward the bright sky, the wind plucking at his short white hair.

"Justice," he whispered, then pushed the man back onto the bridge, straight into Logan's arms. Days later, Logan would still be wondering if that move, or what followed, was intentional, for just then, the Snowman's feet slid from the icy railing and he tumbled to the sharp rocks waiting below.

There was a wet crunch, and then silence.

The injured dog stepped forward to join his master, and

Logan left them to comfort each other. He glanced over the rail at the broken body. The sharp angle of the neck left no doubt that the Snowman was finally dead.

Jean walked slowly toward him across the bridge. "Oh, Logan, it's terrible. Once he was psychically healed, the Snowman couldn't live with what he'd done."

"Who could, darlin'? The kid?"

She shook her head and sniffed. "Gone, I think. That makes two lives sacrificed today."

He put his hand on her arm. "And two saved. Prob'ly more. You did good."

But Jean drew away, turning her attention to the fallen man. She knelt next to him, picking his dark glasses up from where they'd fallen in the snow.

He moaned softly, and his eyelids fluttered. The dog whined and licked his face. He chuckled softly and started to push the animal away. Then his eyes opened, "You're hurt," he said to the dog. He gingerly explored the dog's injuries with his fingers, but there was more than that.

"You can see!" she exclaimed.

"I can see," the man parroted flatly. He repeated the words with more emotion, like an infant trying his second spoonful of ice cream. "I can see. I can't believe it." He climbed unsteadily to his feet, refusing Jean's offer of the glasses. He picked up his white cane, perhaps merely as a familiar comfort, since he seemed at a loss as to what to do with it.

Logan watched as the man walked to the far railing, leaning over to look down at the body. Jean followed the man, taking his arm to steady him. "Are you all right?"

"We're better now—both of us." He nodded downward.

"Even he was better in the end." He turned and smiled. "Thank you, Jean, for everything."

"I don't know your name," she said.

"My name is Roger Besda. *Our* name is Roger." He chuckled. "A nice coincidence, isn't it?"

Jean laughed, squeezing Roger's hands.

Logan drifted back, feeling an outsider in this moment of warmth and renewal. He and Jean could never be together. He knew that now. He'd battled the beast today, knowing he could never win. That was how it would ever be.

He stood at the far end of the bridge, looking out into the wild places beyond. That was where his destiny lay, with the inner-beast, and the battle that he must ever fight— alone.

OUT OF PLACE

Dave Smeds

Illustration by Brent Anderson

ank McCoy knew something was wrong, but he couldn't quite pin it down. He glanced at his shoes, brushed a hand across his white linen smock, and lifted his pen off the lined page of the patient medical file in front of him. He stared at the sentence he'd just written, suddenly uncertain that the handwriting was his.

"Is something wrong, Dr. McCoy?"

He turned to the patient on the exam table. The unfamiliarity faded. Of course. Mrs. Wilson. Age forty-one. He'd just removed a mole from her shoulder for a biopsy.

"Not to worry. As I said, your body is positively brimming with puissance and vitality," he said in his most soothing tone. "My apologies. I was thinking of something entirely unrelated to your visit."

Mrs. Wilson settled back into the relief of a person who has just been told the growth she feared was malignant is surely nothing of the kind. She fastened the last button of her blouse and, at the doctor's reassuring gesture, exited the exam room.

As soon as the door closed, Hank stood and gazed into the mirror above the sink. Slowly, unsteadily, his fingers made contact with the smooth flesh of his cheeks, then rode down to his chin, the nubs of his beard resisting the action like sandpaper.

"In the proverbial pink," whispered Hank. Not a single blue hair or elongated canine tooth could he find—just the brown hair and ruddy complexion he'd once owned, before the experiment that gave him his feral appearance. He was staring at a face that belonged in old photographs.

He turned away, hissing between his teeth. He'd been

taunted this way in the past, only to see his human form vanish—the last time stolen away by an evil mutant who called herself Infectia. But hands, not gorilla paws, still jutted from his sleeves, and his body no longer exuded the aroma or held in the heat of a thick indigo pelt. It didn't feel like a trick.

The Beast had disappeared. In his place was a totally different Hank McCoy. He squeezed his temples, trying to force the unfamiliar, vivid memories from the confines of his skull. The office in which he stood was his own, located outside Boston, shared with three other general practitioners. It was not the Brand Corporation labs, and he was not a biochemist. He was just a regular doctor, seeing ordinary patients in a peaceful suburban neighborhood. The memories were complete—all the way back to childhood, up through med school, and into private practice.

Nowhere in that life history was there any manifestation of mutant abilities in high school, no entry into a facility run by Charles Xavier, no charter membership in the X-Men, no details of a thousand incredible events since then. In fact, any recollection of being the Beast was growing muted, as if banished to the same place that had claimed his fur and the points of his ears.

He glanced at his watch. Another dozen people to see that morning. He stepped toward the door, to head to the next room, where another patient was no doubt waiting. Then, with a low, Beastlike growl, he stopped. Such a powerful, persuasive milieu. At every turn it was seducing him into forgetting who he was.

What could this be? Some sort of alternate universe? Another timeline? Certainly the X-Men had encountered those before. Yet every other trip to such places had in-volved a transition of sorts, such as a jump through a portal. Even teleportation left momentary tingles. This time he had simply become aware, at nine fifty-one in the morning, that something was wrong with the context around him.

A dream? Dreams didn't feel like this. The clipboard was firm in his grip, the floor solid, the sunlight out the window crisp and bright. Like his strange new memories, this place had the aspect of reality. Something told him whatever hap-pened here would have genuine effects. This was no fantasy.

Desperate to break the routine that was making this place so compelling, he made his way to the nurse's station, where he found a receptionist whom he'd never met before, yet whom, paradoxically, he'd known for two years.

"Developments have arisen," he said, measuring the words out with forced calm. "Kindly cancel the rest of my appointments today."

"Mr. Grauehe's already in room three," she said.

"My regrets," Hank replied, and turned his back on her worried frown.

Back in the exam room, alone, he slid out of his shoes and socks. Bounding forward, he somersaulted onto the exam table. There. He still had his mutant agility. But his leg muscles quivered, overtaxed by the effort. He over-balanced, and had to hop to the floor to avoid falling. He had congratulated himself prematurely. Yes, his powers were there, but they had faded. Were fading.

He looked again at his human body. Perhaps miracles did occur, after all.

* * *

Scott Summers was walking across the campus when he tripped on the flagstone path. Suddenly the lawns, the landscaping, the vine-cloaked brick buildings of the university, took on a numinous clarity. That was all the more alarming, because he was certain the scene had to be false.

He sat down on a bench, trying to sort out particulars of two separate lives: one as Cyclops, co-leader of the X-Men, the other as Scott Summers, PhD, assistant professor in an excellent, but typical, chemistry department at a modest undergraduate school in Illinois. The former seemed more true, but the latter was more vivid. He recalled verbatim sentences from the class he had just taught; he could cite the names of pupils he'd had over the last several semesters, complete with the grades they'd received. He knew that his excursion was taking him to the library in order to pick up an abstract not yet available by modem. These were all the sorts of evidence he could easily track down and confirm. Their undeniability confronted him.

One fact stunned him more than any other. *He wore no visor or glasses, yet he was viewing the world with eyelids wide open.*

"Can't be," he muttered. He peered at a blade of cut grass lying on the flagstones, examined an individual petal of a flower growing beside the walkway, and scanned a leaf in the nearest tree, a young Japanese elm. Not only did his gaze lack its usual destructive effect, what he saw only affirmed the palpability of the place. He recalled, for instance, that the tree had been planted two years before. The campus's handsome American elms had succumbed to the infestation that was destroying the variety throughout the continent. The details couldn't have been more clear.

Suddenly he began to chuckle. How blue the sky was.

Clouds hung like decorations placed by a divine hand. How fine the architecture of the campus buildings—such handsome lines of brick and mortar, laced with shrubbery.

To see. To see as he had not seen since childhood. It was grand, potent, compelling. . . .

But it was not right. He was Cyclops, and long ago he had become reconciled to living without normal vision. He struggled to his feet, fighting off the complacency this environment evoked.

Keening his mind for the telepathic whisper of Jean or of Professor X, he heard nothing. Was he the only X-Man affected? He reached out, but even his psionic rapport with his beloved proved insufficient to achieve contact.

One obvious test remained. He concentrated on the building site across the quad. The new student union. The structure was unoccupied; the construction crew had suspended work, unable to do more until a state inspector made a visit. There. That spot—where the upper-story window was due to be installed.

A familiar, momentary blindness seized him. He heard the moan of an optic blast. As his vision returned, he saw girders and concrete collapse within the building site. Dust poured out of the window he'd aimed through.

Students nearby gawked and pointed. Fortunately the burst had been too fleeting, and its effects too distracting, to mark Scott as the cause. He listened to the outbursts, taking strange comfort in the tones of dismay, fear, and excitement. The reaction was familiar to the part of him that remembered being an X-Man.

He waited for the inevitable exclamations—"Must be mutants! What are those freaks up to now?" No one uttered them. Instead, the talk buzzed with phrases like, "Political protest?" and "Gas leak?" and "Never seen anything like it."

Brows furrowing, Scott headed for the newspaper dispenser outside the library doors. The headlines contained no references to X-Men or their splinter teams, to renegades such as the Mutant Liberation Front or the Acolytes, or to any mutants at all. He pored through the entire edition page by page. There weren't even any articles about the latest doings of the Avengers, Spider-Man, or the Fantastic Four. The only thing that seemed right was the date on the masthead.

Shifting to the phone booth in the foyer, he began leafing through the Yellow Pages, but under "Attorneys," he found no ubiquitous advertisements by shysters offering to file personal injury claims on behalf of bystanders caught in the crossfire during fights between super heroes and super-villains.

"Can't be," he said again, and called Information.

"What city, please?" asked a voice that might, or might not, have been a recording.

"Salem Center, New York. I want a number for the Xavier Institute for Higher Learning."

"I'm sorry. No such listing."

"Thanks anyway," Scott said, the sinking feeling in his heart advising him not to protest. He waited a moment, breathing unevenly, and punched in the number he knew should work. An obnoxious mechanized voice began, "We're sorry. The number you have dialed . . ." He clanked down the receiver.

The rules were different here. This was a reality in which

mutants, super heroes, and their powers were unknown. He shook his head, trying to deny what his surroundings were telling him, but the more time that passed, the more convinced he was that these new conditions were how things should be.

His optic blast had not been as powerful as usual. Given the amount of focus and intention, it should have pulverized objects that had only been dislodged. The suspicion grew that if he were to try again, his powers would prove to be reduced even further.

Leaving him as what? A human?

If only it could be true.

While there was any vestige of Cyclops left, he couldn't just stand by passively. He had to contact the others. How, he didn't know. Perhaps if he . . .

His concentration faltered. Shouldn't he just go upstairs and pick up the abstract, make some photocopies, and prepare the handouts for his one o'clock class? No, that wasn't right. There was something nagging him—an image of a red-haired woman.

He rose, and instead of continuing into the library, as Professor Scott Summers would have done, he wandered outside, unsure where he was going, or what he was doing.

Jean Grey set her fork down on her plate, swallowed the bite of mashed potatoes she had taken, and tried not to show the alarm she was experiencing.

At the table with her sat her parents, John and Elaine, and her sister, Sara. The familiar walls of her childhood home enclosed her, the dining room arrayed with family photos. It was all as it should have been. She was a lawyer specializing in environmental issues, enjoying a lively but not overly taxing career, home for a long weekend with the folks—a regular occurrence, now that she had passed the bar and set up her practice only a two-hour drive away.

The part that didn't fit was the recurring impressions of another life, far removed from this calm, nurturing scene. She closed her eyes and saw starships explode, buildings crumble, colleagues fall, witnessed a woman with white hair riding the winds, and a man with claws slash through steel cables. She remembered the tug of a uniform against her skin, and the highly trained muscles beneath that fabric. When she asked herself who she was, she was tantalized with names like Marvel Girl and Phoenix.

"Jean? Are you all right?" Sara asked.

Jean flinched. Her gaze roved over her sister's face, noting the tiny mole on her right cheek, the precise shade of her irises, the sheer . . . health . . . of her complexion.

"Sara? You're supposed to be dead."

Sara's mouth dropped open. "Jeannie!" blurted her parents simultaneously. And Jean, blushing, suddenly had no idea what had prompted her throat to produce such a statement.

"I'm . . . sorry. I was recalling a dream I had last night," she lied. "Didn't know I was saying anything out loud."

As the heat dissipated from her cheeks and the meal resumed, the cordiality and sense of security Jean had felt earlier took on a brittle quality. The X-Men identity solidified, and though it was as faint as the nightmare she had invented to excuse her *faux pas*, it didn't waver. It was no hallucination. Jean guarded her reaction carefully, until the plates were cleared and she could excuse herself.

"I think I need a nap," she said, and disappeared into her bedroom.

First, the tests. She gestured, trying to telekinetically lift a chair. It rose. Frowning, she deposited it where it had been. Six inches? She had meant to raise it to the ceiling.

Still, even a minor amount of levitation proved she couldn't be plain old Jean Grey, attorney-at-law, no matter what her memories said. Time, then, to explore the "dream," and come up with some explanations.

She lay back on her bed and focused. Her last distinct memory of her existence as an X-Man surfaced: she and Scott had shared a cup of coffee after breakfast, savoring a little domestic ritual before suiting up for a session in the Danger Room. Professor X was out of town. The X-Men in residence that morning included herself, Cyclops, Wolverine, Archangel, Psylocke, Iceman, Beast, and Rogue.

That group would be easiest to make contact with, assuming they were still in close proximity. If that failed, she could try the Professor or more distant comrades, but given her depleted resources, she didn't want to attempt too much.

Naturally she tried Scott first. All that came back was an odd sort of echo—enough to confirm that he was alive and unharmed, but not enough to permit verbal messages, and not enough to fix his location relative to her.

She sagged back on the mattress, already wearied by the attempt. What was it about this world that sapped her powers so insidiously?

She had to try the others. No choice about that. Either she would succeed, or she wouldn't, but she couldn't go down without a struggle. One by one, she reached for them. . . .

Logan crashed through the front window of the hardware store/lumberyard, landing on the balls of his feet on the sidewalk, deftly avoiding the shards of glass he'd caused.

Flaring his nostrils to take in scents, he glanced about, requiring no more than the span of a heartbeat to orient himself. To his left the main street led to the town square and courthouse. To his right the community trailed off into the taiga forest of northern Canada.

He sped off toward the forest, snarling at the storefront facades beside him, the electric lines snaking from poles to the eaves of the buildings. The call of native, untamed spaces overwhelmed any coherent thought he might have.

A woman passerby backpedalled into the street, shrieking as she caught a glimpse of Logan's savage expression. He ran by, caring nothing about her as long as she wasn't in his way, but ahead, a policeman on the corner turned, saw the commotion, and reached reflexively for his pistol.

Logan closed the gap between himself and the man before the latter could unsnap his holster. Logan swiped, and his claws ripped through the leather, knocking the gun to the concrete. He scooped up the weapon, tossed it onto the roof of the next building, and raced into an alley that led to the fringe of the wood.

The shrill call of the cop's whistle faded as Logan lost himself amid boughs heavy with pine needles and trees higher than the town's tallest building. Finally he slowed, though he was only mildly winded. His first truly conscious act was to bring up the hand that had torn the pistol loose and stare at it.

The hand was scarred, powerful, with fingernails sharp and thick. But no claws protruded, as they had they when he slashed at the holster, no matter how fiercely he flexed and squeezed.

He growled, trying to drive from his mind the memories of a life where he was a cutter in the lumberyard from which he had just fled, one of a series of jobs he'd held during a life spent entirely in the Great White North. He'd often imagined such a life—one he might have lived had he not been a mutant, and never been the subject of Weapon X experiments.

The false identity clung to his mind, eroding the essence of his Wolverine self. He had endured many kinds of madness, but this was new. He wasn't sure how to fight it. He had done the one thing that made sense—got out among the trees, away from the stench of civilization. What now?

A weak telepathic voice called from deep in his brain— a shout reduced to a whisper.

"Red? 'Zat you?" He asked aloud because he couldn't remember how to answer mentally.

An image came to him of a face. He knew he should know her, but her name wouldn't surface. He felt that if he tried too hard to recall it, he would forget his own.

The hunter in him recognized that she was *that* direction—over the hills, through more forest, and then who knew what. Far away. Hopelessly far.

Yet lurking here, passively accepting a transformation into a new self, was not something he would tolerate. He needed to take action. Until he could think of something better, at least he could run.

He set off, the trail seeming more faint with every tree passed.

Hank McCoy, still ensconced in his office, unwound the cuff of a blood pressure gauge and tossed the device in its drawer. Once more he checked the printout of the treadmill test he'd performed on himself.

The proof was right there, stark and irrefutable. An hour earlier he had still shown indications of mutant, Beast-like physiology. Now his scores had fallen to levels within the reach of a trained athlete. At this rate another hour would bring the results down to a point that could only be described as "normal."

And it was getting so, so hard to recall why that should bother him.

Bobby Drake lifted the ice cream cone to his mouth. How fascinating the cold felt as it caressed his tongue. The flavor almost seemed superfluous. Temperature mattered far more.

On the other side of the parlor, the freezer case beckoned. He had half a mind to crawl right in there among the tubs of Rocky Road and Orange Sherbet. Was that weird? Quickly he checked the faces of the servers and the other customers. They weren't looking at him.

He laughed inwardly. Who the hell would care what off-the-wall ideas he had, as long as he kept them to himself? No one. Strange, then, that his paranoia lingered. Some part of him was accustomed to people staring at him, attacking him, or running as fast as they could away from him. The eerie depth of the perception sent chills up his spine.

Chills were good, though. He relaxed. *Get real, Drake. Just who or what do you think you are?* The windows reflected back the image of a healthy, young, all-American guy. Nothing strange whatsoever.

Just hanging out, having a cone. A zen moment. Life didn't get much better.

He licked again, letting the dollop of full-sugar, all-the-fat Mocha melt on his tongue until nothing remained but a tiny speck of ice that had crept into the mixture. Now, what was so hypnotic about *ice?*

The carousel sounds and popcorn aroma of a carnival surrounded Rogue as she took a place in line for the fourth time. Beneath her feet, straw kept the dust down; she liked the way it tickled her bare feet. The sun of the Deep South kneaded her skin—and there was a lot of that showing around her halter top and cutoff denim jeans. She treasured the heat with a fervor that verged on nostalgia. Now, why should that be? She'd lived in Dixie her whole life, hadn't she?

"Back again?" asked an old lady with a wink.

Up ahead a sign read "KISSES—$2." Rogue blushed, then grinned. "Can't seem to get enough," she admitted.

"He's quite a hunk, isn't he?" remarked the matron.

The dark-haired, muscular occupant of the booth, just then lending his wares to a plump lady in a summer dress, was indeed a fine specimen of manhood, but Rogue didn't really care about that. It was the kissing itself that compelled her to fork over her cash so generously. The contact of flesh against flesh, even in such a relatively chaste, public way, gave her an indecently intense satisfaction.

The hunk finished with his chubby customer and, scanning down the line, saw Rogue. He winked.

She grinned back. Funny thing, after their first kiss, he'd seemed rather pale. She'd thought he might faint. But the color was back in his cheeks. The second and third times had been fine.

Why did that make her feel so good? So . . . forgiven?

Scott stood at a revolving display rack in a drugstore, trying out various pairs of sunglasses. He felt like a kid let loose in a toy store, though why all these silly little plastic shades should appeal to him so much he didn't quite understand. After all, he'd never needed prescription lenses in his life. He could have bought any style he wanted at any point in the past—what was the big deal about them now?

As he selected a gray-lensed, bronze-frame aviator pair and set them on his nose, an image of a great-looking redhead popped into his mind. He hardly paid attention, since her description didn't match any of his friends or acquaintances. Then he remembered that this was the fifth or sixth time he'd thought of her that day.

And then he remembered much more.

Steeling himself against the delicious contentment he'd been feeling, he finally succeeded in framing a reply to Jean's psionic query: "How many of us are here? Is anyone missing?"

In the bedroom at her parents' home, Jean Grey heard Scott's question. Though it was a reply to her own, it came back as if it were nothing more than television-show dialogue overheard from the living room, having nothing to do with the here and now.

A cozy, soothing mood possessed her. She wanted to go downstairs and play cards, or simply indulge in the companionship of her family, especially with Sara. What a silly question, anyhow.

Is anyone missing? The voice said it again, insistently.

Jean frowned, got a grip on her X-Man self, and laboriously combed her chaotically jumbled memories for the answer. Yes, other members of the team were "here" in this reality. She'd touched their minds, even if the brief comments of Logan and Scott were the only distinct examples of contact.

Or rather, she'd touched six out of seven. She'd completely failed with . . . Psylocke.

A cold sweat burst on her brow. Psylocke was another telepath. With the exception of Scott, with whom Jean shared a psychic rapport, Psylocke should have been the easiest to contact, even with weakened powers. Jean brought what little reserves she had left to bear, and from the place in her mind where she should have received a response— nothing.

"That's the key," Jean murmured to herself, and realized then how little time she had left to do anything. This new world had almost swallowed her true identity, and those of the others. If she were going to save the group, she had to find the answer to a puzzle quickly.

One option made the most sense. Before she lost track again, she broadcast a set of insistent telepathic instructions, but this time it was not toward Psylocke.

* * *

Warren Worthington III was flying a small airplane, and having a great time doing it. Barrel rolls and sudden swoops—they felt like second nature to him. His aircraft behaved like an extension of his body. He laughed out loud as he climbed through a layer of thin, scattered clouds, regaining altitude in order to try more antics. He couldn't remember an hour in his life when flying had seemed so grand. As an heir of wealth, he had always enjoyed taking the plane up; it got him away from corporate boardrooms and obligatory high-society gatherings, out where he could be himself. Today, though, his piloting skills seemed almost more than human.

The "almost" part struck him as particularly important. The seat beneath him, the cockpit around him, comforted him with their separateness from his body. It was a strange emotion, but he didn't dwell on it. He had only a few more minutes until he'd have to land and immerse himself once again in the details of his busy life.

Warren! called a voice so clearly that he looked behind him to see if he had a stowaway. Only when it came a second time did he realize it was in his head.

"Jean," he said. The knowledge of who Jean Grey was poured into him, and with it arrived the memory of being Archangel.

Go to Betsy, Jean said. *She's . . . she's . . .* The voice fell below the level of intelligibility.

Warren wasted no time. He wasn't sure how long he could retain this sense of his proper identity. He brought his plane down low over the landscape. As his altitude plummeted, that landscape began to shift, becoming the familiar settled woodlands surrounding the town of Salem Center.

A large set of buildings emerged from the leaves. *Emerged* was precisely how it appeared. He was certain the structures hadn't been there until he willed them to be. He banked the plane and straightened to attempt a landing.

As he settled in, the aircraft dissolved. His back tingled fiercely. The wings used to land himself on the broad lawns were no longer propeller-driven. Down and on his feet, he flapped them twice just to reinforce his mutant identity.

The ivy-encrusted walls of the Xavier Institute wavered, threatening to fade out of this world once more, but Warren didn't let them disappear. He rushed inside, making straight for the quarters of Elisabeth Braddock.

Psylocke woke on an exam table in the infirmary. Warren was leaning over her, his somber expression easing as they made eye contact. Several other X-Men hovered in the background. The Beast switched off a monitor, having obviously tended to her.

"How do you feel?" Warren asked.

"Awful." She coughed. Her muscles seemed to be slung on her bones like overstuffed luggage, and her skin itched as if bathed in grit and insecticide. Even lifting her tongue to form words proved taxing.

"You had a tremendous fever," Warren told her. "It created some interesting effects."

"I think I remember," Betsy said. "It was like I was doing psi-probes of each of you. You were in places you have tucked deep in your minds. Except you weren't there by choice. You had been forced there . . . by me."

"That is our working hypothesis," the Beast confirmed. "While in the midst of your fever, instead of simply reading minds, you projected something—call it a fervent wish—into everyone in the building. Thanks to the abundant vigor of your psionic abilities, you overlaid alternate realities upon us all, each one a mixture of your own desires and those of the individual affected."

Added Jean, "The illusions were so strong that we couldn't break free of them until my telepathic red alert to Warren shook him awake here, in the real world, where we had all been rendered unconscious. He woke everyone up, then Bobby iced you down. We carried you to the infirmary, and Hank's treatments brought your fever down the rest of the way."

"I'm . . . sorry," Betsy said. "I didn't have any control over it. I don't even know how it started. I've often had dreams where I was living in a world where I wasn't a mutant—where no one was. But I always woke up, same as ever. I had no idea anything like this would develop."

"It was a narrow escape. This occurrence, thanks to the fever, activated a variation of your psychic knife," Jean added, referring to Psylocke's ability to telepathically "carve out" a person's memories. "Those false memories we all experienced were given such a boost, they would have soon taken root permanently in our brains."

"But when Warren realized that I was in distress, he found a way to get to me," Betsy said, turning to gaze at him again. They clasped hands.

"Least I could do for my favorite ninja," he replied. The words were flip, but the tenderness in the delivery was like a cool cloth on her forehead. It brought a romantic smile to her lips, and worked to ease the guilt at having endangered everyone.

"Jean and Professor Xavier will do some scans of us all during the next few days, and make sure any residual effects are minimized," Cyclops said.

"Well," Iceman said, "I guess we can consider it a case of 'no harm done.' "

Most of the group filed out, leaving Psylocke to recuperate. Archangel remained with her, trying out a joke or two to further revive her spirits.

No harm done? wondered Hank McCoy as he sequestered himself in the med lab next door. In the gleaming metal of a cabinet, his blue-haired face projected back, as brutish as ever.

A narrow escape? questioned Rogue. Bobby strode beside her down the corridor. She wanted very much to be able to take his arm in hers, laugh a little at another rescue accomplished, maybe even give him a peck on the cheek. All without having to restrain herself for fear that her power would drain him of things it shouldn't.

In her and Scott's bedroom later that day, Jean Grey picked up the picture of her sister that she kept on the dresser. She traced the edges of the frame, and sighed. A pair of tears fell from her lashes.

AUTHOR BIOGRAPHIES

ELUKI BES SHAHAR also writes as Rosemary Edghill and is the author of over fourteen books (like eluki's "Hellflower" series and Rosemary's Bast novels), even if you don't count her upcoming X-Men novel *Children of the Atom*. From earliest infancy she has suspected mutagenic influences in her environment, and bought *Uncanny X-Men* #1 off the stands, thereby changing the entire course of her life. She thinks Scott and Jean should have gotten married *years* ago and has always thought the green costume with the skirt was silly.

TAMMY LYNNE DUNN is a thirty-year-old native Texan who became hooked on the X-Men characters when her children started reading the *X-Men Adventures* comic books. In her "normal" life, she lives on a small ranch two hours north of Houston where she and her husband raise assorted animals and children (the animals are assorted, not the children). This is her first published short story.

KEN GROBE is an editor and writer living in New York City. His first comics work was with Eclipse in 1992, where he co-edited *Hot Pulp*, an anthology of 1930s "spicy" men's magazines, and assisted on the *AIDS Awareness Trading Cards*. Grobe's editorial credit can be found on such comics as *The Hitchhiker's Guide to the Galaxy; Life, the Universe, and Every-*

thing, Roger Zelazny's Amber (all from DC); and *Ray Bradbury Comics* (Topps Comics). His short fiction can also be found in *The Ultimate Super-Villains,* and he is the writer of a new comics series copublished by Rock-It Comics and Capitol Records. Grobe is also an accomplished songwriter and musician, and has appeared on national television in this capacity. Okay, it was *The New Gong Show,* but that still counts.

GLENN HAUMAN has ten years of experience in publishing, including work for Random House, Simon & Schuster, and DC Comics. He is the president of BiblioBytes, which publishes and sells electronic books on the Internet (http://www.bb.com). Glenn has worked as a graphic designer, an editor, a story consultant for films, the promotions manager for New York's largest science fiction convention, a stand-up comedian, and a radio show host. In what's left of his spare time, he enjoys challenging unconstitutional laws in court and banging his head into chandeliers.

ANDY LANE lives three separate lives. On the one hand he has a degree in physics and works for the British Civil Service. On the other hand he writes TV tie-in fiction, including four *Doctor Who* novels and one *BUGS!* novelization. On the third (Venusian) hand, he is the author of various serious SF and fantasy short stories in anthologies such as *The Ultimate Witch, The Ultimate Dragon,* and *Full Spectrum 5,* as well as in the British magazine *Interzone.*

STAN LEE, the chair of Marvel Comics and Marvel Films and creative head of Marvel Entertainment, is known to millions as the man whose super heroes propelled Marvel to its prominent position in the comic book industry. Hundreds of legendary characters, such as Spider-Man, the Incredible Hulk, the Fantastic Four, the Silver Surfer, Iron Man, Daredevil, and Dr. Strange, all grew out of his fertile imagination. Stan has written more than a dozen best-selling books for Simon & Schuster, Harper & Row, and other major publishers, and he has previously served as editor for *The Ultimate Spider-Man*, *The Ultimate Silver Surfer*, and *The Ultimate Super-Villains*. He is the creator of *Stan Lee's Riftworld*, a fictional universe that has spawned three novels and two forthcoming comics series. Presently, he resides in Los Angeles, where he chairs Marvel Films and is co-executive producer for Marvel's many burgeoning motion picture, television, and animation projects, including the animated series *Spider-Man*, *X-Men*, and *The Incredible Hulk*.

Having spent her childhood living on an Israeli kibbutz, in a caravan, and in a converted barn that used to be a pigsty, **REBECCA LEVENE** has chosen to spend her adult life in London, England. She used to work at the House of Commons for the Shadow Agriculture Minister but decided she wanted a job that had more to do with the real world, and is now SF Editor at Virgin Publishing.

Born in Germany and a long-time resident of the American Southwest, **ASHLEY MCCONNELL** has also lived in the Midwest and North Africa. She has published poetry, short stories, and nonfiction, as well as two original horror novels, five tie-in books for *Quantum Leap* and one for *Highlander*, and the first two of her Demon War series, *The Fountains of Mirlacca* and *The Itinerant Exorcist*. The third in the series,

The Courts of Sorcery, will be released in early 1997. She has always felt a certain kinship with mutants, probably due to spending far too much time with her cats.

JENN SAINT-JOHN was left as a changeling in her parent's nursery. Being kind folk, they kept her, and she lived a perfectly normal childhood . . . for a mutant. Now that Jenn's an adult, her human mother constantly wonders where she went wrong. Currently living in the wilds of Milton, Florida, Jenn is the slave to Trip and Sugar, two representatives of an advanced alien civilization who masquerade as dogs whenever another humanoid is around. Her work as a writer takes her into a variety of worlds and dimensions, most recently as a storybuilder and developer in the mysterious land of computer games, including *Modus Operandi* and the *Erasmotron.* Only her e-mail address is in this timeline: JENN@CHENEY.NET.

EVAN SKOLNICK jumped headlong into the world of professional publishing at the tender age of fifteen, and has never looked back. After graduating from the University of Connecticut in 1988 and doing a short stint as a newspaper reporter, Skolnick landed an editorial position at Marvel Comics. During the course of his six-year run at Marvel, he was involved in properties ranging from the innocuous *Alf* and *Count Duckula* to the more hard-hitting *Doctor Strange* and *Ghost Rider 2099.* In 1995, Skolnick left the Marvel staff to energetically pursue the freelance writing career he had been nurturing for years. He has written such comics for Marvel as *Iron Man, Excalibur, The Incredible Hulk, Spider-Man Unlimited, Venom, New Warriors, Nova, Web of Scarlet Spider, William Shatner's TekWorld, 2099 Unlimited,* and many others.